BOOKS BY [illegible] SE

JOSH KAVANAGH THRILLER SERIES
The Patriot Oath
Never for Glory

STANDALONE THRILLER
Running with the Enemy

HISTORICAL FICTION
suspense, thriller, action, adventure, romance
My Splendid Concubine

STANDALONE MURDER MYSTERY
The Redemption of Don Juan Casanova

MEMOIR
Crazy Is Normal

JOSH KAVANAGH THRILLERS

NEVER FOR GLORY

LLOYD LOFTHOUSE

A Three Clover Press Book
Published in the United States of America

Cover, editing and launch promotion by Imbue Editing
https://imbueediting.com

Three Clover Press
Pittsburg, California 94565

"All gave some, Some gave all."

CHAPTER 1

AFTER THEIR FIRST HALO jump together in 2002, Josh and Cheéte vanished into the Hindu Kush Mountains, a rugged area covering 160,000 square miles. Their orders had been to search for targets of opportunity, and for weeks they worked alone with little or no support.

Now, in 2019, seventeen years later, they were doing it again. This time, their C-130 belonged to The Oath Group, and it was 30,000 feet over Venezuela.

Getting ready for another drop was like déjà vu. Back then, they were Marine Corps scout snipers serving in Operation Anaconda against al-Qaeda, Taliban insurgents, and members of the Islamic Movement of Uzbekistan. That had been their last mission together. Cheéte retired a few months later in 2003.

"I can't believe my ghillie suit still fits," Josh said. "It feels the same, hot and heavy. It was perfect last summer for our sortie in Montana."

Cheéte grunted as he finished squeezing into his old camouflaged ghillie suit. Once he had it on, he looked like an unkempt yeti that needed to lose some weight. "Well, some of us don't always get what we want. You've been out for less than a year, so I'm not surprised your suit fits, but I think mine is going to eat me like a starving anaconda."

They were talking to each other through their helmet's military-grade communication units.

Josh grinned as he fastened a g-suit around his abdomen and legs, covering most of the camouflaged outfit he wore underneath. Then he manually inflated the g-suit's five air bladders. The pressure around the muscles would prevent blood from pooling in the feet and legs and push blood pressure up to the heart and brain. The last thing he did was attach the oxygen mask and tactical goggles.

With a frustrated sigh, huffing and puffing, Cheéte did the same thing. Once they were on the ground, they'd ditch the gear required for the HALO jump. Their ghillie suits concealed them from prying eyes.

Like most Marine Corps snipers, they'd made their own unique disguises by hand and when not in use stored them in sealed, plastic boxes lined in cotton and kept dry with silica gel packets.

"I'm worried my Christian Crow wife knows about my two other common-law wives," Cheéte said, interrupting Josh's thoughts.

Josh did a double-take and stared at his old friend. "Whoa! Where the hell did that come from?"

"In case I don't make it home, I want you to know what's going on in my life. My Christian wife said the only reason for sex is to create children for God. When I said no more kids, she cut me off. There's no way I'm going without for the rest of my life. What about you?"

"I have nothing to confess to anyone," Josh replied.

"Ah, what about Rachel and Mia?"

A green light came on, signaling it was time to jump. The C-130's ramp yawned open, depressurizing the cabin and causing the temperature to drop more than 70 C, too far below freezing.

Josh stood, ready to go.

"Well?" Cheéte asked.

"I haven't had sex with anyone since they shot Rachel in San Francisco, and she's still in the hospital. So, I'm not that desperate." Finished, he walked off the aft ramp and dropped from sight, falling 30,000 feet toward the ground.

"Sheesh," Cheéte hissed. "That's not what I wanted to hear." Then he was dropping with his belly pointed toward the ground, his chin lifted, and his arms and legs spread out for stability.

As Josh fell hard and fast, he thought about Rachel and Mia. He'd lied to Cheéte. He was desperate, which explained why he was losing a lot of sleep. But he disagreed with the crap that sexual frustration was normal. So, shrug and take it in stride...

Bull shit! He couldn't remember ever being celibate this long before.

The temptation to keep both of his lovers, as Mia had suggested, was almost overwhelming. But when he thought about going through with it, he heard Dr. Tate's voice telling him that would be wrong. Then there was the Christian guilt his mother instilled in him as a child with the Seventh Commandment, "Thou shall not commit adultery."

He still didn't understand why his mother started preaching that to him when he was seven. It couldn't have been because of his crush on Rachel in second grade. He told no one about that. There was no way his mother could have known.

To escape the jumble of depressing thoughts stirring up trouble inside his head, he gave himself over to the plunge. Jumping from 30,000 feet felt more like flying than falling. It was windy, loud, and intense. Josh's senses became wildly alive. That was why he had an obsession with HALO jumps. The thrill lasted about three times longer than a basic skydiver's altitude.

With a stable belly-to-Earth position, the fastest speed he'd reach was 120 mph. If he wanted to fly faster, he'd shift position, his head facing the ground and his feet pointed up. Then he'd drop at 180 mph. Josh had always wondered what it would be like to die like that. He'd been tempted every time he jumped.

Checking out of life also offered him an easy way to avoid deciding between Rachel and Mia. The main chute was set to open automatically at 1,900 feet because of the high altitude, low open insertion. If that failed, the reserve chute deployed at 1,000.

The best way to bail out of life would be to use one of his keen-edged combat knives and cut the straps that held the two chutes to his body. He had about a minute left to make that decision.

Was there a better way to die if you were doing something you loved? He started laughing and realized he sounded possessed.

Still, there was Damian Bran, the man they were hunting. He was the one responsible for Rachel living in a hospital, trapped in a coma. Wasn't that a good enough reason to hang on?

Bran had been a heartless CIA agent for thirty years before leaving the agency in 2009. They also knew him as the Strawman because of his tall, thin stature. Soon after he retired, he'd joined a white supremacist neo-Nazi militia in Montana and ended up working for a ruthless libertarian billionaire, a match made by Mephistopheles.

Josh had been hunting Bran since his thugs had shot Rachel. His efforts to find the former CIA agent had started by putting the man's wife under surveillance. There had been no calls or texts in or out. Instead, she hadn't budged from their home in a remote area of Minnesota and didn't seem to care if she ever saw her husband again.

After the Oath Group's successful raid in Northwest Montana on that neo-Nazi training camp, Charles Tweet, the billionaire who financed the militia, revealed it was Bran who introduced him to the profitable sex trade. It turned out that the former field agent had trafficked children years before he left the agency.

Most of the young sex slaves Bran sold to Tweet had worked in massage parlors spread across the United States. But some of the most beautiful had suffered a worse fate. If one of them was unfortunate enough to catch the billionaire's eye, they were doomed.

His last intended victim had been a seventy-six-pound thirteen-year-old Ukrainian girl. The billionaire had slipped a plastic bag over the child's head while he was raping her. When Cheéte had burst into the underground room where it was taking place, Tweet was suffocating the girl, a method known as sexual asphyxiation that helped his orgasm become more intense.

Later, during his interrogation, Tweet revealed that Damen Bran had introduced him to that risky erotic method. When the billionaire accidentally murdered his first victim, Bran had shrugged it off and said, "Females were created for two purposes. To give men pleasure and, if they survive, to make babies. Besides, when you're kidnapping children and selling them for a profit, expect to lose a few. Think of it as collateral damage, a business expense."

Tweet accepted that justification as gospel and had murdered more than a dozen young girls over the years that followed. Now the billionaire was in court, fighting to avoid spending the rest of his life in prison. The judge had not approved bail, but his lawyers were claiming the evidence was inadmissible.

The information that pinpointed Bran's location in Venezuela had come from Mia Belle-Chanson, one of Josh's best friends and a former lover. To her fans, she was a singer-songwriter and a documentary producer. What her followers didn't know was what she did away from a studio or stage. Because someone had kidnapped her in Haiti at fourteen to become a sex slave, she now operated a secret network that rescued abducted children all over the world. Josh had met Mia when he and Cheéte had rescued her and several other girls.

Venezuela was the perfect country for a brute like Bran. After Venezuelan President Nicolás Maduro rose to power in 2013, sex trafficking and child sex tourism had become common, and it was getting worse.

The intel from Mia's rescue organization reported that Bran was living on an isolated cattle ranch in Venezuela's savanna southwest of the Rio Apure River.

Having second thoughts about dying, Josh checked his altimeter to determine how much time he had left to decide.

CHAPTER 2

ABOUT AN HOUR after their parachute landing, Josh and Cheéte approached the clearing where they expected to see the dark outline of a Vietnam-era Huey sitting there like a dead relic, the rotor blades motionless. On the ground, it was muggy, and a heavy silence surrounded them.

Mia's people had arranged for this bird to pick them up and carry them the rest of the way to their destination, wherever that was.

Dressed in their hot and oppressive ghillie suits, they'd blended into the brush-covered terrain. With heavy backpacks and carrying sniper rifles, they'd walked, according to their GPS devices, about five klicks to reach this spot. The night was darker than usual, making it impossible to see anything of their surroundings.

Adding all of that up caused Josh to wonder if they were walking into a trap, something Damian Bran was known for.

There were no doors on the helicopter's passenger compartment, just a pitch-black opening in the bird's side. When they stopped a few yards away, a darker, fuzzy silhouette moved inside, and the hairs on the back of his neck bristled.

This better not end up being a clusterfuck, Josh thought as he flipped off the safety on his HK MP7, a compact, accurate 9mm submachine gun fitted with a suppressor. It had a 40-round magazine housed in the weapon's pistol grip. He heard a similar snick from Cheéte's weapon. They also had assorted knives, explosives, flashbangs, their scoped sniper rifles, the 9mm SIG Sauer P226, the Special Operations pistol used by Navy SEALs, and his backup Glock in the ankle holster.

Cheéte placed his back to Josh's and searched the darkness around the chopper with his night-vision gear. "Doesn't look like an ambush," he said in a low tone. They were using tactical throat mikes with earbuds for audio. "I'm not seeing any heat signatures, so who's the hairy beast in the bird?"

They were both wearing the latest bullet-resistant clothing under their camouflage. They'd planned for this possibility and had agreed to die fighting before ending up a prisoner of the Strawman, an expert at torture.

"We'll figure that out soon," Josh replied. Then, to lighten the sense of menace in an iffy situation, he changed the subject. "I've been thinking about what you said before the jump. If you have other women, does that make it okay for your wife to have other men?"

After a moment of silence, Cheéte replied in a hiss, "You want to continue that conversation now?"

"Why not? I regret not letting you have more time to confess. It's apparent you needed to get that burden off your chest, and I was too dense to see that then."

Cheéte sputtered. "That wasn't a conversation. It takes two for that, and all I remember was me doing the talking. You've been too mute, and that was telling me you have something stuck in your head. I wanted to help you, not me."

That was when the bird's turboshaft engine started with a whine that grew louder as the rotors spun faster, churning the air. Josh didn't know if the camouflaged figure in the cargo compartment had heard them or even knew they were there. It was that dark. As the rotors became a whopping blur, his ghillie suit felt like it was being buffeted in a hurricane until the burlap flaps and jute twine on his head were thrashing about like a tree being battered in a hurricane.

Well, so much for trying to change the mood, he thought. As a seasoned warrior, Josh's combat mindfulness was on full alert. Time stretched and the seconds slowed, becoming as long as minutes as his senses ramped up. A dim red light came on inside the cargo area. A naked hand appeared out of the darkness, and a sexy index finger pointed at him.

His heart drummed as adrenaline and cortisol flooded his brain, preparing him for fight or flight. The barrel of his MP7 was aimed at the figure's center mass. He almost pulled the trigger, but what he saw on the back of the hand stopped him. It was the tattoo of a white rose that glowed in the dark. He doubted that there were two people on the planet with the same tattoo.

Time froze, and his mind flashed back to the day Mia and he had visited the oldest flower and bird market in Paris for the first time.

"This is the heart of Paris," Mia had said. The market was on the Isle de la Cite, a stone's throw from Notre Dame.

With Mia holding his hand, and the fragrance and colorful vividness of millions of flowers and the songs of thousands of exotic birds surrounding them, Josh felt as if he'd been transported to another world.

"This market had been here since 1809, dedicated to flowers and birds," his lover had said. Then she handed him an exquisite white rose with pearl-shaped dewdrops clinging to the petals.

Mia continued, "The white rose is the 'flower of light,' and it represents loyalty, purity, and a love stronger than death."

He'd held the rose to his nose to smell its sweetness. A black ladybug with red dots had slipped out of the petals where it had been hidden and flew into his nose. He'd snorted, and it set the ladybug free. While Mia giggled, sounding like a musical chime, they'd watched it flutter out of sight.

A few days later, a perfect tattoo of that rose and its one dewdrop had appeared on the back of her right hand. He'd asked her why. She said to remember that moment forever. Over the years, other tattoos had appeared on her radiant caramel-colored body, each one a precious memory she didn't want to forget. Most of them represented something they'd done together.

Snapping back to the present moment and with time moving again, Josh turned his head to the side and shouted into Cheéte's ear. "Stand down, first sergeant, and mount that bird. We're with friends."

As they slid into the cargo bay, they discovered Mia was wearing a four-piece ghillie suit similar to theirs. There was the mask that covered the entire head and shoulders, the jacket, and the pants that had hidden pockets. The fourth piece covered the rifle.

After they sat, a dim red light came on inside the cabin, and she took off her headpiece, revealing her stunning features and close-cropped, curly hair. Josh sat on the bench to her right, and Cheéte took the spot on her left. The bird lifted straight up, spun ninety degrees, and flew southwest.

Cheéte saw the rifle resting between Mia's legs with the muzzle pointing at the ceiling, and he held out a hand. "May I?"

She nodded. Once he'd identified it as an FR F2, the standard sniper rifle of the French military since 1986, he handed the weapon back. Then he leaned closer to her ear. "The last time I saw you was eighteen years ago, and you haven't aged a day."

"You're still full of nonsense." Her pure grin revealed what she was thinking. "Josh wasn't supposed to tell anyone about us being together."

"I'm not anyone," he said.

"I know. If you were a woman, I'd be jealous."

Cheéte glanced over her shoulder at Josh, but his straight-shooting partner was facing the other way, ignoring them. Cheéte could tell by his stiff shoulders he was struggling with his emotions.

"He's angry," Mia said with the patient tone of someone who knew her man.

Cheéte shrugged. "He'll deal with it. You know he can hear every word we're saying through our tactical comm gear."

With a slight nod, she showed she knew Josh was listening.

"And," Cheéte continued, "from what I've heard, you two have been in some pretty tight spots together. The way he talks about you, I thought you might be Wonder Woman."

She laughed. "It will be nice having someone I can trust with our secrets," she said.

"You can count on me," he replied. He nodded at her rifle. "Is it safe for me to assume you know how to use that?"

Josh thought, *Of course she does*. Once Mia does something, nothing stops her, even if it might get her killed. That pissed him off even more.

"I've learned from the best. The children of several snipers who belong to the National Gendarmerie Intervention Group (GIGN) are my fans, and their fathers were thrilled to teach me until I was as good as them. I also know Savate. Do you know of this sport?"

"What color are your gloves?" he asked.

"Silver," she said.

"That helps," he replied.

Josh wanted to join in but wasn't ready. He knew this unique style of fighting, with sweeping high kicks, had been developed in the south of France by sailors after they'd witnessed Chinese Kung Fu masters in the late 19th Century's Boxer Rebellion. He also knew Mia had earned those silver gloves the hard way. He admired her dedication.

"I am also learning Krav Maga," she said, referencing the Israeli Defense Forces martial art. Learning this self-defense and fighting system emphasized awareness and avoidance of dangerous situations. "Josh was teaching me before he left France and married Rachel."

Since Josh told him Mia knew about Rachel, that didn't surprise him. "I trained in French kickboxing for about a year," Cheéte replied. "But that was a long time ago, and it isn't much use to me now. I'm not as flexible or as fast as I was back then."

Josh felt it was better to let Cheéte keep her occupied while he listened in and worked on his roiled emotions. Mia had pulled stunts like this before, and he knew why. She enjoyed breaking down the facade of calm he'd cultivated over the years. By getting him to lower that defense, his performance in bed was off the charts. That warned him what to expect when they reached the end of this flight, and he didn't know what he was going to do yet.

Josh had learned the hard way that speaking when antagonized made situations worse. Dr. Tate, his PTSD counselor, had taught him how to recognize when his temper was triggered and how to manage it. That was why every morning he meditated with a focus on maintaining control when the unexpected happened. That was also how he kept a lid on his thoughts, but that didn't always work, explaining why he took so many risks in combat, gambling with his life.

Mia loved it when his wild side was released. Over the years, Josh had learned that being sexually active was a defense against the self-destructive side of PTSD, something they both lived with. Being intimate with someone he cared deeply for pepped up his mood and helped erase stress with a short-term high.

He wouldn't tell Cheéte this, but he understood why his friend and mentor was sneaking around with other women after his wife cut him off. Too bad he couldn't bring himself to do the same thing, to release those feel-good chemicals in his brain with a woman he loved. With Rachel still in a coma, that left only Mia.

Damn, what a fix he was in, trapped between guilt and temptation. He preferred going after the Strawman than dealing with those emotions.

CHAPTER 3

WHEN THEY REACHED the film camp and Mia's air-conditioned, forty-eight-foot trailer, she pointed to the left and said, "Your bedroom is that way, Cheéte. It has a small refrigerator filled with bottled juices and water. It also has a bathroom. If you want coffee, there's a single-cup pod machine too."

The custom-made trailer had two bedrooms, one at each end, with a room in the center for the cooking and sitting. All three areas had slide-out sections that expanded the size of the rooms.

Mia's household manager, Aya, was waiting behind the marble-topped kitchen island in front of the gleaming stainless-steel refrigerator and cooking area. She was old enough to be Mia's grandmother and had two grandchildren, both young girls who lived near Paris with their parents.

"Hello, Aya," Josh said as he slipped off his ghillie suit's head mask, revealing his face. "I've missed your baguettes and that incredible coffee you brew." He loved the older French woman's cooking, and over the years they'd developed a friendship, but something was different. He'd never seen her posture so stiff, her face that rigid, and her eyes so troubled.

"Are you hungry?" Aya asked, avoiding eye contact. "I made a vegan hazelnut-cream chocolate parfait."

"Thank you but maybe later, Aya," Mia replied. "Take the rest of the day off. Your granddaughters will leave for school soon. Call them and say hello for me."

Josh noticed the stress lines around the older woman's eyes tighten with fear when Mia mentioned her granddaughters. He thought he saw fresh tears glistening in her eyes as she hustled past him and out of the trailer without another word. She hadn't even glanced at Cheéte, who looked like Sasquatch.

Cheéte said, "No coffee. All I want is sleep." He dragged his feet to his bedroom and closed the door behind him.

"He'll sleep in his ghillie suit," Josh said, his mind churning with thoughts of Aya. Her body language was setting off alarms. Josh was accustomed to her being friendly and full of energy. Something wasn't right. In fact, he suspected something was horribly wrong.

Josh took Mia's hand and towed her into the master bedroom. The attached bathroom held a hot tub for two next to a roomy walk-in shower.

Mia's carnal smile suggested what she was thinking.

While he was turning on the shower, she was wiggling out of her pants. When she stepped out of what now looked like a pile of dirty rags, she was naked from the waist down. She hadn't been wearing any clothing under her factory-produced ghillie suit.

Turning toward the hot tub, he saw Mia pulling the suit's shirt over her head, revealing smooth dark skin, toned abs, slender arms, and firm breasts. For an instant, he was tempted to pull her into the shower, because it might be their last chance to make love. Every mission came with a high risk of death.

Instead, he turned on the hot tub's noisy bubblers and jets, and for good measure flushed the toilet. Done, he turned in the tight space and faced a naked, waiting Mia, and her eyes said it all. *What the hell are you doing? We can't fuck in the hot tub and shower at the same time, and why are you still dressed?*

"Did you irritate Aya?" he said.

"Why would I do that?" she replied with a snap. "I love Aya. She's like family." Without warning, she grabbed his crotch. Discovering his erection, she fumbled with his pants to remove them.

"Stop!" Josh placed both hands on her shoulders and gently pushed her away from him. "This is serious. Have you noticed anything different about Aya's behavior since you arrived in Venezuela?"

Mia's expression changed to uncertainty. She shrugged. "That's how she's been since we got here. I thought it was the humidity and heat. If something is bothering her, she knows I'm willing to listen and help, but it's up to her. I'm never intrusive."

"We don't have time to play around. Please get dressed before I change my mind." He shook his head. "Jeez, I must be crazy." Turning away from the temptation Mia offered, Josh found his encrypted satellite phone in one of the ghillie suit pockets, pulled it out, and activated it.

Mia's eyes went to the phone. "Merde," she said and covered her mouth with a hand, her eyes growing wider. When Josh used that thing, it was almost always serious.

Stepping back to the pile of cloth on the floor, she pulled

the pants on first. "What's going on? You're scaring me." She reached for the shirt.

"I'm calling France to talk to our friend in the DGES," he replied.

"Why call him?"

The DGES was France's most powerful intelligence agency, known as the Director General for External Security, that had several thousand agents and an unknown number of voluntary spies, French nationals who lived abroad and did not appear on the government's list of civil servants.

Josh was calling a man high in the DGES's Security Intelligence Service. It helped that his three adolescent children were on Mia's most-devoted fan list. She'd learned from Lady Gaga, Beyoncé, and Taylor Swift that you treated this group special. When she held a concert in Paris or released a new documentary, they always offered them the best seats in the house, completely free.

"I want him to check on Aya's granddaughters and make sure they're home and safe. His people will be discreet, and no one will notice."

It took a moment for Mia to figure out what he meant. "This Strawman you are hunting would do something so horrible that he would use children like that?"

"He's known for his dirty tricks. All of his operations with the CIA were covert and off the books for that reason. When we questioned his team in Montana, we learned that using children as hostages to get a parent to do what he wants is one of his favorite tactics, that and throwing his victims out of planes without parachutes."

Alarmed, Mia turned to leave the trailer. "I must go to Aya and offer her my comfort and support."

Before she could take a step, Josh's arm shot out and grabbed her shoulder.

"What?" she asked, turning to meet his eyes.

"You can't do that. I think Damien Bran knows about your rescue operation and has infiltrated your film crew. He's setting a trap to grab you and sell you to someone like that Russian who offered a half million to make you his sex slave when you were fourteen. Now that you are a popular singer in the EU and South America, your value has gone way up. The Strawman never recruits just one victim when he infiltrates an organization. There will be at least three if not more, and for sure they bugged this trailer. There's probably a hidden camera in your bedroom. Since you sleep naked, he was watching."

"No," she said, her eyes full of shock. "None of my people would betray me."

"I agree when it comes to your bodyguards and the combat team, but not your film crew."

She shook her head. "Aya would never do that to me."

"She isn't being disloyal. If they kidnapped her granddaughters, she's doing what she can to save them. If you were her, would you let them die out of loyalty to your employer?"

She stopped shaking her head and chewed on her lower lip, staring at the floor and thinking.

"We are in Venezuela, Mia, one of the most dangerous countries in the world. Damien Bran has to be here with Maduro's approval, and I won't be surprised if Maduro profits from Bran's illegal sex trafficking enterprise. Maduro probably has a story ready for Venezuela's major newspapers to tell the world how you and your film crew were slaughtered by criminals and that all of your bodies were burned beyond recognition."

"Impossible," she said. "They would not dare to harm me and my people. I have fans here."

"Think again," he said. "Venezuela is a path to the United States for illegal drugs out of Columbia. The Cuntrera-Carunana Mafia owns hotels and businesses in Caracas and Valencia, and a ranch in Barinas near the Columbian border. We're in hot water that's going to boil, and my people are too far away to help. All we have is you, your twelve-man team, your three Israeli bodyguards, me, and Cheéte."

Looking like he'd bludgeoned her, Mia collapsed on the toilet seat and stared at the marble floor between her bare feet. While she thought, Josh flushed the toilet again and called Jean-Bernard in Paris, who picked up on the second ring. Josh explained what he suspected, and the French agent said he'd assign several of his best people to discreetly gather the information Josh wanted. Before Josh hung up, Jean said, "My children would hate me forever if I let anything happens to Mia. They love their père and mère, but they worship her. If you want support, I have assets in French Guiana that can reach you in a few hours."

Josh accepted the offer and gave Jean their GPS coordinates. "I'll call back with updates," he said.

"My people will be on the way to your location as soon as possible. Mia is a French treasure. France will do all that is possible to protect her."

"Don't forget that her film crew is all French nationals too," Josh said. "Is there any way for you to contact Juan Guaido and ask for his help?" Guaido was the opposition leader that wanted to replace Maduro as Venezuela's president.

"I will see," Jean replied.

It was early May, humid with heavy rain clouds moving in that were going to dump an inch of rain on the state of Amazonas. Most of the inhabitants of that state lived in the northwest corner of Puerto Ayacucho, the state's capital, almost two hundred miles from Bran's ranch. Josh had planned the assault to take place during the rainstorm. He ended the call.

"What are you thinking?" Mia asked.

"How were you going to transport the children you rescued out of this country?"

"The Brazilian Air Force promised to send one of their planes," she said. "They promised one to me."

"Let me guess," Josh said, smiling. "The Brazilian Air Force general in command of those planes is a fan of yours."

"Not him, his grandchildren, seven young girls ages ten to twenty, and they worship me. General Costa also supports my rescue organization. All of his grandchildren are beautiful, and so are his three daughters. When I was planning this operation, I called him, and he was more than willing to assist in the rescue."

When Josh had been with Delta Force, his team had worked with Costa once. The man's rank in Brazil was equal to a lieutenant-general in the U.S. Air Force. He was an honorable man and a competent general.

Josh noticed the communication bud in her right ear. He tapped his ear and asked, "Does that thing give you a direct link to your bodyguards and your strike team?"

She nodded.

"Contact them now and tell them what's happening. Your strike team must gather the film crew without revealing what's going on and start out on foot toward Brazil. Tell them not to let any of the film crew out of their sights and make sure they confiscate any mobile phones, letting no one make a call. They may have to get tough."

Mia activated her ear piece and started talking.

When she finished, Josh handed her his satellite phone. "Call General Costa and tell him that the schedule is being moved up. Explain the mess we're in and that we'll need his bird early tomorrow morning, not tomorrow night. That means we have to be in position and ready to hit Bran's ranch before dawn. That gives us less than four hours. Tell him procrastination will be lethal to you and everyone with you."

"He hates Maduro," she said, "and Brazil publicly supports the uprising against him but won't intervene militarily."

"This won't be an intervention," Josh replied. "It will be a rescue operation. When I was in Delta, I worked with him, and I know he has friends in Brazil's Special Operations Support Battalion."

Brazil had the second largest military in the Americas, including well-trained special forces units.

"I will find out." Mia took the satellite phone to make the call, but Josh stopped her.

"One more thing," he said. "I want your raptors to come with us. Have them prepped for some serious action. Don't go into detail. We do not know who might be listening." Mia had three Israeli female bodyguards who went everywhere with her when she was working or out in public. They were all former Mossad field agents, fearless and lethal.

"Why do you want them?" she asked.

"They're going to help us take the ranch, rescue the children, and hopefully grab the Strawman."

"You're crazy." Mia had an incredulous look on her face. "We can't take that ranch with only six people. I'm hoping you're wrong, and this will be a big joke we can laugh about later."

Josh shook his head. "I want to be wrong, but in a few minutes Jean-Bernard is going to call back and tell us Aya's two granddaughters haven't been to school for the last couple of weeks and her parents are also missing."

"Then we must wait for his call to make sure."

"We don't have time for that, Mia. Bran's people will attack your camp before dawn in about three or four hours."

"How do you know that?"

"It's what I'd do. For tactics, I know how he thinks, because I was trained to think the same way. When the Strawman arrives, your film location must be a ghost town. He'll think we're attempting to escape his trap and suspect one of his reluctant spies told you. His focus will be to find us between here and Brazil. Make the calls. The clock is ticking. While you're doing that, I'm going to wake up Cheéte and tell him to brew lots of coffee. Soon after your raptors arrive, we have to leave."

"This Bran's mind is out of control," she said.

"No," Josh replied. "He knows what he's doing, but he's evil and arrogant. That will be his downfall."

CHAPTER 4

AS THEY LEFT the trailer, Mia hooked arms with Josh. "I have a surprise for you," she said.

"Should I be worried?" Her surprises were never boring, even when dangerous.

"Wait and see." Mia's three Israeli bodyguards, Shani, Naomi, and Esther, had left the trailer earlier to make sure it was safe. Years ago, Josh had called them Mia's raptors, and the tag had stuck.

Mia's strike team had reacted fast rounding up the film crew and had headed south toward Brazil over an hour ago.

Once Esther gave the all clear, Shani took the lead through the empty camp with Mia, Josh, and Cheéte wearing their ghillie suits.

"What do you think the surprise is?" Cheéte asked Josh. "I'm hoping it has something to do with Shani."

All three of Mia's Israeli bodyguards had dark hair and complexions, but Shani stood out because of her gray eyes, high cheekbones, and dimples that appeared even when she wasn't smiling. All she had to do was speak.

Josh worked hard to suppress his laughter and to sound seriously judgmental at the same time. "You already have a wife and two girlfriends. Why do you want another one?"

"I can't help myself," Cheéte said. "It's in my DNA. I'm like an alpha lion that wants his own pride."

"You're not a lion." Josh couldn't see his friend's face, so he didn't know if he was being serious or not.

"I'm a Crow war chief, same thing."

"That thinking is so lame," Josh said. "There are no lions in Montana."

"There are cougars."

"Cougars are solitary animals. They avoid other cats except during courtship."

"That's me. I'm a solitary cougar, always on the prowl. Better than being known as The Badger."

"Cougars don't get married and don't help the females raise the cubs," Josh shot back, ignoring the dig about his Badger tag, fearless in battle, risking death at every opportunity.

"What can I say?" Cheéte replied. "I'm a woman magnet. What do you think my chances are with Shani?"

Shani was several yards in front, leading the way as they left the ghost town of tents and trailers and out into the open savanna. Naomi and Ester brought up the rear, spread out to cover both sides.

"Be careful, Cheéte," Mia said. "Shani is the jealous type. When a man earns her trust, he better be faithful, and you have already failed that test, even if she doesn't know it yet."

"Haven't you noticed how she's been checking me out?"

"You're still wearing your ghillie suit and look like a giant Sasquatch?" Josh said. "She hasn't seen your face yet."

"That hurt. What's wrong with my face? I'll bet she likes

older men who have milage on them, and I know how to treat women right."

Hidden behind her ghillie mask, Mia rolled her eyes. "You're right about her liking older men, but..."

They'd left the film camp's location behind. Shani was keeping them close to trees and brush and avoiding the savanna's wide-open spaces as much as possible. She held up a hand and stopped. She had her night-vision goggles down, and without saying a word she pointed southeast of their position and then kneeled to create a lower profile. The others copied her, activated their night vision gear, and looked in the direction she'd showed.

What they saw in the distance was an Austrian-made Pinzgauer high-mobility all-terrain vehicle parked behind a shield of trees and brush, and there were others on its far side. Venezuela's military had hundreds of them. Not counting the driver and co-driver, the all-wheel-drive vehicle could carry eight to twelve troops.

Shani pointed southwest. Their heads swiveled, and their night-vision gear revealed the green glow of the troops the vehicles had carried already moving toward Mia's deserted film camp.

Josh leaned closer to Mia and kept his voice low. "Is that the surprise?"

Her answer was an elbow jab in his side.

"I guess that means no." He grinned. Only God knew how much he'd missed Mia, and that thought triggered a twinge of guilt, followed by a vivid image of Rachel in her hospital bed trapped in the arms of Morpheus.

Mia's warm breath caressed his ear. "Your sixth sense was right again."

Shani glanced over her shoulder, capturing their attention.

Then she pointed north. Both Mia and Josh nodded. Shani led them through the brush and in the opposite direction, away from the troop carriers.

Mia's raptors carried suppressed 9mm Bullpup submachine guns with thirty round magazines behind the trigger group. That weapon could fire 750–950 rounds a minute on full auto. They each had ten extra magazines and a holstered Glock 19, a semi-automatic pistol used by Israeli Special commandoes. The girls also had a variety of throwing daggers and knives stowed from ankle to waist, forearm, and one thirteen-incher in a scabbard fitted against their spines below their necks.

With hardly a sound, they continued moving at a fast pace for another hour until Shani signaled another stop. Josh estimated they had to be at least five klicks from the film camp. Mia's strike team and film crew had been on foot moving south for over two hours, and Josh hoped they'd reached the Serranía de la Neblina National Park. Once in the park, they had over five thousand square miles to vanish in, and a lot of it was heavily forested. But the park also provided cover for drug traffickers and guerrilla groups.

Mia's three raptors waded into some thick brush and dragged branches out of the way, revealing a diesel-powered Toyota Hilux light truck that had been modified and painted to blend in with the local terrain. Even the tires had a camouflage pattern.

Mia held out a hand to introduce the Hilux. "That is the surprise."

Josh couldn't see her face hidden under her ghillie suit's mask, but he imagined her brilliant smile. "Did you know this truck has been used by ISIS and other Islamic terrorist groups so much it has become identified with them?"

"Of course," she said. "Just because ISIS is evil does not mean they are stupid. This is a sturdy and reliable truck. In fact, if we run into a military checkpoint, we can take advantage of the Hilux's reputation, and I'm betting your Strawman, this Damien Bran, knows my film crew didn't have one of these."

"Good," he replied. The Hilux had a custom-made mount for a belt-fed M240 machine gun fitted on a roll-bar behind the truck's cabin. They had replaced the normal headlights with infrared lamps to be used with night vision. All interior and exterior lights had been removed, and it had antennas for VHF, UHF, and satellite communications. The suspension had been upgraded, and they'd outfitted the truck with ballistic armor.

When Josh said nothing, Mia continued, "I know what you're thinking, that one of the reluctant spies has bugged this truck with a GPS tracker, but no one knows about it except for my raptors. It was delivered miles from our camp, and Naomi drove it to this location and hid it here. I didn't want anyone else to know because it was to be a surprise, so you and the ancient lion with you will not have to walk forty miles to reach the Strawman's ranch."

"Hey," Cheéte replied. "I'm not that old." They heard soft laughter from the Israelis.

"That's not the reason I'm concerned," Josh said. "We don't know the extent of Bran's surveillance abilities. On foot, we have a better chance of avoiding being detected. In the Toyota, we might lose that advantage." He sagged. "But I don't see that we have a choice. If we're going to have a chance of drawing Bran and his troops away from your people before they reach Brazil, we must hit that ranch sooner than later."

"Ah, yes," Mia said, "now I understand. We're going to be the decoy to help save my people. I like that."

Josh waved everyone toward the truck. "I want you and the raptors inside the cab where you'll be safer. Cheéte and I will ride in the open bed and man the M240 if we run into trouble."

Mia shook her head.

Now what? Josh thought. "What are you thinking?"

"The raptors will ride in the open bed, and I will be in the cab with you and your cougar that wants to be a lion."

The others had gathered around, and there was more snickering from Mia's bodyguards.

"I'll drive," Cheéte said.

"No!" Josh said.

"I second that," Mia said. "Josh told me about your driving skills, and I'm the better driver."

"I'll have you know no one has died in any of my accidents over the years. If you want to get there fast, I'm your man."

"Cheéte, how fast can you drive backward only using the rearview mirrors?" Mia asked.

"Ah...I don't know. Never did it. When I retreat, I turned the truck or car around so I could see where I'm going."

"And you still hit things," Josh said.

"I have learned defensive and evasive driving," Mia said. "Take off your mask and show us how far you can turn your neck to look over your shoulder. Neck pain is common in old lions."

Without taking his mask off, Cheéte said, "Okay, I surrender. No need to test me. I admit I can't turn my head as far as I did a few decades ago, and my eyes don't adjust to the dark like they did back then, but I want to ride with the girls."

"Not unless you look as sexy as they do," Mia said.

"Huh?" Cheéte watched the three tough Israeli women change their camo jackets for skimpy halter tops before climbing into the bed of the truck, which was just enough to reveal their incredibly sculpted upper bodies. If they ran into an enemy check point, no man would open fire with them looking like that, but that look might set off a stampede that turned into a gang rape, a high risk in a violent, crime-ridden, corrupt, authoritarian country like this one.

"What about the machine gun?" Josh asked. "Oh, I see." The girls turned the weapon so its length lined up with the roll bar and then covered the M240 with a form-fitting piece of canvas fastened with Velcro straps.

"Best camo I've ever seen." Cheéte couldn't take his eyes off the three drool-worthy young women and was glad they couldn't see him staring.

"Mia, I want to show you the route we're going to take." Josh spread a waterproof map on the hood of the Toyota, and she joined him.

Cheéte took advantage of the moment and stepped closer to the bed of the truck. He pulled off his mask and caught Shani's attention. The other two raptors noticed. "Why did you join the Mossad?" he asked.

Shani cocked her head at an angle and studied his face. From a lot of experience, Cheéte had learned that the safest path to a woman's heart was to get them to talk to you and not to flower them with praise of their beauty. It was a struggle for him to keep eye contact with her, because his eyes wanted to explore every square inch of her exposed body.

"Do you think the Mossad is not a place for women?"

From the tone of Shani's voice, he knew what she was thinking, that he assumed he was superior to her. "I'm a Native American, and in my tribe both men and women hold positions of leadership in the tribal council. Our traditional healers are both men and women. Crow women are very important and may earn high status. Some even become chiefs." He suppressed the desire to brag about how he'd become the tribe's war chief. When he'd been in Afghanistan with Josh during a raid with a squad of Recon Marines, he had achieved a series of war deeds, or coups, that earned him the honor.

If he hadn't outranked all the other Marines on that raid, he wouldn't have qualified.

To become a Crow war chief, the first one since Joe Medicine Crow in World War II, Cheéte had to accomplish four tests: touch a living enemy, steal one of the enemy's weapons and a horse, and successfully lead a war party. With the rest of his combat team as witnesses, he snuck into a Taliban camp, touched one of them with his coup stick and stole a knife and one of their horses while escaping. Once Cheéte accomplished all that and rejoined his team, they opened fire on the Taliban, killing most of them before withdrawing.

"Are you saying there is no glass ceiling among your people?" Shani asked.

"Is that why you joined the Mossad?" One skill Cheéte had learned was to answer a question with another one. The idea was to keep the woman he was interested in talking about herself.

"In the Mossad, they consider women among the best agents," she said.

"What caused you to leave that agency then?"

"You ask a lot of questions." It was obvious she didn't want to answer that one.

He nodded and kept his mouth shut. It was getting harder to maintain eye contact. Her body was a super magnet, but he'd been a Marine for almost half of his life and was confident the discipline he'd learned wouldn't fail him. If he was going to overcome the age barrier with this woman, he'd have to be persistent and always know what he'd say before he opened his mouth.

Startled, Cheéte turned when he heard what sounded like throats being cleared behind them. Both Josh and Mia were watching. How long had they been there? His face heated from the blood rushing into his head.

"It's time to go," Josh said. There was a ghost of a smile on Mia's lips that said she knew what he was up to.

Cheéte nodded and slipped his mask back on to hide his embarrassed expression. It was obvious Mia was a mind reader! Maybe he should never take his mask off around her. Now he knew why Josh loved her like he did. She was not only stunningly beautiful but also perceptive, smart, and tough. The perfect formula for his friend.

A moment later, they were racing northeast across the flat grassland, weaving to avoid trees and brush. It was a jolting ride, and the Israelis had to hang on to the roll bar.

The plan Josh had mapped out for Mia meant driving north and around the ranch's perimeter before turning south. Once they were on the other side of the ranch, as far from the film camp as possible, they'd hide the truck. Then the fun would begin.

CHAPTER 5

I'M TOO OLD for this, Aya Nicolet thought as she huddled with other members of the film crew. After hours of stumbling through the dark, they'd stopped in a rainforest clearing, miles from where they'd started. During the dark morning trek across the savanna from the camp and into the rainforest, she counted sixty-three in their group, and a dozen carried weapons.

When the armed men had roused the camp and gathered the film crew, she'd been half asleep and groggy. If she'd known what was going to happen, she would've taken some of her precious things with her, especially the photos and DVDs of her daughter's family that included Aya's two granddaughters. Just thinking about them filled her with guilty grief.

The armed men had been part of the film crew, but it was apparent now that they weren't. Instead, they were brutes who might work for her family's kidnappers.

Sore, exhausted, confused, hungry, thirsty, and filthy, she focused most of her misery on her two granddaughters. They were probably dead because of her, and she wanted to die too. To save them, she'd done exactly what the kidnappers wanted and spied on Mia, her employer, a woman Aya loved and respected. That treachery gave her another reason to die.

Aya hadn't seen Mia since the armed men had rounded up the film crew. She prayed her employer was better off than her. If Mia had been with this group, Aya would've confessed what she'd done and asked for forgiveness before they were all executed.

Hearing a noise from the sky, she looked and saw an armed helicopter with French military markings as it drifted into sight above them.

"Where did that come from?" she heard the film director ask.

One of the boom operators replied, "It must have come from French Guiana to rescue us from our tormentors." With a smirk, he glared at the silent armed men surrounding the film crew.

"If they fire on our captors, we'll also get hit," the director said.

Someone hidden in the thick rainforest at the northeast end of the clearing started shooting at them. Streams of tracer rounds reached out from that tree line and hit one of the armed men. Then a cameraman was hit, and his torso exploded in a bloody mist. People screamed and threw themselves on the ground. There was no place to run and hide. Time slowed as Aya sprawled flat in the dirt and weeds. Closing her eyes, she covered her ears and the back of her head with both hands and prayed to God for forgiveness.

She heard a barrage of deafening gunshots much closer. Aya looked and saw that the men who had forced them at gunpoint to leave the film camp were returning fire at their assailants.

Feeling the downdraft from the Eurocopter hovering above them, she rolled over and watched it turn ninety degrees until its nose was aimed at the spot where the unknown attackers were located. She gasped, and her heart leaped into her throat when the helicopter fired several rockets from two exterior pods mounted below and in front of the sliding side doors. Machine guns protruding from the small rectangular openings above the rocket pods also opened fire. The darkness vanished in bright flashes of blinding light and explosions, causing her to lose most of her vision and hearing until she only saw spots of light with a loud ringing in her head.

Her vision cleared enough to see another armed helicopter appearing above the clearing. It dropped to the ground like an elevator, but this one had Brazilian military markings. Behind it were others.

Confused, Aya didn't know who to trust. Nothing made sense.

What she didn't know was that France and Brazil had established a formal strategic alliance in 2008. Because of that, Brazil was very French-friendly. When Mia had called the Brazilian Air Force general, other calls followed from Brazil's leader to France's president. French Guiana was the only territory in the Americas still part of a European country, and France kept over two thousand troops stationed there.

Mere minutes after Josh had called Jean-Bernard in Paris, the French Air Force platoon stationed at the Felix Euboea Airport outside the coastal city of Cayenne in French Guiana had received orders and scrambled to comply. In the military, the troops didn't question orders, and soon that Eurocopter was airborne and skimming the treetops to stay below radar as they flew toward Brazil. Once over the border, the helicopter turned west, following the border past

Suriname and Guyana to Venezuela before entering that country's airspace.

Aya jerked in fear when one man who had treated them like sheep started prodding them to move out of the way, to make room for the helicopters to land. *Has the world gone mad?* she thought.

The armed men had confiscated their mobile phones back at the camp when this nightmare started. She'd seen the film director attempt to make a call with his satellite phone, and Aya thought the armed men were going to shoot him, but after a warning the director had dropped the phone as ordered and held his hands above his head to show they were empty. It was obvious the director had been terrified, because he'd wet his pants.

Then everyone in the film crew had been searched as if they were criminals. Burning with humiliation and weeping, Aya had to strip. The man who searched her groped under her underwear with probing fingers. A few members of the film crew became hysterical, and another armed man gave those people shots with a syringe that calmed them down. During the relentless march from the camp through the night, those film crew members had stumbled along with numb expressions and glazed eyes, needing help from the others to keep moving.

Aya knew nothing about her employer's past before her life as a French songwriter, singer, and producer of documentaries. Aya didn't know that her employer funded and operated a secret global organization that rescued trafficked sex slaves. She didn't know that Mia had been born in Haiti and had been one of those sex slaves when she was fourteen or that Josh and Cheéte had saved her and others from a horrible fate.

"You," one of the armed men shouted at her, "get on that one." He pointed at one of the Brazilian Eurocopters that other members of the film crew were already boarding. Dazed, Aya stumbled toward the open doorway and thought once that helicopter was high in the air, she'd end her misery by jumping out and letting the fall kill her. After what she'd done, she didn't deserve to live.

A man inside the helicopter dressed in a Brazilian Air Force field uniform with his head covered by a flight helmet helped her climb inside the cabin. There were benches on both sides, and the only open spaces were near the rear. The Brazilian pointed at a spot, and she sat there. Once the cabin was full, the sliding door was closed.

Aya stood and watched carefully so she'd know how to open that door when the time came to pay the price for her disloyalty. Then she sat and buried her face in her hands and let her pain and guilt out in a flood of tears and racking sobs. She felt an arm drape itself across her shoulders to comfort her, but she didn't care.

CHAPTER 6

JOSH DIDN'T LIKE what he saw. Damien Bran's compound was surrounded by apparent killing fields. From where they were concealed, they had to cross about a hundred yards of open space to reach the nearest building, and surveillance cameras monitored that area.

"The children are in that outbuilding," Esther said as she indicated the largest structure, a barn about fourteen feet high. She was using a see-through-wall thermal-imaging camera attached to a smartphone. Although the camera worked through thermal energy, an app transformed what it saw into a visible image on the phone's screen. A shotgun microphone with help from another app allowed them to hear what was going on inside the building, all labored breathing and occasional moans.

The see-through app allowed them to see that the children had been crammed in tiny cages with legs folded against chests, heads jammed between knees, and no room to move. Their arms were also restrained behind their bowed backs.

"The men who did that are monsters," Esther whispered.

"A world that allows such wickedness is the reason I don't want children," Mia added.

As former Mossad Kidon agents, Mia's Israeli bodyguards were highly skilled, each one an expert assassin. But that wasn't all. Shani was a bomb-disposal specialist. Naomi was a sniper as good as they came. Esther was a tech genius. She'd programmed the apps that enhanced the camera and mike.

On the far side of the target building, Bran's house was surrounded by a wraparound covered porch. While the house Josh grew up in looked similar, Bran's was a third the size. All the roofs were covered with overlapping, wavy sheets of tin, the type that made a lot of thundering noise when it rained.

Apparently, the house was built about three feet off the ground on a sturdy foundation of large cement blocks. Knowing Damien as he did, there was probably a basement beneath the single-story residence. His underground bunker would have an escape tunnel.

While Josh studied the buildings, he thought about the oath he'd taken as an officer in the military to defend the U.S. Constitution against all foreign and domestic enemies.

Damien Bran also took that oath when he became a CIA agent almost fifty years earlier. Still, he'd demonstrated repeatedly over his career, and even after he'd retired, that he couldn't be trusted. Bran should've been arrested for his crimes, but it was apparent that someone higher up was enabling and protecting him.

The Department of Justice was supposed to investigate and prosecute the Constitutional violations of federal employees like Bran. If found guilty, it was a felony conviction. But establishing the intent required proof beyond a reasonable doubt that the bad guy knew what he was doing, knew it was wrong and against the law, and did it anyway. Everything the CIA did was monitored by several government agencies, but in Bran's case they'd apparently ignored him. Why? The answer was above his pay grade.

"What are we waiting for?" Mia asked, interrupting Josh's rambling thoughts. She stood. Without hesitation, both Esther and Josh pulled her back to the ground.

"What?" Mia asked as she turned to look at each one.

"We don't know all the risks yet," Josh said.

"Correct," Esther added. "It's too dangerous to proceed without knowing what is between us and the barn. There's also this." She scrolled back to another saved image on her smartphone and enlarged the picture to show the equipment in the main house. She indicated one item. "That is a night-vision scope. They are well equipped, and we must take all precautions."

"I don't understand," Mia said, staring at Josh. "There's no one in the barn guarding those children. Even though the main house and the bunkhouse are occupied, none of those buildings have a line-of-sight between us and that barn. Even their night-vision things can't see us here. Those children are in cages built to hold small animals. I want to liberate them now."

"It's what we don't know that we must discover." Esther's voice made Mia turn to look at her again.

"And we can't afford to assume no one is in the barn guarding them," Josh said. "Bran is a tricky bastard. When he was still with the agency, his trademark was killing people from a distance, and not with a sniper rifle. Even that method was too close for him. He usually was long gone before his target died from a lethal dose of poison or explosives blew them up. Until we cross that open space between us and our objective, we won't know all the risks."

"Then what are we waiting for?" Mia asked. "How long will it to take to gather this information before we can free those children?"

Josh took out his waterproof map, unfolded it, turned it to the blank side, and spread it on the ground. The others crawled closer to watch until they were in a circle. The back of the map offered an empty white space. He used an erasable marker to map out the ranch buildings. Changing from black to red, he placed four large Xs on the map and drew lines between them. Finally, he used green to mark their current location. He then wrote a name beside each X: Mia, Cheéte, Esther, and Naomi.

He looked in turn at the four faces that had their names next to an X. "Those four locations will allow you to pin down anyone inside an occupied building while covering each other. Never stop scanning with your night-vision gear. Since the walls of those buildings are all cinder blocks, focus on the windows and doors. Don't shoot at the blocks. Esther's camera revealed that the hollow spaces are filled with something, maybe sand. No one on this ranch except the kids in those cages is innocent. That means when you squeeze your trigger, every shot counts. Shoot to kill."

"Why is my name by one of those X's?" Mia asked. "I'm not afraid of taking risks. You all know I don't like to be treated like I'm fragile. I'm as tough and dedicated as anyone here."

Esther put an arm across Mia's back and squeezed to gain her attention. "None of us think you're a coward, Mia," she said. "But if there are traps between us and that barn, and probably inside it too, Josh and Shani are the best ones to deal with them."

"Like what?" Mia asked.

"Like explosives, poisonous stakes, or venomous snakes hidden in holes you don't know are there until you step in one," Cheéte said. "One misstep and you're dead."

Mia shuddered. "Seriously, I think you're just trying to scare me!" She jabbed her index finger toward the cluster of buildings. "While we've been doing nothing, I've seen several of Bran's men moving about between the other buildings. If there were traps out there, they wouldn't be walking around freely like that."

"Did you notice that the few men we saw doing that stayed away from our objective and never left the compound?" Josh said. "I watched one of them take the long way around his bunkhouse to reach the mess hall. If he'd taken the shortest path, he would've shaved off a few hundred feet. He went the long way to avoid going near the barn holding the children."

Mia's eyes swiveled to the others, who all nodded. She looked embarrassed. "I'm sorry," she said. "I didn't notice."

"There's nothing to be sorry about," Naomi said. "You have dedicated yourself to learning martial arts, defensive driving, and to become a sniper, but the one thing you don't have is the combat experience we've had in dangerous situations like this one."

"That's not an excuse," Mia replied, breaking eye contact and staring into the distance.

"Mia, you're being too hard on yourself," Josh said, and he saw the restrained tears moistening her eyes. He knew her better than most. She was eager and depressed at the same time. She lived for moments like this—to free children destined for sexual slavery. "I know you've killed no one before, but this time you might have to." He tapped her X on the map. "From that position, you cover part of the bunkhouse the other three can't see from their locations. Do you have any doubts that might stop you from taking a life?"

He watched her sense of despair vanish to be replaced by resolve. "No!" she replied. "Those bastards deserve to die."

"Good!" Josh looked around the tight circle of faces. "Any problems with this plan of action?"

No one said a word.

"Shani and I will wait until we hear that you four are all on your spots, and then we'll cross no-man's-land to reach the objective. I suspect the approach to this side of the barn will be the most dangerous area to cross, but we have little choice. To approach the barn from any other direction would mean we'd be exposing ourselves to shooters from inside the other buildings."

Shani added, "It's possible there's a hidden shooter we haven't discovered watching this side of the barn. He might be out there, away from the buildings." She pointed at the area behind them. "He could be in any of those big trees we can see from here. If we can see the tree, he might see us once we're in the open."

Josh nodded. "It's what I'd do. There's a good chance someone's out there. That's why I want Mia to give Shani her ghillie suit. You two are about the same size." He turned to study the open space between them and the barn. "That's a long crawl, and we have no choice but to take our time doing it. The faster we move, the higher the risk we'll be spotted and shot at if there's a sniper."

"We should go one at a time," Shani said, "and I'll go first. I'll use Esther's electronic-nose device to detect any hidden explosives between this location and the barn. Once I reach the objective and find cover from those trees behind us, Josh will follow my slug trail. Then we'll find another way to enter the barn. We won't use any of the doors. We'll cut through a wall or climb up and cut our way through the tin roof. We have everything we need to get inside that building and search for any traps before we release anyone from those cages."

Mia whispered she'd do it, but her eyes said something else. She frowned. "I don't like it, but I understand. I promise to do nothing stupid that will get us all killed."

"Mia, no one thinks you're going to do something stupid," Josh said. "But sometimes your courage causes you to take unnecessary risks." He leaned closer and whispered in her ear, "I'm selfish. I love you and don't want to lose you."

"If you lose me, you still have your other lover, your wife Rachel."

Josh thought he'd heard some hurt in her voice. He grinned. "Seriously, you're talking about your secret sister who's still in a coma. If something happens to me and you make it out of here alive, I want you to watch over her, okay?"

Without breaking eye contact, a long silence followed until Mia nodded. "You can count on me," she finally said.

CHAPTER 7

"CERCHIAMO IL CAMPO e non troviamo nessuno," one of Bran's louts said in horrible Italian, meaning "we search camp and find no one." His men's English was worse.

Hearing that, Bran wanted to breathe fire on someone. He'd taken a dozen of his men and a company of Venezuela's National Bolivarian Militia on the raid of the French whore's film camp. A Russian, his biggest client, would pay a lot of rubles to own or get rid of that bitch.

Now Bran was using Mia's trailer as his headquarters. "I want to know where they went. No excuses!" He replied in a rush of fluent Italian and didn't care if the man understood. He then sipped wine from a long-stemmed Waterford Crystal Balloon glass filled with 2009 Chateau Lafitte Rothschild. There was an excellent selection of quality wines in the trailer. He'd searched Google and discovered the most expensive one on the list, opening it first.

Only the best was good enough for him, and the French slut he hunted had provided the treat. If he couldn't catch her, at least he had her wine. He was also considering taking her trailer back to the ranch since it was more comfortable than the house he lived in.

Bran held up the glass and studied the shifting colors of the liquor as he turned the cut-crystal goblet between his fingers. "Did you know this wine is a blend of Cabernet Sauvignon, Merlot, and Petit Verdot?"

His bully boy's expression went blank.

Bran stared at his brown monkey man and thought Trump was right when he said countries like this were shitholes. Taking a sip, he smiled. Most of his men were stupid, but they knew how to torture people, rape, and pillage. That was why he'd hired them, that and they came cheap.

In the 1970s, when he'd joined the CIA, his mentor had been a former Nazi who'd worked for Hitler at the infamous Wannsee Institute, the SS think tank involved in planning the Final Solution that exterminated over seventeen million people. The CIA hired hundreds of these Germans guilty of war crimes, helping them avoid the Nuremberg Trials.

Damien Bran had retired from the CIA the day before President Barack Obama took the oath of office. He'd left because he wasn't about to work for a government led by Islam's Trojan Horse. He agreed with Trump that Obama wasn't eligible to be president.

Since his failed operation in San Francisco a few months back, he'd been hiding in Venezuela, where no one called him Strawman, an alias he hated. Still, Bran was proud of his decades as a relentless and efficient CIA agent.

One of Trump's lawyers had recently contacted Bran. During the call, the man said the president was thinking of pardoning Bran, avoiding Senate confirmation, and appointing him as the senior official performing the duties of the director of the CIA. That lawyer said, "President Trump wants someone he trusts in that position before the 2020 election, a true patriot loyal to him."

Bran focused on the dumb third-world monkey standing in front of him and said, "Get out of here and discover where they went. One of our drones checked this site late yesterday afternoon, and the place was still occupied. That many people do not vanish without a trace."

His goon fled the trailer.

"We will catch them," Captain Thiago said. He was a Maduro loyalist and the commander of the militia company. The captain was sitting in a recliner outside the kitchen area, sipping from a cold liter bottle of Polar, Venezuela's most popular beer. He always had a cooler packed with bottles and chipped ice.

"And how do you plan to accomplish that, Captain?" Bran asked.

"As soon as we found the camp empty, I sent patrols out and called for an Air Force helicopter to help with the search. It will arrive soon."

"All of their vehicles are here," Bran said. "That means they're on foot and can't have gone far."

"That depends on when they left," Captain Thiago replied. "It's been over ten hours since the last drone flyover. If they went south toward Brazil, all they needed was a few hours to reach the Serrania de la Neblina National Park, where they will have over 13,000 square kilometers of rainforest and mountains to hide in. Even with our troops patrolling the border, they still might escape. It's rugged terrain with much cover."

"We must catch them before they reach the border," Bran replied.

"Easy to say, my friend," Thiago said. "On the other side

of the border, the rainforest continues in Brazil, and it covers an even larger area. That's a lot of difficult territory to search. They could be anywhere."

"I will not accept that excuse, Captain," Bran replied.

The captain shrugged and took another long drag from his chilled beer. His portable radio purred, and he answered. When he signed off, he turned to Bran and said, "One of my patrols found a fresh trail."

Damien Bran left the stool he was sitting on and started pacing behind the kitchen's island counter. He wanted to catch this slut. His stomach was a boiling pot because of her.

The leaders of several Russian mafia groups wanted the French blister and her organization eliminated. Mia and her people were finding and freeing too many kidnapped women and children from all over the world, property that wasn't theirs to take. That's why Bran preferred being a middleman who concentrated on children between ten and fifteen. His network collected them from all over South America. And now that Charles Tweet was in jail, the Russians had become his biggest clients.

The global sex industry was always hungry. Of the 600,000-800,000 slaves trafficked across international borders annually, most were females and children. A child might be sent to the local market to buy milk and vanish. Since many only survived a few years, that created a never-ending demand for replacements. This French singer and her group's success were generating even more business for him. Still, this French woman was worth a fantastic amount of money from the Russian mafia.

Thanks to the years he'd spent as a CIA field agent, Bran knew a wealthy Russian mob boss willing to pay almost forty million rubles for her. Once she was in the oligarch's possession, she'd vanish without a trace. Instead of collecting art, fast cars, and yachts, this billionaire bought beautiful women and kept them on a remote private island in the Indian ocean. The only way in and out was by air or by boat. It was a luxurious prison built to feed the lust of one very wealthy man who thought, like Bran, that women were things to use and throw away. When the Russian lost interest in one of his sex toys, Bran knew he fed them to the sharks surrounding his island. Watching them struggle and scream as they were being tossed overboard excited the man. The one time Bran had witnessed this, he'd been stimulated too.

"How did this French woman discover we were coming?" Thiago asked. "The leak came not from my troops. None of them knew that this film camp was our target. They thought we were searching for criminals not loyal to President Maduro. We have been doing a lot of that lately along the border with Brazil."

Bran stopped pacing and stared at the ceiling in thought. Then his head came around, and he made eye contact with the captain. "I had two spies in the camp, and one of them placed a call to me a few hours ago. Before we talked, the call was lost. My other spy was an old woman." He waved a hand at the surrounding room. "Her job was to cook and keep this trailer clean. I had her plant several hidden cameras in the trailer, but they stopped working last night. I think the French whore's Israeli bodyguards found them. And I suspect this old woman was the one who warned her boss. The other spy was easy to buy, but I used another method to recruit the old hag."

"A bribe or blackmail?" the captain asked.

Bran shook his head. "No, terror, fear, and despair. I had her two granddaughters kidnapped. Most of the time that works much better. This time I think it failed. No matter, those children will be sold to the highest bidder and end up working in some bordello in Russia, China, or India."

"You said the disconnected call was several hours ago. If that's when they left, they might have reached the rainforest and are that much closer to Brazil." The captain's phone throbbed again. He picked up, listened, and grunted several times.

As soon as he disconnected, Bran said, "Good news, I hope."

"One of my patrols found the group we were hunting, but my men had to retreat when a French military helicopter arrived and opened fire on them. Then Brazilian Air Force helicopters carried them across the border."

Bran hated the idea of telling his Russian contact in Caracas that they'd lost Mia Belle-Chanson. He knew little about this French singer and actress. Still, French and Brazilian military helicopters sent to Venezuela to rescue her people revealed she had friends in high places. "Maybe the bitch wasn't with them. We'll keep looking until we've exhausted every possibility." Bran hated to lose, and someone was going to suffer horribly if he did.

This time it was Damien's phone that warbled, and when he picked up, his breathless ranch foreman said, "We're under attack, trapped in different buildings and can't escape. These people are very dangerous. Every time one of our men is stupid enough to peek through a window or open a door an inch, they're shot at, and some were killed or wounded. What do we do?"

Bran had left two-dozen men to guard the ranch and his latest child harvest. A wicked grin split his thin, colorless lips. "Stay where you are and let them have the barn where we keep our livestock. If you followed my previous orders, none of my men are in that barn where the children are, right?"

"That is correct, but we risk losing this shipment if we can't defend the ranch."

"Well, we can't win all the time," Bran replied. "There will be other girls and boys to scoop up and sell. The world is full of them, all ready to be plucked like ripe fruit. Do as I say. Tell your men to stay put. Before we left, I had that barn booby-trapped. As soon as we finish this call, activate those explosives. You know what to do. I showed you before I left."

"Yes, sir."

As he hung up, Bran's acid reflux worsened. If this French slut was at the ranch and survived the explosions, she might be damaged. Then his Russian friend would lose interest in adding her to his beauty collection. Her dead head wasn't worth as much as her living body.

CHAPTER 8

SHANI STUMBLED AND weaved across the open space toward the barn. She was covered in blood. Wearing only a flesh-colored bikini, she looked nude.

"Ayuadame!" Help me. Her tone was loud, pleading, desperate. "Por Favor!" Please. She stumbled and fell to her knees with head hanging between her shoulders. Her body contorted like it was racked with pain. She sobbed and made sounds of desperation. Then she was on her feet again.

Josh and Mia, hidden in the brush at Mia's x-spot, held their breaths and watched as Shani took a few more unsteady steps before collapsing again. She held out one hand toward the barn as if she were reaching for salvation. "Ayadame!" she called. "Estoy muriendo." I'm dying. "Mis hijos son masacrados." My children are slaughtered. "Mi marido decapitado." My husband beheaded. "Los salvajes me quieren comer." The savages want to eat me. "Tener Compasión." Have mercy.

"I know she's faking it," Josh said, "but her acting is so

realistic I want to rush out there and save her." He placed a hand over his heart. "I'm ready for anything. Adrenaline is turning me into a cheetah."

Mia slipped one of her hands over Josh's free one and squeezed. "That is a good thing, yes?" She felt a flutter of jealousy, something she'd never felt before. She knew Josh only fell in love with strong women like her and Rachel. And Shani was a very strong, ruthless, and tough woman, someone she knew Josh admired. Shani was also beautiful in a rugged way.

"No," Josh said. "I fight better when I'm calm without a heart that's acting as if it's going to turn into a cruise missile and blast out of my chest."

If Bran had a sniper inside a blind in one of those distant tall trees watching Shani's performance, the sentry couldn't see that she was holding a small device, an electronic sniffer, in the palm of her left hand. It had been developed by scientists at Tel Aviv University, and Esther had improved it. The device was more sensitive and more reliable at detecting explosives than any trained dog.

What looked like the rambling, stumbling walk of a desperate, nude, bloody woman was really Shani avoiding the land mines she was discovering. doing all she could to leave an easy trail for Josh to follow.

"I think you should help her find an acting job," he said.

"If she can repeat this in front of a camera, she will end up being nominated for a French César Award for best supporting actress and win. Of course, it will have to be the correct role. Then I will have to find another bodyguard to replace her." She frowned. "It will not be easy to replace any of my raptors."

"Did you forget I recruited them for you?" Josh said.

"When the time comes, I'll find replacements too. Nothing lasts forever."

"All I want to do is rescue more trafficked children," Mia said.

They were so close to each other, their bodies touching, and Josh sensed Mia's emotional furnace. He knew the cause and said, "She's not my type."

"She is a genius," Mia said.

"I know, and so are you." He cleared a path through his ghillie suit's shaggy face mask and, leaning forward, pressing his mouth to hers, savoring the smooth heat of her lips.

A moment later, he drew back and asked, "What's on your lips? It tastes like heaven."

"Desert Light-Brown Lip Ink," she replied. "I only buy vegan products. What did you expect?"

"I didn't expect that. Let lips do what hands do." He kissed her again. *I shouldn't be doing this*, he thought, but it was so good. *Oh, hell, why not?*

When her body responded, he broke contact and leaned away from her. "I've always wanted to say that." His voice was husky. "Now I can check that off my bucket list before I join Shani out there."

Her sensual eyes were smoking when she asked, "Why are you quoting Shakespeare and kissing me like that at a time like this?"

"Who knows, this might be a comedy or a romance. I'm voting for romance."

"You are such a clown," Mia said, smiling.

Josh handed her his satellite phone. "Keep in touch with your Brazilian general. Once we have secured the barn, I'll let you know. That's when you will call and tell him it's safe to send in that C-130 he has orbiting close to the rainforest canopy on the other side of the border. If Lady Fortune is on our side, we should be out of here before Bran returns from the film camp with his people. We don't want to be here when that happens."

"How do you know he will return that fast?" she asked.

"Once the shooting starts, he'll be notified and know we're here. He won't waste time."

Then they watched Shani turn her face toward the night sky and shout. "Querido Dios." Dear God.

"That's my cue," Josh said, half-joking. "Hope I don't forget my lines."

Mia squeezed his left hand and shook it. "This is not a joking time."

"This is how I calm down in situations like this or I'll make a mistake out there. I can't let emotion make my decisions for me." He pointed at the building. "And we are on camera. There are four security cameras mounted under the barn's eaves, and someone is watching. Hopefully they'll be so focused on her they won't notice me."

He resisted the urge to kiss her again, and his expression turned serious. Searching the depths of her eyes, he said, "Never forget that I love you." Then he was gone, out in the open, moving like a snake with Shani's gear and weapons stuffed inside Mia's empty ghillie suit that was strapped to his back.

Mia shifted her gaze to the security cameras and whispered, "I hate you." After the shooting started, Cheéte was going to take out the cameras and the spotlights that turned the open space and this side of the barn into the day.

Mia pulled her sniper rifle closer, moved into the proper shooting position, and placed her sights on the building she was responsible for. When she spotted a face peering out of a window, she gently squeezed the trigger and saw the glass shatter and the head explode. Her stomach flip-flopped, and she struggled to control the sudden unexpected nausea. She'd killed someone for the first time.

Cheete's x-spot was to her right and in her line of sight, but she couldn't see him. In his ghillie suit, he had merged with the vegetation. He was not only watching the buildings he was responsible for, but he was using an invisible laser beam to discover a sniper in the trees a few hundred yards out. He'd said if there was a shooter out there, the hide should be about ten to fifteen feet off the ground.

Mia prayed that Cheéte's searching laser would soon find the glass lens of another scoped rifle. She wouldn't see the flash of the reflection, but Cheéte was wearing goggles with colored lenses that would, and if his laser beam hit the glass lens it would also damage that shooter's eyes.

She heard Cheéte fire but didn't know if he'd fired at a building or a tree. Then she heard a scattering of shots from Esther and Naomi's positions. Mia struggled to resist watching Josh and Shani and focused on the area she was responsible for. When she saw a door crack open an inch, she fired and hit the door dead center. The door slammed shut.

Before Shani reached the barn, Cheéte took out the cameras and the security lights. He didn't miss. After he shot out the last light, the open space plunged into inky darkness.

Mia turned her scoped rifle toward Esther's x-spot to her left and scanned the area beyond that location with her night-vision gear. When she didn't see anyone sneaking up behind Esther, she shifted to check Cheéte. They were doing the same for her.

It didn't take long before she was focused back on the building. She looked for heat signatures to reveal another target to take out.

Mia thought this was sort of fun and immediately had a guilt attack. Josh had said, "Killing someone who wants you dead is serious shit and not a movie or a video game. If you start having fun, that's a dangerous sign you might get carless. That can get you killed."

She didn't want that, so she forced a serious expression on her face and fought against the thrill she'd felt.

The satellite phone beside her vibrated. Without taking her eyes off her targets, she blindly groped for it with one hand and answered.

"Josh." Mia recognized the voice. It was Jean-Bernard in Paris, the French DGES agent.

"It's me," she said in a hushed tone.

"Mia?"

"Oui."

"We have found your housekeeper's two grandchildren with the man Josh thought was holding them," Jean replied. "Tell her the girls are safe."

"What about her daughter and son-in-law?"

"We have them too."

She said, "Dieu mercie." Thank god.

Cheéte fired another round. Then Mia saw a shadow of movement behind a window and fired as well.

Jean heard the shots and asked, "Is your status hazardous?"

"Très." Very.

"Help is on the way. Brazil sent a small team from its Rapid Action Force." The call disconnected.

"We're on the roof," she heard Josh say through her earpiece.

Elated, Mia thought the plan was working. Then, remembering something else Josh had said, she sobered. "Just when you least expect it, the best plans will blow up in your face and turn everything into shit. Never forget that. Take nothing for granted. Stay focused. We don't do this for thrills or glory. We're doing it to save lives."

Filling her lungs with a shuddering breath, Mia hunkered down and stared through her night-vision scope at the area behind Esther and then Cheéte before returning to her assigned targets. Josh had also said that during an operation, time might move with lightning speed or crawl like a worm. Right then, she sensed the seconds crawling like worms and worried it was taking too long.

"Stay focused," she said to herself and kept repeating that in her head as she covered her areas of responsibility. She itched to know what was going on inside the barn.

CHAPTER 9

IT WAS A half hour after Damien Bran had taken the call from his ranch and heard his people were under attack, trapped, and unable to fight back. A Russian-made Mil Mi-17 helicopter with its engine running was sitting near Mia's trailer.

Captain Thiago stood beside Bran as they watched a Ford F350 back under the front of Mia's forty-eight-foot-long travel trailer, linking it to the truck's hitch plate.

"Since it was her fault that our raid on her camp failed, I appreciate the French floozy donating her truck and trailer to make up for my losses," Bran said. "I must thank her as soon as the opportunity presents itself. That is if the cock-tease still has her head."

Thiago studied Bran's emotionless expression. "You baffle me, Senior Bran. Your ranch is under attack, yet you seem to care more for this trailer."

Bran's eyes were hidden behind reflective gold-lenses. His thin mouth twitched, reminding Thiago that snakes had no lips. The captain wanted to take a couple of steps away from the pale gringo, just in case he had a forked tongue and fangs. Once this operation was over and he returned home, he planned to go to his church and pray to Our Lady of Guadalupe for forgiveness.

"Why should I be concerned?" Bran didn't bother to look at Thiago.

"I don't understand."

Bran slipped off his Vuarnet Pilot Edge aviator sunglasses. Slowly, he swiveled his head to stare at Thiago. The haughty look in Bran's eyes reminded the captain how creepy this American was.

"Isn't it obvious, Captain? That helicopter only carries twenty-four troops, and you need every able-bodied man to rescue my Mucuchis. I love those dogs." He spread his arms wide until his body made the shape of the cross. "Look at me. I'm an old man. It would be a waste of space to include me on that chopper." He tapped the side of his head. "All I have left is my intelligence. I'm a genius for running covert operations, but as much as I hate to admit it, I have no brawn left."

The Mucuchi was a Venezuelan breed. They were descended from dogs introduced by the Spanish conquerors at the end of the 16th century as watchdogs and herders. The ability to herd cattle or sheep had been lost, but they were still excellent guard dogs, and Bran treasured them for that ability.

Bran had little use for people unless they were women, who had one purpose: to accommodate his sexual needs. After he'd been forced to flee the U.S. and leave his two beloved German shepherds behind with his useless wife in Minnesota, he'd adopted three aggressive Mucuchies. He didn't miss his wife but often thought about his shepherds.

That reminded Bran of Josh Kavanagh, the man he blamed for losing his CIA retirement pay and the dogs he'd been forced to leave behind. He resented the fact that when Josh was graduating from high school in 1994 Bran had already been serving his country for twenty-five years as a field agent in the CIA.

If time travel were possible, he'd go back and strangle Josh in his crib before he grew up and join the Marines. But first Bran would've forced the boy to watch as he used a rusty, single-edge razor blade to turn the boy into a eunuch. His experience in the field had taught him many creative ways to torture a prisoner and punish those who didn't do what he wanted.

Bran was an avid science fiction reader and had read several of his favorite books more than once, *Hold Back This Day* by Ward Kendall, *Bedford* by Ellen Williams, and *The Turner Diaries* by William Macdonald.

Macdonald's book was about a young white man who joined a white supremacist group called The Order that was launching terrorist attacks designed to incite a wider race war, something Bran often imagined doing.

Then, once his imaginary time travel op was successful, Bran's life in the altered future would return to its glory days when he literally did no wrong.

When he'd been with the CIA, the agency used national security to hide his justified brutality behind a top-secret label. He had no choice, because the libtards with their idiotic left-wing political views would never accept that kind of collateral damage. Those bleeding-hearts didn't understand that to protect capitalism innocent women and children who lived in shit-hole countries had to be sacrificed.

That reminded Bran why he loathed men like Kavanagh. Not because of what Josh had done to him but because that Tier 1 Operator was one of the few people on the planet he feared.

What kind of man in his right mind spent over twenty years of his life doing what Josh did? He'd started out as a Marine sniper. From there he'd become a Navy Seal. Years later, he'd left the Navy to join the Army's Green Berets before transferring to DELTA.

If it hadn't been for Josh's sister letting Danny Tweet rape her, he'd probably still be in the military as a full-bird colonel, and Bran would still run the CIA's counterintelligence center at the George Bush Center for Intelligence in Langley, Virginia. The billionaire's younger son should've killed the girl after he was done with her. That was what Bran would've done. It was stupid to let a victim survive. If you didn't want a potential problem to come back and bite you in the ass later, eliminate it.

Bran knew assassins who worked for Mexican-American drug cartels that dissolved their victim's bodies in chemicals, leaving no evidence behind. They used sodium hydroxide or potassium hydroxide, commonly known as lye. Heated to three hundred degrees, a lye solution turned a body into a tan liquid with the constancy of mineral oil in a few hours. It was an easy way to get rid of evidence that way. Bran had done it a few times over the years. Once the liquefied remains cooled, he'd poured them down the drain into the sewer. Problem solved.

For an instant, Bran wished Josh was in Venezuela and was his target instead of the French singer. Then he had second thoughts and changed his mind. If he knew Josh was here, he had to be honest with himself.

When he thought of how dangerous Kavanagh was, the waste in his bowels felt like it was turning to dry ice. No, he'd never go hunting for someone like Josh, and he was too frugal to pay professional assassins to do it for him.

Instead, he'd move to Argentina, where he had a few former Nazi friends his CIA mentor had introduced him to. Their families would help him disappear again. If Josh was in Venezuela hunting for him, Bran wouldn't be wasting his time taking the French cunt's truck and travel trailer and hunting for her, no matter how much she was worth to the Russian. Bran valued his own skin more than money.

Noticing Thiago's shocked expression, Bran left his brooding thoughts and shook his head. He wondered how long the captain had been watching him like that. "Don't be concerned, Captain. My Mucuchies are not your responsibility. They can take care of themselves, and I'll be following you on the ground once all of our troops have returned to this camp. Expect us to reach the ranch by noon or soon after. By then, we will be finished with this troublesome woman and the few people she has with her. Since we have verified that most of her film crew fled to Brazil, we have the advantage."

An interruption inside the camp distracted them. Two of Bran's men were fighting over a Blackmagic URSA Mini Pro, a six-thousand-dollar digital camera. It was a shoving match. The camera was on the ground in the dust, looking like it was going to get trampled. Their faces said they were going to swing fists soon.

Thiago was jolted when Bran bellowed. "Toss a coin to pick a winner. If you ignore me, both of you will be executed." Since Bran always talked in a dull voice, the captain hadn't expected that. It was as if Bran had flipped on a loud switch. Breathing hard, the two angry men stepped back from each other, and a third man slipped between them to toss a coin. The loser roared his displeasure and hurried off looking for more loot.

Bran was disappointed. The camp was being picked clean

like a homeless shelter's Thanksgiving turkey. There wouldn't be anything left to blow up. He turned back to Thiago and continued, "It's going to be worth your while to get there before me. Once you have the woman, I promise to share some of the money the Russian will pay for her. If you can't capture her alive, just cut off her head. It isn't worth as much as her alive, but there are other Russians who will pay me if we prove she's dead."

Thiago stood straighter. "I won't cut her head off. She's a woman. I respect women."

"Then you must have a weak stomach." Bran revealed a wicked grin. "No problem. I've already planned for that task. One of my men at the ranch will do it. He might rape her first, but that's okay. Don't get in his way. All you have to do is make sure he doesn't take the head to the Russian in Caracas and sell it for his own gain."

Thiago was surprised. "You don't trust your own man, but you trust me?"

"Of course. You're an honorable man loyal to President Maduro, and I also serve him. If you cheated me, that would be like stealing from your own president. You have a family, right?"

Thiago nodded. "Yes, a wife and five children." It took a moment before he realized what Bran was implying. He almost shuddered from the fear that rushed through him, but hid his reaction.

"And you love them, right?"

"Yes, doesn't every father love his children and their mother?"

Bran turned back to stare at his new trailer and slipped the sunglasses back on. "Goodbye, Captain. It's good that you love your family. I'll see you again when I reach the ranch with my men and the rest of your company."

Dismissed, Thiago hurried to the helicopter to join his twenty-three troops already on board. He should've felt insulted by Bran's disrespect but wasn't. That man had no soul. Just sharing the same air made the captain feel dirty, and he wanted to take a shower. Too bad he couldn't scrub his lungs out too.

CHAPTER 10

THE AIR INSIDE the barn was blistering and smelled of fecal matter and fear. From the beam where Josh squatted, he studied the spot to land when he jumped. His target was the top of a heavy-duty mesh pet crate holding one of the kidnaped teens. He estimated the distance to be fourteen feet from the beam to the cage.

He'd counted enough children in the barn for the C-130 transport to carry them out in one flight, with little room left over. Their only break had been the fact that Bran hadn't rigged the beams, joists, and rafters under the barn's roof with explosives.

After snipping two square holes through the tin roof to expose the interior of the barn, Shani had used the bomb-sniffing scanner to pinpoint the locations of all the explosives. Lying prone on the roof beside the hole with only his head hanging inside, Josh watched as she scampered back and forth on the rafters.

Every time she spotted a bomb location, Shani glanced his way and pointed. She'd wait for his nod, signaling he'd seen it too. It didn't take long to discover that there was a predictable pattern, that a perfectionist had rigged the explosives. The biggest, about five pounds of C-4, was attached to the double barn doors. The way that cube of plastic was rigged, once the door moved an inch or two, the explosive would blow.

The walls were rigged with one every meter. Black-coated electric wires ran through lag screw eyes screwed into wall studs. The wires were about two feet off the dirt floor, attached to fuses stuck in what looked like one-pound blocks of plastic explosives.

The barn was fifty-two feet long and thirty-six wide. He estimated there were three dozen blocks of C-4. *Jesus, Bran, why the overkill?* he thought. *You're a demented anal maniac!*

They hadn't been equipped to discover the wires from the outside. If they had cut through a wall instead of the roof, that would've triggered the bombs. If the explosion didn't kill them, the spray of splinter shrapnel from the barn's structure as it disintegrated and the roof collapsing would have shredded them. Every child would have been obliterated too.

Once Shani finished searching, they made eye contact again. The only piece of the bushy camouflaged suit they did not have on was the face masks. Shani nodded, giving him the okay, and Josh pushed off the beam and slid down the rope he'd rigged for the drop.

He was using a method known as an Australian Rappel, in which a six-foot section of rope had been wrapped twice around his waist and the snap link was attached to the center of the small of his back. To stop, all he had to do was raise the hand holding the waist rope to his chest.

Halfway down, he stopped and hovered. With an Uzi in the other hand, he moved in a lazy circle searching for targets, someone waiting to ambush them. Finished, he made eye contact with Shani again and nodded the all clear. She nodded back.

Because of all the explosives, they hadn't expected anyone to be inside to ambush them, but you took nothing for granted.

Shani was on another beam closer to the double barn doors. Before dropping, she put on her face mask. When she slipped off her beam, she didn't stop as he had. She slid all the way to her target cage and braked just as she reached it, so her feet barely contacted the top of the sturdy wire mesh. Then she gently lowered herself until she was perched on the cage, scanning the inside of the barn with her Uzi moving in tandem with her eyes.

The rule was to check twice just in case one of them missed something. When she finished her silent inspection, she nodded.

That was his signal to put on the face mask and drop the rest of the way. Moments later, he squatted on top of a cage, looking through the metal grid at the painfully bent back of a slender girl. She didn't have enough room to turn her head to see what had landed on her cramped prison cell. He heard her whimper, but some teens in their cages watched, their eyes glued to him or Shani.

He saw Shani place an index finger in a "stay quiet" gesture to where her lips were hidden inside the mask. She also held out her Uzi so the kids could see the weapon.

Josh did the same thing and made sure every eye watching him saw the gesture for silence and the weapon. Eyes that had been filled with misery and fear now reflected a spark of hope.

He scanned for surveillance cameras inside the barn and

counted ten. He knew Shani was doing the same. Every portion of the interior of the barn's floor area was under observation. There were no blind spots. If the cameras were hardwired and linked to a remote location, the watcher might trigger the explosives and blow up the barn.

If there was a trigger device and it was wireless, they were safe because the rest of the team was using jammers to block all the signals around the ranch buildings. There was only one frequency that wasn't jammed, the one linking the six of them together.

Finished counting cameras, Josh held out one hand for Shani to see. He flashed all the fingers and the thumb twice to show he'd counted ten. She replied with the same gesture, so they agreed.

He pointed to his right, showing he'd take out the five on that side of the barn. She nodded. The Uzis were overkill, so they used their automatic pistols and started shooting. Since they didn't miss, they only used ten rounds. Every bullet not wasted was a bullet that might save or end lives later. They knew the risks. Freeing these kids would not be easy or fast, and Bran might return in force.

Touching his right ear, Josh activated his earbud and throat mike and gave a brief report. When he finished, he said, "Mia, call your Brazilian general and tell him to send in that C-130 and any other available assets."

Shani was already moving across her row of cages toward the double barn doors, where she'd disarm the explosives there. Josh started at the back and worked his way to the front. Once the walls were clear, they'd both clear the aisles between the cages.

Shit, Josh thought. The path through the minefield was marked, but the kids wouldn't know that. They could use another person to escort them from the barn to Mia's location, the spot closest to the dirt airstrip where the C-130 would land. He had to trust Shani to solve that problem.

What they were doing seemed impossible, but the impossible had always been a challenge he welcomed. He'd never failed before, even if he always ended up injured. It was amazing how every time he was in a tough situation similar to this one all of his demons retreated into their caves and stopped howling. Sex offered some relief but didn't last as long. Dr. Tate had said that was why he was addicted to this kind of danger, to escape those relentless voices in his head, explaining why he only felt peace when he was closer to death.

Taking his time, Josh moved across the cages until he reached the back of the barn, stepped to the ground, and squatted near one of the visible bombs attached to the wall. Earlier, Shani had indicated there was one blast mine buried in front of each block of plastic explosives.

He opened a black-tactical butterfly knife and used the blade to scrape away the dirt, exposing a pressure plate where he expected it to be.

Once stepped on, seconds later, the mine detonated. Hollywood movies created a false concept that if you didn't lift your foot, you survived. Wrong. All it took was that one contact and boom, you lost at least one leg, if not both, and maybe your life.

After removing the dirt on top of and around the mine, he identified it as Russian made. A moment later, he had the mine out of the ground and unscrewed a plug in its side to reveal the detonator. He removed the firing pin, making that one safe.

With one down and more to go, he looked to see Shani's progress. She'd already cleared three blast mines and the explosives attached to the doors and had the first child out of one cage. They were huddled, talking. He couldn't hear them, but it was obvious she was telling the girl what her responsibility was going to be.

Damn, Shani was good.

He'd known her and the other two raptors longer than he'd known Mia. The Israelis were in their early forties, but they looked younger. Before meeting Mia, he thought maybe Shani would be the one because of the nonverbal language he'd detected between them during a joint operation in Iran.

By the time Josh had removed the detonator from the first block of C-4, the double barn doors were open, and Shani and the girl had slipped outside where he couldn't see them. Shani would show the girl the trail through the minefield.

Josh moved to his second blast mine.

He heard an aircraft, and it wasn't the C-130. It sounded like a chopper. He keyed his throat mike, "Mia, is that helicopter our or theirs?"

"It isn't ours. No one called me on your phone to let me know it was coming."

"Cheéte, take charge out there," Josh said. "If you guys can't identify the chopper, disable it."

"Will do," Cheéte replied. "Hey, everyone, shoot at the tail rotter. It's critical for stability. If we hit one blade and break it off, that will throw the craft into a spin. Once you gain the target, don't wait. Start shooting. If the thing keeps coming, aim for the cockpit and take out the pilot."

Josh keyed his mike. "If that thing is an armed transport with troops on board, we'll be outnumbered and outgunned. Don't miss."

"It's an armed transport!" Cheéte replied.

Finished with the second block of C-4, Josh moved to the

third blast mine. The chatter of machine guns and reports from other weapons revealed that Mia and the others had engaged the bird.

They were in trouble.

He quickly scanned all the cages with kids still in them. Fuck. He couldn't let what was happening outside distract him. He squatted and used his knife to dig up the next blast mine and noticed that Shani was back disarming explosives. And the girl she had instructed was taking three other kids out the door.

Josh had no choice. He had to remain calm and focused. One mistake and they'd all be dead.

CHAPTER 11

AYA NICOLET THOUGHT her two granddaughters had been murdered, and it was her fault. In a cowardly attempt to save them, she'd betrayed Mia, her employer, a young woman she respected and loved. Convinced that Mia was also dead because of her treachery, Aya wanted to end her life.

There were twenty-eight other refugees on board. Aya sat near the end of the bench farthest from the door near the tail of the sixty-four-foot-long helicopter.

After being rescued and airlifted out of Venezuela, the helicopter's doors had been closed. For what felt like forever, Aya stared at them, stressing out over how to get them open without being stopped. Then one of the crew members had turned off the chilly air conditioning and slid the doors open to let the outside air in, and she thanked God.

The Brazilian saw her watching and said, "We're over Brazil now. It's safer. No need to keep them closed."

She nodded and felt relief when he accepted her response with a smile. Now all she had to do was stand on aching, rubbery legs and walk between the people sitting on both sides of the narrow aisle to reach the opening. The forced march from the film camp to the clearing in the rainforest where they'd been rescued had been exhausting. But it would only take a few steps to reach it and step out into the sky. Without a parachute, death would arrive fast.

With her family and employer gone, Aya had no reason to live. Closing her eyes, she imagined the sweet faces of her two loving granddaughters, twelve and eight, and of her daughter and son-in-law. The kidnapper said that if she didn't do exactly what he demanded, the girls would suffer a fate worse than death.

What could be worse than death? She had thought and didn't want to know.

Trapped in Venezuela on location during the production of Mia's next film, Aya had no one she trusted to ask for help.

"Tell anyone," the voice on the phone had said, "and you will never see your family again. If you attempt to confide in Mia Belle-Chanson, we will know." His muffled, accented, raspy voice had sounded hideous, and it had become a fixture in her nightmares. Every time she fell asleep, she heard him again and awoke trembling and drenched in sweat. It had gotten so bad that she feared sleep, and exhaustion had become her constant companion, muddling her thoughts, causing her to contemplate suicide.

After all, Aya was Catholic, and she'd been raised to believe that suicide was one of the gravest sins a person can commit. When you took your life, you were bound to spend eternity in hell.

But didn't she deserve to suffer that fate forever?

The heat and humidly made it difficult to breathe, draining what little strength Aya had left. There was no difference between summer and winter in the Amazon Rainforest.

Without a dry season, it rained all year, and the high humidity made it feel hotter than hell. Her body and eyes felt heavy, but she fought the temptation to sleep. It didn't help that half of the film crew already slept while the other half kept yawning. Every time she saw someone yawn, another kilo added to her heavy eyelids.

The Brazilian military pilot flying the lead helicopter had led the flight of five Eurocopters low over the Rio Negro River to take advantage of the cooler air rising from the water. With the doors open, a warm, moist breeze flooded the compartment, and the fresher air helped Aya stay awake.

That river was the largest black-water river in the world, and it wasn't shallow. Its depth started about 66 feet and plunged to 330 feet at its deepest points.

The helicopter's firm, narrow bench hurt Aya's bottom. No matter how many times she shifted position, she couldn't find comfort. She missed the Divano Roma recliner in Mia's travel trailer that, as the household manager, she'd selected for her employer. Alone in the trailer after cleaning and cooking, she often took naps in that chair. If she'd been given a choice, that was where she wanted to take her last breath.

To end her life, she had to force her sluggish body to stand and walk to the nice crew member who helped her board the helicopter. She planned to make eye contact with him and pretend that she wanted to ask him a question. He had kind eyes. Maybe the man would treat her like his grandmother. When she reached him, she'd leap out of the helicopter before he stopped her.

The river reminded Aya of her family's annual trips to the magnificent beach at Biarritz on France's Basque coast. Her son-in-law, a financial adviser, loved surfing. While he was in the ocean with his favorite board, she'd accompanied her daughter and granddaughters on strolls along the beach toward Bidart. She remembered tamarisk trees, music, outdoor tables, tapas, and Champagne. Those memories caused a wave of depression and nausea to wash over her, because that perfect life was over. She liked her son-in-law. He'd always treated her nicely. Her daughter had been fortunate to find a man like that. Tears filled her eyes, and she used the back of her hands to sweep them away.

Another doubt surfaced. If she died, who'd remember them? Aya reached into one of her pants pockets, searching for a tissue to soak up her tears, and her fingers touched a tube of lip gloss, sending an electric shock filled with guilt up her arm. Chloe was the twelve-year-old, and the week before Aya had left for Venezuela the young girl wanted her grandmother to teach her about makeup. They'd gone shopping and bought two tubes of Summertime Peach Lip Gloss. Showing the girl how to use hers had been the last thing they'd done together. Aya promised that when she returned, eye shadow would be next.

Her resolve to die returned with a vengeance.

The Brazilian military Eurocopters were flying to the town of São Gabriel da Cachoeira, located one hundred and twenty-six miles south of Venezuela. With a cruising speed of one-hundred-and-seventy-seven mph, they'd reach their destination in less than an hour. The town had a population of about thirteen thousand, and most of them were Brazilian Native Indians. The town's non-Indian residents were mostly members of the Brazilian army. Surrounded by the Amazon Rainforest, the town could only be reached by boat along the river or by air to a small airport that had flights to and from Manaus, a city with a population of 2.5 million located over five hundred miles southeast along the river further into Brazil.

The monotonous drone of the helicopter's engine and the moist, warm air were like a tranquilizer. Aya felt her head sagging until her chin touched her chest. She was so tired; she ached. Ever since that first phone call from the kidnapper, she had not had one full night of sleep. If she allowed herself to fall asleep now, maybe she would die and never wake up. She had read once that sleep deprivation could kill you.

A half hour later, she said, "No!" Her head jerked up. She felt stupid for hoping that she might die in her sleep. It would not be that easy to pay the price for her sins. With an effort, she forced her reluctant body to stand. Feeling dizzy, she reached out and placed a hand on the bulkhead behind the hard bench that she had been sitting on.

The man next to her, one of the few who forced the film crew at gunpoint to evacuate the camp, looked at her. "Are you okay?" he asked in French.

"I feel sick." She held her free hand over her mouth like she was going to vomit. Taking a step, Aya moved closer to the open door and the kind-looking crewman near it. Her body felt like concrete even as her heart struggled to beat faster because, yes, she wanted to die, but she feared death. Those mixed emotions had released a flood of glucose into her bloodstream, giving her more strength.

Another doubt flashed through her mind, and then she took a second step. The crew member pointed toward the rear of the cabin, showing he wanted her to return to her seat and strap in. With her hand still over her mouth, she bent forward from the waist and made a loud gagging noise in her throat. She puffed out her cheeks as if her mouth was full and ready to erupt.

The few film crew members on the benches who were still awake tucked their feet under the benches while pressing back against the bulkhead to put more distance between them and Aya.

The crew member's expression revealed concern. He found a vomit bag and started toward her.

He now blocked her passage, and she couldn't let him stop her. She thought, *O Lord, Jesus Christ, Redeemer and Savior, forgive me for the sin I am about to commit, just as You forgave Peter's denial and those who crucified You.*

Desperate and fighting back tears, she turned her head to the side to hide the two fingers she stuck in her mouth, touching the roof at the back of her tongue to trigger her vomiting reflex.

Since her stomach was already twitchy, she turned her head and spewed like a flame thrower, hitting everyone in front of her. The crew member leaped back to avoid the cascade of greenish-yellow bile, but some of it splattered his boots and pants anyway. That set off a chain reaction as the others heaved, and Aya took advantage of the turmoil to rush forward and step through the open door and outside of the helicopter, where she felt herself drop like a log toward the dark water below.

The last thing she heard before hitting the water was a voice inside her head that said, "I have heard your prayer. I have seen your precious tears."

CHAPTER 12

"CHEÉTE, TAKE CHARGE out there," Josh said, which Mia heard through her earbud.

Then, as the helicopter appeared in the distance, Cheéte said, "Mia, when it's in range, shoot for the tail rotor."

When she first spotted the helicopter, it was miles out on the other side of the ranch buildings. She knew that even on a clear day, you rarely saw over twelve miles, and it was probably closer. She watched until it dropped out of sight. If it didn't land over there somewhere and didn't change course, she guessed it was going to cross over the barn holding the children. Once the helicopter cleared that structure, it would cross the mine field about thirty yards to her right.

"Mia, make sure you're using armor-piercing rounds," Cheéte said. "You have the best line of sight for the rotor, but you'll lose the advantage once the bird clears the barn. If you miss, it will move parallel to my position, and I'll target the pilot once it's over the minefield."

She didn't change magazines since the one in her rifle already held armor-piercing rounds. Mia tensed. She heard the aircraft's engine and rotor noise increasing as it closed the distance toward them like a grim reaper. Her eyes darted from the buildings she was watching to the open entrance of the barn. She saw the girl Shani had selected to help, escorting three other teens through the killing field toward her prone position in a shallow ditch.

The dirt Mia had excavated with her folding shovel had been piled and compacted in front of her, providing some protection from return fire. Her French sniper rifle rested on its bipod. It was a bolt-action firearm with a ten-round detachable box magazine. The 7.62 sniper round was heavier and more streamlined. If she hit anywhere inside that tail rotor, there was going to be some serious damage; the aircraft would crash.

After Mia's training by French military snipers, she'd performed several sold-out concerts in Canada. While there, she learned more from two of that country's top sharpshooters.

Her nerves were on edge as the thrumming of the helicopter's blades increased in volume as the aircraft drew closer. It was apparent now that it wouldn't land on the other side of the ranch buildings, and since the dirt airstrip was behind her location, she expected the target to appear any second.

When Naomi and Esther started shooting from their forward positions, Mia felt her stomach flip-flop, and her body quivered when heavier caliber machine guns from the helicopter returned fire. Naomi and Esther were using smaller 5.56x45mm cartridges from their Israeli bullpup assault rifles. She prayed that her two raptors survived uninjured.

Her eyes widened in shock as she realized the four teenagers were only halfway through the minefield, and once the helicopter cleared the barn, its machine gunners would spot them. Those children didn't stand a chance. Mia's heart thudded like a jackhammer.

Shifting her gaze back to the barn's roof, Mia settled the crosshairs of the telescopic sight on the spot where she guessed the helicopter was going to appear. If she was off too much, she might not have enough time to shift her aim. Only Cheéte had another sniper rifle, and it fired a larger round, but from his position he wouldn't have a clear shot at the target until it was too late. The kids would be dead, and she'd be next.

I love you, Josh, she thought and then fought back tears that threatened to blur her vision. The first time Josh had asked her to marry him, she should've said yes. Then he wouldn't be married to Rachel, his childhood sweetheart. What a fool she'd been! The pain in his eyes when she had said no would haunt her for the rest of her life.

What am I doing? Now was not the time to examine her past mistakes. It was going to be up to her to save those teens and her own life. She breathed deeply. Once the helicopter appeared, she'd empty her lungs, hold them that way, and shoot between heartbeats as she'd been taught.

Then she heard the familiar sound of a C-130 behind her coming in low from Brazil for a landing on the hard-packed dirt airfield. The whine of the plane's four turboprop engines drowned out the helicopter. She'd been counting on the rotor noise to figure out where and when it was going to appear.

"Putain de merde!" she hissed in French. *Fucking shit!*

Taking control, she forced her heart to beat slower before the helicopter appeared exactly where she thought it would but closer to the roof. Without thinking, she shifted aim slightly, fired, and operated the bolt, ejecting the spent casing before loading the next round in time for a second shot.

JOSH AND SHANI were inside the barn, working the same wall. Between them, in that aisle, there were still several landmines and plastic explosives to disarm.

Finishing with another buried landmine and the pound of plastic explosive attached to the wall above it, he slid on his knees toward the next pair and froze when he heard a high-pitched command behind him. *"Pare! Pare! Pare!"*

That meant "stop" in Portuguese. He understood the language better than he spoke it.

Turning, he looked at the face of a lovely young girl trapped inside one of the animal cages. His first guess, she was twelve years old, and her dark skin was a match for Mia's. He noticed the child had twisted her head and shoulders into a painful position to see him.

Her vivid, pale-green hazel shaded eyes locked with his, and what he saw was like a red flag warning him that something horrible was about to happen if he moved another inch. A voice in his head said to ignore her and move on. Time was running out, and Mia was in danger. But his gut told him to heed this child's warning.

He nodded and saw relief flood her hypnotic eyes. Her beauty was probably what landed her in this barn inside a cage at such a young age. He didn't think his loathing of Damien Bran could get any worse, but seeing this child made Josh swear to God that he was going to hunt Bran down and take his time to make him pay before a fallen angel appeared to drag his rotten soul to hell.

He took a moment to come up with the Portuguese. *"Mostre-me." Show me.*

The child's eyes swiveled in the direction he'd been moving. His own eyes followed the path she was carving out, and he saw the thin, clear invisible monofilament fishing line running from below her cage to where it had been stapled to a wall stud closer to the ground. The monofilament was tangled in some strands from his ghillie suit. Without moving, he followed the fishing line toward the wall and then back to the girl's cage. The pressure he'd already put on the line had bent it. There was no telling what it would take to trigger the explosive that must be under her cage.

He slowly slid the leg that was in contact with the trip line back, but the line was stuck to his outfit. "Shit!" he said.

The girl replied, *"Pior que merda." Worse than shit.*

The matter-of-fact, light tone of her voice filled his belly with laughter. With an effort, he smothered it. Any movement might set the bomb off. *"Menina engracada,"* he said, as he mangled the words that meant funny girl. "Now is no time for humor," he added in Portuguese.

"Desculpa." But the sparkle in her eyes said she was anything but sorry. *"Voce e meu heroi."*

What an incredible girl, Josh thought. Then, with a twinge of mixed regret and guilt, he remembered the two young adults he'd had with Rachel who he hadn't known existed until the day he first met them the previous year. He was their father and had missed their entire childhood. If he ever had a child of his own to raise, he wanted that boy or girl to turn out like this one. Here she was, naked, locked in a cramped dog cage on her way to a life of abusive sexual slavery that often ended in a premature death, and she acted like it was nothing to be concerned about.

"What is it?" Shani asked as she disarmed another pair of explosives and moved closer.

"Stop!" he said, and she froze. He pointed at the stud where the fishing line started, following it with his finger to where it was tangled in his ghillie suit, and to the bottom of the cage where it vanished. "Bomb!"

"Fuck!" she said.

"My sentiments exactly," he replied.

Shani studied the two meters of space between them. "This is going to add more time to our work. Not good!"

"No shit!" Josh looked at the girl. "Do you speak any English?"

"Um Pouco."

"Your name?"

"Adrienne Odelette Avice," she said, pronouncing the French words without an accent even though it was apparent her first language was Portuguese.

"When we free you, your parents will be thrilled to get you back," he said.

A cascade of distasteful emotions flashed across her face. She said, "They *divórcio* me. *Minha desracado pai* selled me to *sequestradores*."

That jolted him, and he spoke before he had time to think. "If we survive, my girlfriend and I will protect you."

Shani cleared her throat. Josh and Adrienne looked and discovered that Shani was one more pair of explosives closer to them. "Now is not the time to be talking about protecting anyone," she said, repeating the sentence in flawless Portuguese.

"But...will...she...*aceitar* me?" Adrienne asked in broken English, her eyes glued to Josh.

Shani answered, "Yes, she will, and you will love her too. I have no doubts, but first we have to make it out of here alive and stay free."

"Obrigado," the child said.

Josh bit his upper lip to stifle a reply and waited for Shani to reach him and untangle the fishing line. Then they'd have to figure out how to disarm the explosive under the cage. There was no way Josh was going to leave this place without this girl. Once they were free and gone, he'd learn more about her.

Looking at her, he said, "Do you like music?" he asked, and Shani shot him a disapproving look that said, *Not now.*

Josh shrugged, and Shani frowned, shaking her head.

"I play *pai's* guitar singing in Sao Paulo," Adrienne replied. "It is how I get *turista* money to pay for surgery. I have YouTube page too. *Muitas* fans." She smiled, revealing white teeth. There was a slight gap between the two upper-center teeth, and her lower left canine was tucked behind the tooth to its right.

The word surgery stopped him. Does this poor child have cancer or something worse?

Sao Paulo was Brazil's biggest city with twenty million people. The music of São Paulo existed first on the streets. In particular, the metro stations where the buskers worked their craft, and if Adrienne had been surviving by busking, she might be good at it.

"Who is your favorite singer?" he asked.

"Okay," Shani said, startling Josh. "I will do all the work. Don't move!"

The raptor was so close he could smell her intoxicating musky scent. Merely inches away, their eyes met, and he couldn't help but stare at her lips.

She noticed. "Me too," she said. "Now let's find out what's hidden under this cage." Looking down and away from him, she used her largest knife to carve out the dirt from beneath it.

When they heard the crack of rifles before the rat-a-tat of

the helicopter's machine guns, Shani paused her digging and said, "They have engaged the bird." With one cheek pressed against the dirt floor to see under the cage, she continued digging, and soon said, "This is not good. It is a Russian thermobaric explosive device rigged like a grenade. The firing pin has almost been pulled out. It looks like we are a quarter-of-an-inch from death."

A fuel-air explosive device consists of a container of fuel, usually very toxic ethylene and propylene oxide, and two separate charges. The first explosive charge bursts open the container and disperses the fuel in a cloud that mixes with atmospheric oxygen. The cloud of fuel flows around objects and into the structure. The second charge detonates the cloud, creating a massive blast wave capable of destroying reinforced buildings. Anyone near the ignition point would be vaporized. The United States had developed this type of explosive and first used it in Vietnam.

Seeing their expressions, Adrienne asked, "Are we...ah, to die?"

Shani shrugged as if there was nothing to worry about, and said, "If we do, there will be no pain."

The girl said, "*Obrigado*. Me...no regrets."

"Well," Josh said, and both girls glanced at him, "I have regrets. So let's not blow up."

Shani sighed. "I'm very good at what I do, but you two are making me crazy. Now, shut up!"

Adrienne giggled, and Shani frowned. "You are both hopeless, just like Mia is sometimes." She groaned. "Oh, the headaches we are going to have protecting this new family. Maybe I should just tug this line and end it all now." She reached for the transparent monofilament.

"No!" Josh and Adrienne both said.

CHAPTER 13

DAMIEN BRAN WAS having trouble reading his foreman's text. At eighty-one, his eyes had trouble seeing small letters, and he didn't know he could increase the size of the print on the 8.3-inch iPad screen.

"When the shooting started, we lost all wireless communications," his foreman texted from the ranch. "None of our mobile phones work. We also lost the ability to dismantle the holding pen where we keep our livestock. We're still trapped inside the bunkhouse. If it wasn't for the underground cable, we wouldn't be able to call you." Bran believed in covering all bases. That explained why his ranch had cable, a satellite phone, a dish antenna, and wireless.

When communicating long distance, "livestock" was code for the kidnapped children being sold into the illegal sex industry. The word "dismantle" meant "destroy."

Bran never knew who might be listening. He also did not trust the dark web and thought encrypted calls unsafe, preferring situations he controlled. He'd do and say anything to achieve his goals. It was easy for him to fake being interested in what someone else had to say if it meant he'd get what he wanted.

Bran texted his foreman to repeat the message. Then Bran's thoughts traveled back decades to better times. In recent years, he'd been doing that a lot.

This time he thought about his long-dead mentor, teacher, and father-in-law, Reinhard Gehlen. If the Office of Strategic Services (OSS) had obeyed President Truman, Bran would've never met him. When Truman formally approved Operation Paperclip at the end of the war, he'd expressly forbidden the hiring of anyone like Gehlen, who had been a member of the Nazi Party and an active supporter of Nazi militarism.

After World War II, when Gehlen was forty-three, the OSS recruited him. About two years later in 1947, The National Security Act turned the OSS into the CIA. His Nazi father-in-law continued working with the CIA for over twenty years until 1968, when they forced him to retire. He died in '79.

When Bran was first assigned to Germany as an agent, meeting Gehlen turned out to be the best thing that ever happened to him.

Gehlen had been a major general in the German Wehrmacht and a close confidant of Hitler's. Because he'd been in charge of German Army intelligence on the Eastern Front, William Donovan, the head of the OSS, decided Gehlen was too important to reject, so he disobeyed Truman and not only recruited the man but took his entire Nazi intelligence organization.

By 1949, Gehlen's former Nazi spy network had grown to several thousand people working out of West Germany. His group made up almost a third of the CIA, effectively influencing the US agency to operate more like a Nazi organization.

Gehlen and Bran had many things in common, like

Evangelical Protestantism, which was the religious choice of most German and American white supremacists.

Bran had been born and raised in Mississippi. His father had been one of the Seven Furies in the Ku Klux Klan where they lived. By the time Bran turned fifteen, he'd taken part in dozens of cross-burnings and helped hang several black men. Bran's father often bragged about his part in the infamous lynching of Mary Turner in May 1918. Her mistake was publicly denying her murdered husband had been involved in the killing of Hampton Smith, an abusive white plantation owner. Bran's father led the mob that tied her ankles, hung her upside down from a tree, doused her in gasoline and motor oil, and set her on fire.

His father claimed he split open Mary's abdomen with a knife and watched her unborn baby, still attached to its umbilical cord, slide out and fall to the ground. Then he stomped and crushed the child.

They also riddled Mary's burned body with hundreds of bullets.

Damien had heard that story so many times; he almost believed he'd been there doing the stomping and shooting himself.

When he knew his foreman had sent another text, repeating what he had written the first time, Bran texted back, "Has Captain Thiago arrived?"

A moment later, his foreman replied, "I didn't know the captain was on his way."

Right, Bran thought, *I didn't tell him I was sending reinforcements, did I?* But he wasn't sure. Maybe he had. "You didn't need to know," he replied. "The good captain should arrive at the ranch by helicopter at any moment. Text back once he gets there."

"Yes, sir."

"And, before you call, tell him that if he finds this Mia Belle-Chanson woman alive, I want him to hold onto her until I arrive. Oh, what's happening inside our livestock pens?"

He'd just decided he was going to take this black woman's life the same way his father had killed Mary Turner in 1918. After all, the Russian in Caracas only needed to see Mia's head to verify she was dead. The challenge was to figure out a way to make sure her face didn't get burned beyond recognition, just the rest of her. And he didn't want to decapitate her before setting her on fire. If he did that, she wouldn't be alive to suffer. He wanted to do something worse to the French singer than what his father had done to Mary Turner.

He nodded. Yes, Gehlen and his father would be proud of him if he did that, but his men would have to move fast. To get it right, he'd have them practice on a few of the other children. His men would do all the work, but he'd light the match.

Bran stared at the phone as a moment of irritating silence slipped by. "Well, why haven't you told me what you saw happening in the livestock pens?"

Then, as if he'd heard Bran talking to himself, the foreman sent another text with the answer. "Two people wearing monkey suits cut their way through the roof and shot out all the security cameras. We didn't see who they were because we couldn't see their faces, sir."

The tone of insubordination he sensed in that text irritated Bran. When he'd been younger, he would've slapped the foreman around, but at his age that risked damaging his hand. The last time he had a physical, years ago, the doctor had warned him that his bones were becoming brittle because of his lifestyle choices.

"That's bullshit!" Bran shouted at the text and his memory of the doctor he'd seen years earlier.

"Sir, do you have any orders for us?" the foreman texted.

Feeling satisfaction, Bran replied, "Never mind. Just do what I told you."

The doctor had said he had to take walks, lift weights, and eat lots of green, leafy vegetables for the calcium. He hated lettuce, so he ignored the doctor's advice and stopped exercising the same year he left the CIA. No one was going to tell him how to live his life.

"Did you capture any video of the monkey suits before the cameras stopped working?" he texted. "If so, attach them to an email and send them to me."

A moment later, Bran was watching the short video of two figures in ghillie suits that the U.S. Army, Marine Corps, and special operations snipers wore when they were in the field.

"This is not good," he said to the empty room. There was more to this French singer than he knew. Maybe the Russian didn't know either. He leaned back in the overstuffed chair and closed his eyes. He needed time to rethink his plans.

The two in the ghillie suits were not amateurs. They moved like special forces troops. Bodyguards for singers and actors like this French bitch were usually muscle-bound, steroid-pumped bodybuilders with skills nowhere close to that level of training.

The more he thought about the two figures in monkey suits sliding effortlessly down ropes from the barn's roof, and then their skilled shooting, he felt a bag of chipped ice invading his guts.

Without knowing it, Bran had fallen asleep, and he jerked when he heard a loud knocking from the trailer's door, followed by a voice speaking heavily accented English. "Senior Bran?"

Startled, he responded gruffly. "What is it?"

"Everyone is back," the man said. "Your men and my company are ready to move out."

With a grunt and some effort, Bran climbed out of the chair and turned toward the trailer door to see that the officer on the other side of the screen had a two-star insignia on his uniform's collar, showing he was a Primer Teniente, a first lieutenant, and the second in command of Thiago's militia company.

"Then move out, lieutenant," he said. "March your men to your vehicles and return to my ranch to assist your captain." Then he lied. "He's waiting for you before attacking the enemy. It seems there are more of them than we expected." He didn't know who was attacking his ranch and how many of them there were. The two ghillie suited figures inside the barn had changed everything.

"Captain Thiago said you would lead us back to your ranch."

Bran flapped a hand in dismissal. "Those plans have changed. My men are not military and will slow you down. Your captain needs you as soon as possible. We will follow later."

The lieutenant didn't move and continued to stare at him.

"Well, what are you waiting for?" Bran snapped. "You have your orders from Captain Thiago. Get moving!"

Minutes later, Bran was instructing his explosives expert to rig the trailer and its truck. This was the same man who turned the barn holding the sex slaves into a death trap. "Pavlo," he said, "I don't want you to use explosives this time. What do you have that kills painfully and slowly?"

Bran had recruited Pavlo from a group of Russian militants in Ukraine loyal to Putin. The man knew how to set traps, and innocent civilians killed as collateral damage didn't bother him.

The Russian's face brightened. "I have my toxins," he said. "I will set hidden traps that will slowly kill anyone who comes in contact with them. Some of them will be aerosols, and others will work like a punji trap with sharpened stakes coated with my deadly potions."

"Good! Get busy," Bran said. "I plan to be gone before dark. Make sure your little traps are not easily discovered."

Bran found a shady tree, sat on a camp chair, and watched his men working.

He regretted losing the custom trailer but couldn't take it with him where he was going. And that luxury mobile home might be the carrot that lured the French bitch back here. Once her death was confirmed, he'd claim responsibility, and the Russian would pay him. How could she resist the bait? And maybe those two figures in the ghillie suits would end up dead too.

His only regret was the loss of his precious Venezuelan guard dogs. He couldn't risk going back for them.

CHAPTER 14

MIA COULDN'T BELIEVE she'd done that with two shots.

Cheéte's voice came through her ear bud. "You just earned a Marine Corps sniper's Hog Tooth," he said.

The helicopter was spinning out of control. It looked as if an invisible monster was slinging the sixty-foot-long aircraft in circles. With the tail rotor damaged, there wasn't much the pilot could do.

The bird tilted forty-five degrees to its right and drifted over the open space south of the barn between her and Esther's position. Mia's mouth dropped open as the centrifugal force of the spinning aircraft spat men out of the open side doors.

One body hit what was left of the twelve-foot long, still-spinning tail rotors and was demolished, as if it had been fed through a wood chipper. If she hadn't seen it, she never would've imagined how horrifying that was. That image would haunt her for the rest of her life. With a metallic clang, she heard another body hit the roof of the barn, and the others started smashing into the ground as the chopper drifted away from the building further over the minefield.

Then the helicopter tilted on its side and dropped. The main rotor blades hit the ground first and tore into the earth, tossing up a cloud of dust. With the wind blowing toward her, Mia buried her face in the dirt at the bottom of her body-length, shallow trench and covered the back of her head and neck with both hands.

The earth trembled as land mines started exploding under the aircraft. An instant later, a wave of heat washed over her as a tremendous explosion tore through the main cabin and cockpit, sending shrapnel and flames flying in all directions, destroying everything in its path and anyone still inside. The only possible survivors were those who had fallen out, if the impact on the ground hadn't killed them.

When the debris from the explosions stopped falling, she glanced to see if the four children had survived. She relaxed when she saw them flat on the ground, covering the backs of their heads and necks like she'd done. They were two-thirds of the way from the barn's open double doors to her location. The helicopter had crashed on the south side of the barn. Because the children had been in front of the east end of the barn, the building had shielded them.

With a shaking hand, Mia tapped her earpiece and asked, "Are you okay, Esther?" The helicopter had crashed closer to her. A ringing sound was filling Mia's head, and she wasn't sure she was going to hear the reply if one came.

The earbud crackled with background noise, followed by Esther's muted, tinny voice. "I'm good. Can't say the same for that bird."

The four girls were on their feet again, slipping through the minefield toward her. Mia stared past them at the brush on the far side of the cleared area. "Did your shot bring it down, Cheéte?" she asked through their team link.

"Nope, that's your kill. Your second round hit in the target area too and did even more damage."

"How do you know that?"

"From what I heard."

"But it couldn't have been me," she replied. "I'm not that good." She was silently praying that he'd take the credit for killing all those men.

"I didn't have a clear shot. You're better than you know, Mia."

The thought that she'd just killed all those men sent chills through her. Numb, her stomach heaved, and she barely had time to turn her head to the side before vomiting. She continued to heave until she was gasping for breath.

"Are you okay?" a young voice asked.

Mia used the back of her left hand to scrape away the wet, chunky stomach chaff from her lips and chin. She ended up smearing the mess around, and the wet, sour-smelling discharge mixed with the dirt sticking to her skin. A small hand touched her right shoulder, and the child's warm breath caressed her exposed ear. Their eyes made contact, inches apart. The sweet-looking girl had amber eyes, and she was braced on her right knee. She must've been in her early-teens. The other three, including Shani's guide, stood behind the kneeling girl.

Before Mia could reply, she heard the staccato burst of automatic rifles from in front of her position and watched as the young girl was hit, spraying blood everywhere, a lot on Mia. The other three flung themselves to the ground.

Mia watched in horror as the petite body collapsed.

Trembling, she focused on her target building. The door was open, several men outside on the covered porch, shooting at her.

She chambered a round and fired, hitting one man who

was standing sideways. Another man, looking shocked, turned to run inside, but Mia worked the bolt and fired another round, hitting him in the back.

"Bastards!" Mia heard herself shouting after each shot. She fired a third time, hitting the back of another man's head. She felt a round brush her ear and another one tug at her right sleeve. She fired a fourth round, sending an AK-47 flying with a severed hand still holding it. Two survivors made it inside and slammed the door shut.

Mia kept working the bolt, firing one round after another into the door until it was full of holes and hanging crooked from one of the three hinges. She'd taken out the other two hinges, chunks of concrete from the block wall, and pieces of the door's metal frame.

"Stop, Mia," a stranger's voice said from behind her in heavily accented English. "It's over. You're covered in blood. If you're wounded, you need medical attention now!"

Sounding hysterical, Mia stared at the young girl's body. "Her death is my fault. If I'd been doing my job, she'd still be alive."

"No, Mia. You didn't kill her," the old man said. "You saved the other three." He took her by an arm and guided her away from her firing position along the trail through the brush toward the dirt airstrip.

"What are you doing?" She didn't have the strength to resist. "I have to watch that house and keep anyone from escaping and shooting more children."

"My men will take care of that," the old man replied and kept leading her along the path. Then a single-file line of heavily armed men moved past her, headed toward the barn. They wore dark camo uniforms with armored helmets and vests. Their faces covered with what looked like the special force's balaclava masks her team wore during rescue missions. Goggles covered their eyes.

The older man was a few inches shorter than her. He was dressed in a camouflaged military uniform with no insignia on it, and his face had dark camo paint blurring his features.

It took a moment for Mia to realize that only two of the three girls were still with her. She stared at them and said, "What happened to Shani's guide?" Her heart felt like it had skipped a beat. "Is she dead too?"

"She is leading some of my men through the minefield to help in the barn," the older man said. "We have little time. My president said we must do all we can to avoid an international incident. That means haste is necessary."

"Your voice sounds familiar," she said, "but your face paint makes it impossible for me to recognize you."

"My seven granddaughters are fans of yours. You called and asked for our help. We met briefly a few times. The first time was after one of your concerts in Rio, but I wasn't dressed like this, and my children took up most of your attention. I mean, I like the sound of your voice and your songs, but they are your, what you call, super fans."

"General Costa?" she said.

"Yes," he replied.

She collapsed in his arms and cried. "Thank you! Thank you! Thank you!"

"No, it is I who should thank you for risking your life to free so many of my country's children from a horrible life of sexual slavery. You are my hero."

The strength drained from her legs, and she staggered. With his help, they reached the dirt airstrip, and the rear of the Brazilian C-130 came into view. The ramp was down and the aircraft was sitting a few yards away from them. General

Costa waved for one of his medics. The man leaped up, grabbed his medical bag, and came running down the ramp, straight to Mia.

She protested. "Tend to the girls first. Make sure they're okay."

The medic looked at the general. "Do what she wants," Costa said. "Then look after her."

CHAPTER 15

JOSH FELT AS if he were at the tail end of a Chinese parade dragon, but this one was naked children and teenagers instead of cardboard, colored tissue paper, glue, tape, and paint. As the single-file column moved out of the barn and across the minefield, Shani, the procession's Pied Piper, looked like an undersized Sasquatch in Mia's ghillie suit. The only thing missing was a flute and drum. For an instant, he was tempted to break out in song and dance his way across the killing field toward the dirt airstrip but didn't think that was a good idea.

The haunted expressions of most of the children revealed the trauma they'd suffered since being kidnapped. All of them had been stripped naked and shoved into cramped cages. All were filthy and smelled as if they'd slept in a septic tank. Some had been raped and tortured in front of the others as examples that disobedience would be punished severely.

The serpentine path through the minefield was now marked by red flags on both sides of the route. The Brazilian special forces troops had added that feature.

"Stay inside the flags," one of the camouflaged, anonymous soldiers had said in Portuguese.

"And put both your hands on the shoulders of the person in front of you, so no one strays outside of the marked path," Josh added, since some children were almost catatonic.

Josh only had one free hand, and it was resting on one of Adrienne's bony shoulders. He couldn't take his eyes off of her thin legs, where the skin was covered with dried and crusted blood down the inside of her thighs. Her torso also had cigarette burns, and there were bruises on both arms and around her throat. It was obvious she'd been selected to be publicly raped and tortured as an example to the others.

How did this child stay sane after going through all of that? He shuddered. Is it possible that her life before being kidnapped was worse?

When Adrienne started limping as if her legs were going to give out, Josh told her to stop. She was more than a foot shorter than him, about four-foot-eight. He turned his back to her, kneeled, and said, "Climb on."

After she settled on his back, he stood, her legs around his waist, her arms around his neck. He thought she weighed less than one of his heavy gear packs, maybe eighty pounds. Her body reminded him of photos he'd seen of the survivors of the World War II Nazi concentration camps. Once he started moving, he felt her relax, sigh, and rest her chin on his right shoulder. If he could carry her pain, he would've.

As they left the minefield and moved past Mia's sniper position that was now occupied by one of the Brazilian special forces troopers, Josh watched the man place a U.S. made M32A1 Multiple Grenade Launcher against a shoulder. Over thirty-inches long, the weapon was a lightweight,

40mm, six-shot revolver-style grenade launcher originally developed in South Africa.

Josh stopped and felt Adrienne straighten. "You're awesome!" He heard her say in Portuguese. In reply, the trooper flashed her a grin.

The grenade launcher fired with a hollow popping sound. Josh followed the shell's flight through the air toward the building that Mia had been responsible for. The bullet-riddled door had been placed back in its fame. They must have piled furniture behind it to hold the door in position.

The first grenade hit the door with a resounding boom and blew a large hole through its top half. The second round went through the hole and exploded with a bright flash, likely killing everyone inside. The trooper then fired a thermobaric grenade through one window. Josh heard Adrienne gasp as the building blew up.

"The bomb under your cage was like that one but larger," Josh said, and he felt her fingers digging into his shoulders.

"Are we going to take prisoners?" Josh asked in Portuguese.

"*Nao,*" the trooper replied in the same language as he fired another thermobaric grenade through the back window of another building. As he reloaded the grenade launcher, he continued. "The general has their commander. The rest must die. We are to leave no witnesses."

"Good! They earned it." Josh wondered what the Brazilian general had planned for the survivor.

The trooper nodded.

Josh looked down the trail through the thick brush that led to the airstrip and saw that the rest of the children had moved out of sight. "Hold on," he said to Adrienne and jogged to catch up.

Reaching the airstrip, Josh discovered that at the base of the C-130's open ramp was a double assembly line. They'd divided the naked children into two single-file columns. Even from a distance, it was easy to see from their expressions and body language that some children were alert and hopeful, a few looked sluggish as if they were drugged, and others were seriously traumatized, their jittery eyes flushed with fear as if this wasn't real.

Troopers moved down each line, handing out pink bubble gum and sweet lollipops to each child.

At the head of each line was a smoothly sanded pine pallet. Josh watched as a child stepped from the dirt to the pallet. Wearing surgical gloves, a trooper dipped a loofah sponge into a large bucket filled with soapy water. He quickly scrubbed the child down, and then a second trooper poured water over her head from a five-gallon can to rinse her off. Dripping wet, she was told to move to the next pallet where two men waited with towels to dry her.

On the third pallet, another man measured the child's feet. He shouted a number over his shoulder and held out a hand behind him. Another trooper rummaged in a plastic container and handed the properly sized flip-flops to the man with the tape measure.

A medic waited beside the last pallet next to a folding table piled high with what looked like cotton t-shirts. There was also a bag of medical supplies. When a clean, dry child stopped in front of him, he had her turn so he could inspect her body for sores and wounds that, if found, he treated with an antibiotic gel and was bandaged when necessary. He then selected one of the white t-shirts and slipped it over her head, guiding her arms through the long sleeves. Josh saw one child's lips tighten around the stick of the heart-shaped lollipop she was chewing on as she scrunched her eyes shut. Her stress and distrust were apparent, even for one of her saviors, a sure sign she had PTSD.

When Josh thought that most of these children would receive no therapy, he felt anger boiling inside of him.

More like a one-piece dress, the t-shirts were long enough to reach past each child's knees. Once dressed, the girl he was watching opened her eyes and literally ran up the ramp into the aircraft, joining the others inside the cavernous fifty-five-foot-long cargo area rated to hold a 72,000-pound load. She quickly joined a group of children inside, and his anger cooled off. There was nothing he could do for her. The PTSD would destroy her life or she'd learn to manage it on her own as he had. But he'd had help from Dr. T.

While the aircraft had been designed to carry ninety-two passengers, Josh knew it could hold more. At the end of the Vietnam War, C-130s flying to Thailand were carrying over 240 refugees on each flight out of Saigon's Tan Son Nhut Airbase. He was confident that this aircraft was going to carry everyone out of Venezuela on one flight.

He spotted Mia at the front of the far column of liberated children. She was soaping down the girls as they stepped up on the first pallet, and Josh joined her. Mia was so focused, she didn't notice him when he stopped beside her. Across from her was General Costa. He had his long camo sleeves folded up past his elbows and was pouring fresh water over each child to rinse them off.

"General," Josh said, "it looks like you also can't say no to Mia."

The general waved a hand at what was going on around them. "You should've seen the shopping list and instructions she texted," he replied. "How could I disobey an order from her? After all, I think her followers in my country outnumber the entire Brazilian military a hundred to one. It's nice to see you again, Colonel Kavanagh."

Mia gasped, dropped her loofah into the soapy bucket, and spun around to throw both arms around Josh. When she realized he had a child sitting on his shoulders, she stepped back, looking up.

"Mia," Josh said, "I want you to meet..."

The child gasped in shock, and Mia said, "Adrienne!" Mia stretched her arms out, and the girl tumbled from his shoulders into her embrace. Both of them started crying as the child wrapped her legs and arms around the woman's slender torso and held tight.

General Costa ordered two of his men to replace him and Mia, then asked, "How do you two know each other?"

Josh wanted to know too.

"She's my idol," Adrienne replied, "but I don't know how she knows me."

"Because you've covered all of my originals, often performing them better. I've been watching your YouTube channel for almost three years," Mia said. "That's why I donated to your surgery fund."

"You did?" Adrienne said, stunned. "I didn't know that." And the girl started crying and buried her face in Mia's short, curly hair. Between sobs, she said, "Were you Purple Tomato?"

"That was me," Mia replied.

A note of awe crept into Adrienne's voice. "You donated over half of the money needed for surgery."

"We'll talk later," Mia added. "We're holding the line up. You must get down so you can be washed and get ready for transport."

But Adrienne didn't let go, and Josh had to pry the young girl from Mia's body.

After Josh set her down, Adrienne said in a shaky voice, "No one is going to touch me but you and Mia. I do not trust anyone else."

"We also have a prisoner to question," the general said.

"I heard about that," Josh replied. "What are you planning to do with him? One of your troopers told me all the traffickers had to die, so there'd be no witnesses."

"He's not one of them," Costa said. "He was the commander of the militia who survived falling out of the helicopter but broke both legs and cracked some ribs."

"But is he responsible for what happened to us?" Adrienne asked, her voice and expression filled with ice.

Concerned, Mia glanced at the girl. "We'll let them do their business," she said. "They will deal with the POW. And we'll be together again on the flight out."

"Where's the captive, General?" Josh asked.

"This way." Costa started toward a tent set up on the other side of the dirt strip, a good hundred meters from the aircraft. Josh noticed Adrienne's eyes shift to the tent and if looks threw knives that tent would have been shredded.

"His name is Thiago," Costa continued, "a captain in the Venezuelan militia, a Maduro loyalist. Mia's bodyguards are already questioning him, and he's been, what you call, spilling the beans about a Russian in Caracas who put a price on Mia's head."

"What?"

The general glanced back. "This Russian knows about her organization that rescues trafficked children and is offering a fortune for Mia, dead or alive."

"And does Thiago know who this Russian is?"

"Yes, and he knows where the man is staying in Caracas."

"Good! I want those details."

The tone of Josh's voice caused Costa to look concerned. "What are you thinking?"

"Later," Josh said, and the two left the C-130 and headed toward the field tent.

As they walked away from Adrienne and Mia toward the tent and their prisoner, Josh heard the girl hiss as if she were a vicious, wild creature.

WHEN MIA FINISHED with Adrienne and slipped the long-sleeved white t-shirt over the girl's head and pulled it down, the bottom hem settled about mid-calf. Mia then placed a hand on the girl's shoulder, made eye contact, and said, "I still have work to do, so I want you to go inside the plane and rest. After we're in the air, I'll find you."

Adrienne didn't protest. She had a plan, and being alone was vital to pulling it off. Wrapping her arms around the taller woman, she hugged her idol before hurrying up the ramp to find another exit out of the cargo area where no one would see her sneak out.

When she saw light spilling across the cargo deck right behind the entrance to the cockpit of the large aircraft, she found her escape route. It was hot, so someone had opened all the C-130s doors to let the breeze in.

Perfect, Adrienne thought as she hurried forward, ignoring the other children already gathered in small groups inside the cargo area. She hated the body-length t-shirt, not because it was uncomfortable but because it was white, making her easier to spot. For her to sneak out of the aircraft, she had to be harder to see, and this t-shirt wouldn't allow that.

When she reached the front of the cargo area and an open door to her left, her eyes widened in victory when she saw her disguise hanging from a hook. It was a large, ribbed, black sweater with long sleeves and a hood. It would be hot, but it would cover the t-shirt and make it harder for someone to spot her. Slipping on the heavy wool sweater, she rolled up the sleeves and pulled the hood over her head before stepping to the open door. She leaned forward and saw that it wasn't that far to the ground, an easy drop and roll. After she'd gone to court in Rio and became legally emancipated from her parents at sixteen, she started taking gymnastics and ballet training and knew what to do.

Until now, she'd never considered that her brutally abusive father had taught her anything. Well, he had. The evidence of his abuse was why the courts had ruled in her favor, and instead of breaking her the bastard strengthened her.

When her *pai* beat her as a child because she didn't want to stay a boy, often breaking that boy's young bones, she had more than a dozen healed fractures as evidence; her pai had even burned that child with the lit end of his Cuban cigars. That torture had toughened Adrienne, preparing her for what the kidnappers had done.

Her *pai* had even threatened to kill her if she ever had the male-to-female gender surgery. That was why after the courts freed her soon after she'd turned sixteen, she'd left Rio and moved to Sao Paulo, where she continued to support herself by busking. Two years later, she was eighteen, the legal age to have the surgery. Once she'd left Rio for the larger city, she also launched her YouTube channel. During those first two years surviving alone, she'd raised enough money through

YouTube and performing on the streets to pay for the surgery, and now that she knew who purple-tomato#82@ was, she knew who her best friend was too.

But her YouTube channel was also how her *pai* found her and followed through with his threat, selling her to the traffickers.

She seethed with hatred for her *pai* and had sworn that one day she'd get revenge somehow. Revenge didn't mean she'd have to kill him. Maybe she'd just torture him like he'd done to her when she'd still been a young boy.

Once on the ground, Adrienne scrambled into the shade under the C-130's wings. From there, she crouched and scurried to reach the brush surrounding the airstrip. Once concealed, she made her way to the back of the tent, where the prisoner was being questioned. Crawling on her belly, she left the brush and carefully lifted the fabric enough so she could hear what they were talking about. She wanted to know everything the prisoner knew about the kidnappers. Once she knew who they were, she'd get the revenge she wanted. That was something else her *pai* had taught her. He'd belonged to one of the most powerful gangs in Rio's favelas as an enforcer.

She also didn't want to get caught and make Mia or Josh angry at her. If Mia trusted Josh then Adrienne did too. That was why she wasn't worried that Josh would condemn her for becoming a girl when she turned eighteen, as her father had.

CHAPTER 16

WITH HER HEART racing, Mia awoke with a scream trapped in her throat. Panting, she looked around, expecting to see headless children and the traffickers she'd killed who murdered them. A hallucination so intense she thought it was real. Even when she realized it wasn't, she couldn't let it go.

How long had she slept? The hypnotic throbbing from the C-130's turboprop engines must have sucked her under into a deep, death-like slumber. Her body was sluggish, her mind numb; she couldn't remember the last time she'd felt that way.

She discovered General Costa nearby, his eyes closed, his back and neck forming a straight line sitting in a Lotus Pose. The backs of his hands rested on his knees with his palms up. He'd created two circles with index fingers touching thumbs, and the rest of his fingers extended. Mia also used yoga to calm her nerves before a live performance.

Not wanting to disturb him, she surveyed the area and saw Cheète with her raptors, huddled against the opposite bulkhead. The cargo compartment of a C-130 was about forty-one feet long, nine feet high, and ten feet wide.

They looked serious, and she wondered what they were talking about.

Taking in the rest of the crowded area, she observed that most of the children were sleeping, and the few who were awake looked zombified. The Brazilian commandos near the loading ramp still had their balaclava masks on, their eyes alert as if they expected trouble to appear.

At first, she didn't see Josh. Fighting panic, she searched until she spotted him sprawled on the aircraft's closed aft loading ramp, possibly out cold as she'd been. He still wore the ghillie suit, his face hidden by the shaggy head piece. She didn't want to disturb him, but she wanted him beside her without that creepy camouflaged outfit on.

With a stab of sorrow, she wondered if he was avoiding her because of Rachel.

Mia blamed herself for Josh marrying his childhood sweetheart the previous year. If Rachel came out of her coma, Mia might lose her man forever. Her fame and wealth would become meaningless. Rachel was fit and still beautiful and had been a significant part of Josh's childhood and high school years before he joined the Marines. Mia had been stupid to think no woman could take Josh away from her. That false sense of arrogance had betrayed her. She'd been a fool.

Struggling with jealousy and guilt, she remembered the only time she'd seen Rachel during that early morning visit to the hospital in San Francisco. Mia had always hated hospitals. The deserted lobby had felt desolate, the elevator a death box. The echoing sounds their shoes made walking the length of the empty, bleak, haunted hallways to reach her hospital room had sent shivers down Mia's spine. Rachel had looked frail and helpless, the top of her head swathed in bandages. There had been too many tubes and wires attached to her.

A flicker of movement pulled Mia back to the present, and she caught Shani watching her. When their eyes met, her favorite raptor flashed a fake grin and glanced away.

What was that for? Mia thought. An uneasy sensation invaded her stomach, and she hated it. Glancing at her Brazilian benefactor, she asked, "General, is everything okay?"

Without opening his eyes, he said, "According to the 14th century Hatha Yoga Pradipika, the Lotus Pose is the 'destroyer of all diseases,' and I am at peace with the world."

A moment of silence slid by before trying again. "General?"

"Yes, child." His eyes opened, and she saw a deep, soothing calm in them.

I'm not a child, she thought. She didn't like when men called her that.

"Where are we?" she asked.

"Over Brazil headed to Manaus. We just turned south, so we're about 750 kilometers from our destination. We'll arrive in less than an hour and a half." The general rubbed his face with both hands before focusing on her. "Do you practice yoga?" he asked.

"I do."

"And does it help?"

She nodded. "Should I be concerned? When we were booking concerts in Brazil for my last world tour, I was told Manaus had a higher murder rate than Rio?"

"There are indeed high rates of robbery, assault, and homicide in some of Brazil's favelas (slums) where security is unpredictable, but that's because of disputes between organized crime groups. The gangsters kill each other and aren't involved in petty crimes that might cause complaints and unrest among the people. There is no reason to worry. The gangs don't want to attract attention. Besides, we'll be landing at a military airbase nine kilometers from the town. There'll be no need to leave the base where you will reunite with your film crew before leaving for French Guiana and, I understand, from there to France. Even if you were a tourist, some areas are completely safe to visit, especially the major attractions."

His face brightened, and he leaned closer. "And," his voice dropped, as if he didn't want anyone else to hear, "if you want to visit our beautiful country as a tourist instead of as a famous person, my family will be more than willing to host you and be your guide." His grin was disarming, meant to convince her, revealing how much he loved his country. "My girls would be thrilled. They'd work hard to keep your identity a secret from their friends, your fans, and the paparazzi."

Not wanting to make a commitment, she asked, "Have you talked to Josh since we left that disgusting ranch? I find it strange that he's sitting over there." She pointed. "Something isn't right. Is he angry at me?" Her stomach tensed, ready to take the blow, if that was the reason.

Sadness appeared in the general's eyes. He lifted a hand and gestured for Mia's raptors and Cheéte to join them. "That answer will have to come from them," he said.

With a spreading sense of dread, Mia watched the four reluctantly cross the space filled with a tangle of sleeping children to reach her. She glanced at Josh's still-sleeping figure in his crappy ghillie suit and asked, "Why can't the general tell me what's going on? Why hasn't Josh joined us?" She started searching for Adrienne. A few of the sleeping children had their backs to her, and one of them could've been her YouTube friend.

"He can't," Shani said, her tone a warning.

Suspicious, Mia studied the five concerned faces around her. Her raptors all reached out at the same time and took hold of her hands. Now she was really worried. Sensing bad news, she felt an anchor drop into her stomach, burying itself in her guts.

"We didn't agree with Josh," Cheète said, and nodded at the general, including him in that statement.

"None of us did," Shani said.

"You make it sound as if he isn't here, but he is." She pointed again at the figure almost forty feet from her, still in that damned ghillie suit. "Are you trying to scare me?" She wouldn't start over with another man. Even with Josh married to his childhood sweetheart, she wanted to be his secret mistress. But if he left her for Rachel's sake, she'd become celibate. After thinking about it, she shook her head. "No, he's not a coward. He'd tell me if he was going to do that. It has to be something else."

"Do what?" Costa asked.

"Leave me for his wife," she replied.

The general raised his eyebrows, a curious expression. "The last time we worked together, he wasn't married. When did that happen?"

Thick silence filled the immediate space, and her raptors and Cheéte turned to her. "You tell him."

"Why me?" Mia's voice sounded defensive. With a sigh, she surrendered and, in a summary, filled Costa in. Finished, she said, "Now one of you explain why Josh is avoiding me."

"With command comes responsibility," Cheéte replied, and the three raptors nodded in agreement as they pinned the general with their eyes.

Costa shook his head in defeat and stared at the ceiling. He said in Portuguese in a barely audible voice, "*Covardes.*"

Then he sucked in a deep breath before looking at Mia to explain what Josh was doing. That he wasn't on the C-130. Josh was still in Venezuela, headed to Caracas to find the Russian that wanted her dead.

"So, who is wearing Josh's costume?" Mia nodded at the sleeping figure at the other end of the cargo bay.

"Josh didn't want you to worry, so he had one of my men put it on," Costa replied.

Mia started laughing, tears flooding her eyes. When she regained control, she said, *"Nom de Dieu! Quel imbécile pour un héros!"* Then she explained, "After we'd been lovers for a few months, he called from Germany to tell me he was going to miss my birthday. He was so sorry and said he was in the US Army hospital in Landstuhl, recovering from wounds. I imagined him without limbs or with his face burned off. Of course, I went to Germany, but I also started teaching myself to stop worrying about him."

She noticed the concern etched on their faces. "Don't worry about me," she added. "I will not fall apart. I'll do what I always do. Find something else to distract me. It's the only thing that works." She scanned the cargo bay again, this time looking for her YouTube friend. "I don't see Adrienne."

After another silence, Shani was the first to speak. "Who's Adrienne?"

Costa cleared his throat. "I was thinking the same thing."

"One of the rescued kids," Cheéte said. "Josh told me about her and Mia."

"Is this the girl who warned us about the hidden explosives?" Shani said. "Are you saying this child is Mia's friend, like your three common-law wives?"

"You have three wives?" Costa said, staring at Cheète, his eyes as big as saucers.

"Did Josh share that with you?" Cheéte asked, turning to Shani.

"No," she replied. "We knew Josh, but we didn't know you, so we did a little digging. Do you think we were going into danger without knowing who you were? Don't worry. Your complicated, secret sex life is safe with us."

The general burst out laughing before adding, "Your soap opera has me hooked. How did someone that close to Mia end up as one of those kidnapped children?"

"If anyone tells you, it should be Mia," Cheéte said. "She knows more than we do."

Shani rolled her eyes. "Then we may never know. Mia keeps secrets better than anyone."

Mia bit her lower lip, deciding to lie. "Adrienne is my half-sister," she said. Everything else she told them was the truth. How Adrienne had been born a girl in a boy's body, the abusive parents, the poverty, her talent for music, the gender affirming surgery. That she looked years younger than someone in her early twenties.

Later, after the conversation fizzled and everyone had retreated to their own space, the sleeping children and the silence triggered an idea for an original song. After she introduced Adrienne to the world as her half-sister, they should have an original song to perform together. She thought a fitting title might be Fairytale.

She vocalized the first stanza.

"Standing on shifting sand.

Enlightened in dreamland.

All things are possible when planned.

Boy born.

Transformed."

She shook her head. No, it wasn't a good idea to hint that

Adrienne had started life as a boy. The idea behind her scheme was to make sure her father never found her again.

Mia would return to that song after reaching France. Shifting gears, she thought of ways to use makeup and new hairstyles to hide who Adrienne was, so none of her YouTube and Instagram fans would recognize her. Maybe a touch of plastic surgery here and there to enhance her beauty would also help hide her from her parents.

Looking for Adrienne, Mia started searching the cavernous cargo area with her eyes again. Eventually, she shrugged, thinking, *Let her sleep. After what she went through, she needs the rest. We'll find each other after we land. Then I'll tell her what I'm thinking.*

CHAPTER 17

AN HOUR AFTER questioning the prisoner, Josh stood by himself hidden in the shade of a tree near the end of the soon-to-be-empty dirt airstrip watching the C-130 build speed until it lumbered into the cloud-streaked sky and banked west. The aircraft would maintain that course until it was over a remote, protected area of the Amazon rainforest occupied by the Yanomami Indian tribe, Brazil's largest remaining isolated tribal group. Then it would fly south.

He thought about the sixty-five-year history of the C-130, an aircraft that had carried him into danger more times than he wanted to remember. Over the decades, they had used it as an ambulance, a gunship, to drop paratroopers, carry cargo, launch drones, and on and on. Now it was rescuing children from a life of sexual slavery.

He'd never been alone in the field without a partner or team before. Even though he'd decided to go alone, he didn't like it.

Cheéte was on that plane, sworn to secrecy. Mia didn't know he'd stayed behind. She thought he was on board because one of General Costa's special forces troopers was wearing his ghillie suit. If she'd known, she would've insisted on going with him. Still, General Costa, Cheéte, and Mia's three raptors had argued that what Josh planned to do was a suicide mission.

General Costa had said, "There has to be another way to protect Mia from this Russian."

Cheéte's protest had also fallen on deaf ears. "You can't do this alone," he'd said. "I'm going with you. We were a two-man sniper team once in the Hindu Kush. We can do that again in Venezuela."

Josh had put a hand on his old friend's shoulder. "No, this is a mission for younger men than me, and you're twenty years older than I am."

"Then why are you doing it?" Cheéte had asked.

"You know why. You'd do the same thing to protect someone you loved if you were in my position. Am I wrong?"

"Shit!" Cheéte had replied, his eyes shifting to the sky beyond Josh's shoulder.

But that conversation was history now, and it was time to move on. After Josh couldn't see the aircraft, he didn't move as he continued listening to the fading whine of the four turboprop engines until he couldn't hear them. Then with a sigh he used the long sleeves of the Venezuelan militia uniform he was wearing to dry his moist eyes. The rank insignia said he was a first sergeant.

Hearing a moan, Josh turned to stare at his prisoner, Captain Thiago, who because of his broken legs and a few other fractured bones was going to have to ride a horse borrowed from Damien Bran's ranch. The rest of the animals had been set free and driven off. Then what remained of the buildings had been demolished with the same explosives Bran had used as death traps in the barn. Thiago probably needed another dose of morphine, but Josh held off on that. Let the bastard suffer.

When he lifted Thiago off the ground, the man screamed with pain. Once Josh tied him to the horse, he stepped back and with a frigid expression glared at the man without saying a word.

"Don't look at me like that," Thiago said, turning his face away.

"What's wrong with the way I'm looking at you?"

"Like you want to eat me."

Josh snorted. "If you were an entrée on a menu, I wouldn't be interested."

Thiago scrunched his face together, looking as pitiful as possible. "I'm begging you. Give me something for the pain."

"Until we reach the safe house General Costa arranged for us on the outskirts of Caracas," Josh replied, "I want you to be alert, not doped out of your mind."

"You're a monster."

"If I'm a monster, what does that make you?"

"I didn't have a choice. When I was being questioned, I made that clear. I was following orders. If I'd refused, my career in the militia would've been over. Didn't you hear me when I said I didn't agree with what Senior Bran was doing with those children or what he intended to do with the French woman? He even threatened my family if I didn't do what he wanted."

"That's not good enough," Josh said. "Try again. Convince me."

Thiago took a moment to think before he replied, "You're a soldier. If they ordered you to do something you knew was wrong, you would've done it to avoid a court-martial or an execution."

"Wrong," Josh said. "When I was in the military, the oath I took didn't include following the orders of a brutal dictator. You're a Maduro loyalist. Why should I trust you?"

Forgetting his pain, Thiago's face bloated with anger as he shouted, "I didn't do it for money! I did it to keep my family safe!"

"You can't fool me, you lying bastard. You were going to take any money Bran was offering as a bribe to do what he wanted. If you keep complaining, you're going to use up any energy you have left and be of no use to me. Do you remember what I said if that happened?"

"That you'll shoot me."

Josh grinned and shook his head. "Good Lord, you weren't listening. I clarified I wouldn't waste a bullet on you. I'll slit your throat and watch you bleed out."

Between General Costa's contacts in the Brazilian Intelligence Agency, the ABIN, and a call Josh made to someone in the CIA he trusted, he'd learned Thiago was married to a distant cousin of his president.

"If you kill me, you'll become a war criminal. International law says that POWs must be treated humanely in all circumstances. I am protected against any act of violence and against intimidation."

"You really think highly of yourself, just like your wife's cousin, President Maduro." Before Thiago could react, Josh jabbed an index finger at one of the captain's broken legs, causing him to cry out in pain.

"First, my country is not at war with yours. Second, I'm a military contractor, a mercenary." He fished up a wicked grin for dramatic effect. "Third, you gave up your rights when you followed Bran's orders to cut off my girlfriend's head and sell it to that Russian in Caracas."

"Your girlfriend?" A look of terror filled Thiago's face.

"Good, you're listening. Think about it. You agreed to cut off Mia's head when you reached the ranch. What would you do to me if I was planning to do that to your wife and children?"

"I refused to cut her head off!" The man was spitting, angry and desperate, an interesting combination.

"But you would've watched as one of Bran's brutes do it after he raped her, and you still agreed to deliver her head to the Russian and collect the bounty for Bran."

Thiago didn't know that his militia company was fast approaching from the west and was minutes from the ranch. One of General Costa's backpack-sized unmanned surveillance drones had spotted them pushing their Austrian built troop transports fast across the rough terrain.

Josh took the horse's reins and led it northeast in the opposite direction toward the hidden Toyota Hilux. "I can't take this!" Thiago said in a strained voice, groaning in pain. "Please, have mercy on me, for my children's sake."

"Shut up!" Josh increased his pace. With all the groans and gasps coming from the good captain, there was no way Thiago was going to hear his troops arriving on the other side of those burning ranch buildings less than a mile away.

By the time they reached the hidden Toyota, Josh estimated that Thiago's troops had been at the ranch for at least a quarter of an hour, and patrols would be sent out soon. He wasn't about to wait and find out. Josh moved the captain from the horse to the Hilux and used rope, duct tape, and zip ties to fasten him to the passenger seat. He did his best to hide the fastenings from casual observations. He stored his packs and most of his weapons in the cramped back seat.

Before he slid behind the steering wheel, he slapped the

horse hard across its rump to get it moving. "Go!" When it wandered off a short distance and grazed, Josh shook his head.

"Dear God," Thiago said after Josh was in the driver's seat. "What am I going to do if I have to *mear y cagar*? It will take an hour to untie me."

"You haven't noticed," Josh replied.

"Noticed what?"

"You're wearing adult diapers. We put them on you after you passed out. You can piss and shit all you want. As the crow flies, we have about 650 miles before we reach the destination that I've designated as the meet-up-point. That means we'll have to stop for fuel at least once, because this truck has a range of about 500 miles on one tank. When we do that, I'll change your diaper."

"You must untie me. It will look suspicious if we're stopped."

Josh laughed. A moment later, he said, "I'm wearing a militia uniform. I'm your driver. I speak Spanish. If anyone tries to stop us and search this truck, I'll shoot you before I shoot them."

"You're a wild animal." Thiago looked like he was ready to spit on Josh.

"You won't get an argument out of me," Josh replied with a grin. "Think of me as a rare, starving and pissed off, six-hundred-pound Siberian tiger." He held up the Seal Team knife they'd awarded him when he'd graduated as a Navy Seal. "If you spit on me, I will slice off one of your gonads."

The captain's face turned ashen as he stared at the seven-inch blade, beads of sweat appeared across his forehead.

"Do you know how fortunate you are that you landed on the barn's roof instead of in the minefield that blew up your helicopter and killed your troopers? Don't get stupid and throw away your life too."

Josh sensed a slight shift in the truck, as if someone had added weight to the almost empty truck bed behind him. With a swift glance, he checked all three rear-view mirrors and caught sight of a flip-flop hanging off of a bare foot before the image slid off the mirror. A heartbeat later, he was outside the truck facing the truck bed with elbows bent, his feet shoulder-width apart and weight slightly forward over bent knees, holding his pistol extended in a two-handed grip, safety off, and ready to squeeze the trigger for a kill shot.

He saw who was staring at him with her hypnotic, pale-green, hazel shaded eyes. "Jeez Louise!" he blurted out in shock. Without relaxing, he tipped the barrel of his 9mm SIG Sauer pistol toward the sky away from her face.

"You forgot my name already?" she said, looking tragic, her lower lip a trembling pout.

"What the hell are you doing here, Adrienne? You're supposed to be on that Fat Albert on the way to Brazil and safety," he said.

"Fat Albert?" she asked. Her heartbreaking expression vanished, replaced with curiosity as she tilted her head to one side.

"That C-130 you were supposed to be on," he replied. He wanted to be angry but couldn't make it happen. "I won't ask how you pulled off your escape from that plane, but I want to know why you're here instead of there." He jabbed his pistol barrel at the sky toward Brazil.

"Well, to survive in favela, I learned how to be sneaky." In a graceful, fluid movement, she stood and took a step closer to him. "I'm good at being invisible. I know how to fight too. After you finished questioning that creep..." She pointed at the truck's cab. "...I heard you talking to my country's general, and he said what you were planning to do to protect Mia from Russian in Caracas was too dangerous for one man, so I decided you needed my sneaky help."

Josh was staring at the pure white t-shirt she was wearing, and thought about the flip-flops, useless in terrain like this. Pursing his lips in thought, he shook his head. *I can't abandon her. She'll never make it. This isn't the favela she learned to survive in. Out here alone, she won't stand a chance.* He wanted to curse, but that wouldn't change things either, so he said, "You can't go with me dressed like that."

With his pistol holstered, he leaned into the cab, lifted one of his packs out and carried it to the back of the truck bed, where he fished around inside while she stood over him, watching. A moment later, he found what he was looking for. A flexible, tight-plastic tube holding a two-piece camouflaged thermal outfit. He pulled out the top and left the bottom behind. Too big for her small size. "Leave the t-shirt on and slip this over it," he said.

Soon she was covered from chin to ankles in his long-sleeved thermal shirt with the sleeves rolled up. He handed her a web belt to cinch around her tiny waist.

"That'll do for now. The first chance we get, we'll see if we can find boots that fit and pants that sort of match." He indicated the bed of the truck with the sweep of one arm. "And you won't be riding back here."

She followed him around as he moved all of his gear from the back seat to the bed of the truck and tied it down. Once she was inside the cab behind the front seats, Josh drove from the depression, where the Toyota had been hidden under a pile of cut brush. In four-wheel drive, he guided the truck northeast across rugged terrain. They had a long way to go before they reached the first decent paved road closer to the Caribbean coast. He'd calculated that it might take three-to-four days to reach the remote beach he'd selected inside Henri Pittier National Park along the coast close to Caracas. He'd designated that spot to meet with one of his six-man Oath Group teams. They were handpicked, spoke fluent Spanish, and would easily blend in once they reached Caracas. He hadn't shared that part of his plan with the general, Cheéte, or Mia's raptors. They thought he was doing this alone. He knew better than to do something stupid like that. They didn't need to know what his plans were.

As he drove, putting miles between them and Bran's ranch, he talked to his captive. "What I'm curious about is why you're not a general? The Venezuelan military has over 3,000 for an active military force a quarter the size of the United States military, and the US has only 920 generals and admirals. It's obvious that you don't need to be good at your job to become a general or admiral in Venezuela, and you're also related to Maduro through marriage. So, what did you do to piss him off?"

Thiago ignored him, staring out the passenger window.

Josh smiled at the back of the captain's head. It looked like he'd touched a sore spot, one he was counting on. Maybe Thiago wasn't as much of a loyalist as the intelligence said he was.

Adrienne had planted herself in the middle of the back seat and was leaning forward, watching them. "I get him to answer your questions," she said. "I good at being a brat when I want to be. I bite and pinch too."

"Thanks for the offer," Josh said, stifling a laugh, "but no. What I want you to do is get some rest. Do you know how to drive?"

She nodded, looking eager.

"Once we reach a paved road," he said. "I'll want you to take over so I can rest, but first you'll have to prove to me you can drive."

Her expression changed, studiously serious now.

Good God, he thought, *this girl is like a chameleon with expressions*. "Show me a face that looks like a terror-stricken, helpless, innocent angel," he asked.

And she did it perfectly.

Maybe she'd come in handy and wouldn't be a burden after all. All he had to do was keep them both alive.

"I'll sing if you want me to," she said. "That will make time pass faster. Keep us awake."

He nodded, and she started singing a medley of songs, smoothly changing from French to English to Portuguese as she sang, while using the center console between the two front bucket seats as a soft drum, she also used a cappella to create additional instrumental sounds of a guitar and flute. Josh thought her voice was better than Mia's.

Glancing at the back of Thiago's head, he remembered the only reason the captain was alive was because the Russian in Caracas expected him to deliver Mia's head packed in ice inside an insulted cooler.

Before the C-130 had left, Thiago had been forced to call the Russian. Following the script written for him, he'd said, "I'm on my way with the trophy that Senior Damen Bran is selling to you. Expect me to arrive in a few days. Please have the proper payment ready when I get there."

"Why is it taking that long?" the Russian had replied.

"During the game to win the trophy, I lost my helicopter. I'll be driving to Caracas from the ranch. If you call the number I provided, you will reach my second in command, and he'll verify we lost our aircraft. You may also tell him I'm alive and the reason I wasn't there to greet him is that I am following Mr. Bran's orders."

After the call disconnected, General Costa took the phone, and Josh holstered the firearm he'd been pressing against a spot behind the captain's ear. "Good boy," Josh said. "You keep that up and you might see your family again."

CHAPTER 18

NO WONDER ADRIENNE was a Brazilian YouTube star. It took a long time for her to get tired of singing. When she did, Josh glanced in the back and discovered she'd fallen asleep. He had to admit that she'd peppered her impressive performance with a wide variety of songs in four languages. There hadn't been a boring moment.

He'd waited patiently for this to happen before using the encrypted satellite phone to call Idaho. Not wanting to wake her up, he gently guided the truck to a stop and watched long enough to ensure she slept deeply. He didn't care if Thiago heard. If Josh had a chance, he wanted to arrange a way to get Adrienne back to Mia, where she'd be safer. What she didn't know she couldn't share with others.

Once satisfied, he made the call. When Forest answered, he said, "After I send the mission details in an attachment, the next time you hear from me it will be a text message after the Dog delivers us to the designated GPS coordinates."

Dog was their code name for a Vietnam vet and bird pilot living in a deep cleft between mountains almost 1,500 meters above sea level in the Cordillera de Mérida, a northeastern extension of the Andes Mountains in Columbia and Venezuela. The only way in and out of his narrow valley was by air. The old man preferred the isolation, but he didn't live alone. He'd gone native and had a family.

"Understood," Forest replied.

A moment later Josh sent the e-mail with an encrypted, compressed data-file to Forest's laptop. After opening the file and reading the instructions, Forest would find what Josh wanted: a trawler yacht for sale in the Cayman Islands. He'd buy the boat and schedule the Oath Group's Cessna Citation Bravo to pick up Josh's handpicked six-man team and deliver them to the Caymans to take possession of the boat, equip it for the mission, and sail to Venezuela, an eleven-hundred-mile journey.

Josh's other instructions were for the Dog.

A few hours later, the Toyota sat in a grassy clearing surrounded by trees on three sides. Josh needed to sleep, but Thiago never stopped complaining.

"You know there are few roads in this state," Captain Thiago rambled on, "and most of them are in the northwest where the state's capital is located. From here, there is no way to reach Caracas in this truck. And why are we sitting here doing nothing? I thought you were in a hurry."

After a burst of laughter, Josh said, "Why should we be in a hurry if we can't get there from here?"

He glanced in the back to check on Adrienne, impressed again by how soundly she slept. For a long time, he hadn't been able to do that. He'd like to know her secret.

They were still in the Rio Negro Municipality, where Bran's ranch was located. It was one of seven districts in the state and had about 2,300 inhabitants. Half were forest-dwelling indigenous natives that hunted and fished for food. Mostly unexplored, Venezuela's Amazonas State was a hot tropical savanna covering an area of about 70,000 square miles with less than one percent of Venezuela's population.

During the rough drive, Josh thought they'd stepped back in time to when humans didn't exist. He'd seen giant anteaters, several capybaras, and heard distant howler monkeys. The isolation explained why Damien had selected this area to locate the ranch he used as a distribution hub for trafficked children, destined for short, miserable lives as sex slaves.

Josh folded the map he'd been studying and put it in the glove compartment with the satellite phone. Then he used the GPS navigation device on his tactile wristwatch to check their location for the fifth time. Nothing had changed.

"Where are we?" the captain demanded.

Josh grinned but didn't bother to look at Thiago. "Where we're supposed to be." Leaning his head against the headrest, he struggled to keep his eyes open. He hadn't slept since arriving in Venezuela and was exhausted. But sleep was a luxury he couldn't afford, not now. He had energy drinks and power bars to deal with this but was saving them for actual emergencies.

Thiago craned his head around, looking in all directions. "There is nothing here but grass and trees. I'm hungry, and I have to *orinar*."

"I'm not changing your diaper for another eight hours," Josh said.

"You're a monster."

"Shut up and listen."

"To what...birds, bugs? The wind? Didn't you hear what I said? I'm hungry."

Josh pointed northeast. "About forty or fifty miles in that direction, there's a Yanomami village. I'm sure they'd love unexpected guests for chow."

"You cannot be serious," Thiago said. "They're savages. They eat the bones of their dead."

"They're not cannibals," Josh said. "I know firsthand that they cremate only the bones and then mix the ash with a soup made from bananas. They believe that keeps the spirits of their dead alive. Now, if you shut up, you might hear our taxi."

Thiago frowned as he squirmed, searching for a more comfortable position. He'd stopped begging for pain killers hours ago. "A taxi here!" He snorted in disgust. "You must think I'm a fool."

"Shush," Josh said with an index finger across his lips.

A moment later Thiago said, "I hear what sounds like a loud motorcycle." He laughed. "A motorcycle cannot be our taxi, not here."

"It isn't." Josh pointed west. "Look where I'm pointing and you might see it. Right now, our taxi looks about the size of a horsefly, but it will grow, since it's fifty-seven feet long and sixteen feet tall."

Thiago leaned forward until the restraints stopped him. He stared for a long time before he said, "I've never seen a relic like that before." The bird had a large, rounded nose and a raised flight deck higher than the cargo area. Any paint that remained was cracked and peeling. The exposed metal airframe streaked with a dull gray film.

"They produced the last Dog in 1970," Josh said, "and the reason you thought it was a motorcycle is its gasoline-powered piston-engine without the original sound dampener."

"We're flying in a dog," Thiago said, shocked. "It looks more like a worthless mongrel."

"Ignore the label. That's what the Marines fighting in Vietnam called it. It's a Sikorsky H-34 Choctaw."

"Are we flying?" Adrienne asked, sounding sleepy.

Josh glanced back to see her stretching, rubbing her eyes, and yawning. "Yes," he replied. "I've arranged for a helicopter to transport us to a location north of Puerto Ayacucho on the other side of the Orinoco River."

Thiago lowered his head until he was peering over the dash, watching the Choctaw drift over the clearing until it was hovering above them. Adrienne had crawled through the open slider window behind the back seat and was standing in the truck bed, gawking in awe. The noise from the Dog's engine was deafening. Someone tossed a harness out of the open cargo area, and it slapped the earth on the driver's side of the Toyota.

Josh slipped out of the Hilux and gathered the tangle of connected ropes. "Adrienne, I want your help."

By the time she joined him, her sluggish expression was gone, and she was glowing with energy. *How did she manage that?* he thought, impressed again.

They climbed into the truck bed, making a lot of noise.

"What are you doing?" Thiago demanded in a shrill voice.

Josh poked his head through the open back window and saw the man couldn't see what was going on behind him. "We're attaching a harness to the Toyota." He tossed two of the thick ropes over the cab to the hood, where they clattered on the metal. There was a rusty metal hook on the end of each rope. Adrienne appeared, took the hooks, and kneeled out of sight in front of the Hilux.

Then a light must have flipped on inside Thiago's head. He shouted. "No! I refuse! I smell gasoline fumes. We'll suffocate."

Josh stopped by the open passenger window and watched the blood rush out of his prisoner's face, turning the man's nut-brown complexion pasty white. "You don't have a choice," Josh said.

Thiago mumbled. "Dear Lord, make me courageous in the presence of these fools."

"Do you want me to fill his mouth with underwear?" Adrienne asked, pointing at the stained boxers on the floor under Thiago's feet where Josh had tossed them.

Josh shook his head, and she looked disappointed. Once Josh climbed on top of the truck's cab, he asked her to hand him the single line at the top of the harness. He slipped the hook fastened to its end onto another one protruding from the belly of the Dog. Finished, he jumped down, backed away from the truck, and saluted the shadowy figures inside the bird's cargo area.

"Adrienne, back seat."

The girl moved fast to comply.

Soon the loud Sikorsky was flying northwest in the general direction of the capital city of Venezuela's Amazonas State. The Toyota dangled below the aircraft. They were so close to the rainforest's canopy that the truck's wheels sometimes caressed the tops of trees, scattering leaves and snapping small branches.

"Are you sure this mongrel will not drop us?" Thiago asked. "We have to be more than a hundred feet from the ground."

Adrienne giggled, and the captain's eyes bulged. "She's crazy like you."

"This Dog can carry an external payload of up to six-thousand pounds," Josh replied.

"But that thing is over fifty years old. How do they keep it running? Parts for a *helicóptero* that old cannot be easy to find."

"My friend machines his replacement parts, and this mutt has never failed. We either get there or we don't." Josh noticed Thiago staring at him in horror as Adrienne started humming a cheerful tune.

Three hours later, the Sikorsky set the Hilux on a dirt road near the Orinoco River forty miles north of Puerto Ayacucho. Josh and Adrienne left the cab and freed the ropes from the truck. A pole with a hook on it protruded from the cargo door, and Josh attached the harness to it.

Then the craggy, bearded face of an old man appeared in the cockpit window, his eyes hidden behind mirrored pilot glasses. A gloved hand flashed the V sign with two fingers. When Josh had been in Columbia with DELTA, Jimbo had been the team's pilot for that black op mission. Josh didn't know the man's last name and suspected he worked for rebels and smugglers too.

Jimbo was a lean, seventy-three-year-old former Marine combat pilot who flew birds like the Dog on thousands of missions in Vietnam in the 1960s, earning the Distinguished Service Cross for extraordinary heroism. Josh also had a DFC besides the Navy Cross when he'd been a SEAL. The only award higher was the Medal of Honor. The pilot loved his country but didn't trust its government. It didn't matter if they were Republicans or Democrats. He thought they were all backstabbing crooked bastards, some worse than others, and he wouldn't speak the current president's name.

The leather-faced combat pilot nodded, slipped off his mirrored glasses, looked at Adrienne and winked, followed by a gap-toothed, lascivious grin. The few teeth remaining were stained a yellowish brown.

The girl's eyes glowed, and she flirted back, throwing him silent kisses.

The old man's grin reminded Josh why he didn't trust Jimbo enough to fly Adrienne to safety. Instead, he planned to wait until they met up with his team in a few days, and then he'd arrange for her to join Mia before he continued with the mission.

A moment later Josh and Adrienne watched the Dog point its bulbous nose west before flying away. Back in the Toyota, Josh retrieved the encrypted satellite phone from the glove box, typed in his password to activate it, and left a text message for Forest in Idaho. "Jimbo delivered. Pay invoice." He put the phone away.

The deal had been simple. Drop them north of the Orinoco River on an isolated dirt road a mile from a paved highway called Troncal 2. The GPS coordinates had been precise. They were now in the next state, three hundred miles from the clearing where Jimbo had picked them up. Josh estimated that San Fernando de Apure, this state's capital, was several hours ahead of them.

"It's your turn to drive, Adrienne. Once I'm satisfied you know how, I'm going to catch some sleep." At least he hoped he'd be able to snooze a bit.

The paved two-lane wasn't in good shape, but he wasn't concerned. The Toyota had four-wheel drive and had been designed for third-world countries. On both sides of the road, Josh saw scattered ranches, farms, and an occasional cluster of houses. Adrienne proved her worth, and he folded up in the tight back seat and was soon asleep to the sound of the girl's incredible voice crooning lullabies he hadn't heard since he was a child.

CHAPTER 19

SOON AFTER THE C-130 landed at Manaus Air Force Base near the banks of the Rio Negro River in northwest Brazil, a colonel in Costa's command appeared and reported that Brazilian intelligence had picked up chatter that a five-million-dollar bounty had been posted on a dark website catering to professional assassins; the target was Mia.

That changed Shani's assessment of the situation to imminent danger. She'd thought they'd be safe once they landed in Brazil, but now it was apparent that her challenge was to protect Mia, who was in no position to decide. Her client looked more like an old woman with dementia instead of an international singing sensation. Since Mia heard that Josh had stayed behind in Venezuela to deal with the threat to her life, she'd convinced herself he was going to die there.

It didn't help that Mia refused to leave until all the children disembarked first. She'd position herself inside the aircraft at the top of the ramp, watching as the children filed past her. If Shani hadn't intervened, forcing Mia to stay in the shadows, she would've been standing out in the open at the bottom of the ramp, an easy target.

Once the last child left the plane, Mia asked. "I didn't see Adrienne. Where is she?"

By then, most of the children were in the nearest hangar, where arrangements were being made to reunite them with their families. The logistics of that operation would not be easy. Shani didn't envy the person in charge. While the traffickers had kidnapped most of the children in Brazil, they'd abducted the rest throughout South America.

"You weren't watching when the first few went down the ramp," Naomi replied, "so maybe she's already inside the hangar."

Shani had tasked Naomi with operating as Mia's human shield as they left the aircraft and crossed the tarmac.

"Then let's get moving," Mia said.

Shani stayed behind with Cheète in the shadows at the top of the C-130's ramp, watching Mia and the other two raptors on either side of her going down the ramp surrounded by the Brazilian special forces troops who had helped rescue the children.

Before they'd landed, there had been heavy rain, and the dark clouds still threatened. Shani shifted her gaze and scanned the airport, searching for the best sniper positions. The maximum effective range of most skilled snipers was eight-hundred meters. Her stomach dropped as she spotted several perfect spots. The best location was a hanger on the other side of the runway, closer to the Rio Negro River. To the left of the C-130's ramp on the tarmac, Venezuelan refugees waited to board. Then there were ground crews scattered everywhere, refueling or doing maintenance on military aircraft. What Shani saw was a recipe for disaster.

Venezuela's long economic crisis had turned into one of the worst catastrophes ever suffered by a nation not at war. Over six million Venezuelans had fled to other countries since 2014, and joblessness was close to fifty percent. Even though the country had the largest oil reserves in the world, there were suffering shortages of food, gasoline, and diesel. And rural farmers couldn't get their crops to the cities where ninety percent of the remaining population lived.

If the chatter on the dark net was true, there'd be many takers in Brazil where the murder rate was three times that of the United States. The intel said the money would be paid to the assassin who got to Mia first and verified the kill. Since chatter was equal to gossip, to check what they'd picked up on the dark web they consulted the CIA along with the Mossad and the UK's SIS. The feedback was not good. All the spy agencies had verified the chatter from different sources.

The offer had been posted on that dark website soon after the C-130 had left Bran's ranch and before the aircraft crossed into Brazilian airspace. Shani didn't know if the mysterious Russian in Caracas Josh was going after had made the offer or someone else. Maybe his target, Damien Bran, had done it.

What concerned Shani the most was the leak inside Brazil reporting Mia's every move in real time. They'd even revealed when the C-130 landed and the minute the first child walked down the ramp and crossed the tarmac toward the hanger.

Another challenge was the eight-mile drive through a city of over two million to reach the waiting-chartered Airbus at the city's civilian airport. Mia's film crew was already on board. The plan had been to land the big passenger jet at the military airbase where security was tighter, but there had been an unforeseen problem. The length of the military runway was two thousand feet too short for the big A350-900.

There could be multiple assassins in Brazil and France, all determined to collect the five-million-dollar bounty. Since this was a competition, the early bird might get the worm, Mia.

Shani expected the first attempt to take place here, with more on the road to the civilian airport. If they survived the eight-mile drive, an assassin might hide a bomb on the A350. After all, the Russian oligarchs were ruthless in getting rid of their enemies, even blowing up and killing an airliner full of passengers to kill one person.

Then there was General Costa's temper. Not much Shani could do about that. Costa had exploded when he was told there might have been a leak in his command staff.

"Impossible!" He'd left in a rage to discover who it was. Brazilian intelligence was already looking into emails and tracking bank accounts of the few people in Brazil who had knowledge of this rescue operation. If Costa had remained calm, he could've helped Shani come up with an alternative plan to throw off the leak, fool the assassins, and to have bomb-sniffing dogs inspecting the A350.

And how was she going to warn Josh since he'd dropped off the grid? If the elusive Russian had arranged the hit on Mia, then Josh might stand a chance. But what if that information had come from Josh's enemy Damien Bran, who might know that Josh had taken Captain Thiago as a Trojan Horse to reach the Russian? If that was the case, the Russian might have been warned, and Josh was walking into a death trap.

Scanning the tarmac around the C-130, Shani spotted one figure in a Brazilian air force uniform walking parallel to the knot of special forces troops packed tight around Mia and the other two raptors. Something about the man triggered Shani's internal alarm, but she couldn't figure out what it was until she saw the square shape of what could be a GoPro clipped to the man's left breast shirt pocket. She focused her binoculars on the object and verified it was one of those cameras.

Was that man one of Mia's paparazzi eager to get photographs to sell or was he working with an assassin? Shani thought the odds favored the assassin since it wasn't public knowledge that Mia was here.

In fact, a video of Mia being killed might be the evidence to cash in on the dark net. And a smart paparazzo earned up to a half-million annually, and some of them were reckless and ruthless. Maybe this guy with the GoPro was planning a double payday for the same video.

The second clue was how the man walked on his toes. Troops were trained to march on their heels and not their toes. This person was not in the Brazilian Airforce.

If Shani was right, that meant the assassin was somewhere inside the airbase. In a situation like this, if she'd been the sniper, Shani knew she'd pick the best position farthest from the target but within range. That way the sniper would have a better chance of escaping and living to collect the bounty. With all the special forces troops surrounding Mia, a close kill attempt had a higher risk of failure, and even if the assassin were successful, he'd end up dead too.

"What are you thinking?" Cheéte asked. He was standing behind her, watching over her left shoulder.

Shani told him about the guy with the GoPro and pointed out the best position for the sniper on a hangar on the other side of the runway. "Tell them to skip the SUV waiting to take Mia to the other airport and get her inside the nearest hangar." She didn't say there might be a bomb hidden there too. In an active situation like this, anything was possible.

Cheéte held a two-way radio to his mouth and shared the info with the other two raptors. An instant later, the group of special forces troops, like a flock of birds, made a sharp ninety-degree turn away from the waiting SUV, and picked up the pace as they hurried Mia toward the hangar where the children were located.

The figure with the GoPro turned in tandem with them, and Shani could see that he was focusing the camera on Mia's location inside the heavily armed and armored escort.

"The GoPro guy is involved!" she said.

"I'll take him out." Cheéte started unzipping his rifle case.

"No!" Shani said, putting a restraining hand on his closest arm. "Do you want to get us killed? The shooting has to be left up to the Brazilian troops. Look at the second ring of security made up of military police." The second ring had surrounded the aircraft and the hangar. "Look at their faces. Like us, this situation has pumped them up with adrenaline and cortisol. You fire a shot, and most of those rifles out there will open up on us inside this plane. They will think we are the assassins."

"Got it," he said and switched the channel on the two-way radio so he could talk to the officer in charge of the special forces troops surrounding Mia. A moment later, three Brazilian MPs peeled off from the outer ring of security and rushed the GoPro guy, tackling him to the ground.

Shani saw the flash from the roof of one hanger across the runway she'd picked as the best place to take the kill shot.

"Mia's down, and someone else was hit with the same round," they heard over the radio and watched in horror as the special forces troops scooped up two bodies and ran with them to vanish inside the hangar.

Expecting the building to blow up, Shani's stomach

clenched, and she held her breath. When nothing happened, she shuddered and filled her lungs.

There was a second flash from the same distant rooftop. This time it hit the GoPro guy as two MPs pulled him to his feet. Shani thought the assassin had taken out a witness that must have known who he was.

MPs piled into a tan Toyota Land Cruiser and raced across the runway toward the sniper's perch. She heard Cheéte say, "Don't shoot me when I fire from inside the C-130. From here, I can see the sniper running across that roof." He was talking to the Brazilian special forces officer in charge of Mia's security detail. "I can take him out."

"Take the shot," came the call over the two-way radio.

Cheéte handed Shani the radio, pulled out his fifty-caliber sniper rifle from its bag, moved into a firing position, worked the bolt to chamber a round, and sighted on the tiny, shadowy running figure he saw through the scope and squeezed the trigger.

"Damn," he said. The assassin had dropped out of sight on the other side of the roof as he'd fired. A moment later, they saw something jaw-dropping.

"What the..." Shani said.

A noisy, ultralight, tiny, single-seat, open-frame helicopter buzzed into view on the other side of the hanger headed to the river. If the shooter reached the Amazon rainforest on the other side, he was home free.

"This shooter is a bargain-basement assassin," Cheéte said. "That's an AW95. I have one back home." Then he took another shot, hitting the little bird, splitting the drive shaft in two.

Shani watched the AW95 drop out of sight. She heard the crash, followed by an explosion and smoke.

CHAPTER 20

WHEN JOSH AWOKE, the first thing he did was check the time. He'd slept long enough for Adrienne to drive about eighty miles, if she'd kept the speed down as he'd wanted. The silence in the cab was so deep that he sat up abruptly to see why and burst out laughing when he saw what was sticking out of Thiago's mouth. Adrienne had followed through with her threat to stuff the captain's mouth with the man's soiled underwear.

"Are we north or south of the La Soledad Bridge?" he asked.

"North," she replied, her eyes watching him in the rearview mirror above the dash.

They were on a stretch of road that curved gently to the northeast. Here, the highway was bordered by thick stands of trees, helping to hide a fifty-three-foot trailer that was slanted across the road blocking both lanes. When Adrienne first saw it, she slammed on the brakes, and the truck shuddered to a stop about thirty feet from the roadblock. The only way around it was a narrow dirt strip on the other side of the road guarded by several armed men wearing bandanas that covered the lower half of their faces. "This not good," she said.

"No shit!" Josh replied.

Thiago had been sleeping, but the abrupt stop jerked him awake. Josh pulled his mouth plug out, and the captain didn't hesitate. "What?" Then, squinting, he panicked and lost his English. "*Maldiciones! Bandidos! Cortar me* lose. Give me a *pistola*."

Three men were walking toward the Toyota from the truck trailer, and they carried AK-47s.

Josh analyzed the situation in an instant. His sniper rifle was in the truck's bed with the backpack that held his gear and supplies. The only weapons he had in the cab were a .45 caliber pistol with a twelve-round magazine in his shoulder holster, his backup pistol in an ankle holster, and a seven-inch fixed blade. He carried three other magazines for the .45 stored in pockets on his vest and several magazines for his sniper rifle. He also had pockets crammed with power bars and a half-full liter water bottle sitting between him and the captain. The light-weight, cheap Venezuelan military uniform Josh wore didn't come with enough pockets or loops to carry much more. The rest of his ammo and gear were in the backpack. That meant he had only forty-eight rounds against several men with automatic rifles, and he didn't know what other weapons they might have or how many were out-of-sight behind the boxy 53-foot trailer.

"Adrienne, we're trading places. You get back here and crawl through the window into the truck bed. Grab my rifle and run for those trees." He pointed. "And stay low! I'll distract them, and hopefully they won't see you." He would've told her to take the pack too, but it probably weighed as much as she did. That much weight would slow her down and probably get her killed. Retrieving the ruck would be up to him.

A moment later, they'd switched places. As soon as she'd crawled through the window into the truck bed, he flung the door open, dove out of the cab, and started shooting before he hit the ground. His first-round slammed into the nearest man, killing him instantly. The next round took out number two. The third man was already trying to escape, but Josh hit one of his legs. When Josh hit the pavement, he twisted his body to the side and rolled toward the rear of the Hilux, keeping a low profile.

The other men watching from the front of the trailer scattered and unleashed a barrage of bullets at the Toyota. Josh felt one round graze his right leg before he turned the corner and, staying low, slid into the truck bed. The back window had already been blown out, and the shattered glass was splattered with Thiago's blood and brain matter. The machine gun attached to the roll bar behind the cab was out of the question. It would take too much time to pull off the canvas cover and connect a belt of ammunition to the weapon and chamber the first round. By then, he'd be dead.

He saw that his M40 bolt-action sniper rifle was gone. *Good girl,* he thought. The weapon had a loaded five-round magazine with a sixth-round in the chamber.

He'd planned to take the backpack but realized that if he did the heavy thing would slow him down and maybe get him killed. With the odds against them, he couldn't afford to be wounded either. Before he left the truck, he switched out his pistol magazine with a full one. Rolling from the truck bed to the ground, he popped up and sprinted down the center of the road, keeping the Toyota between him and the shooters.

When he swerved toward the trees, he'd be exposed, and he wasn't wearing his bullet-resistant DARPA long Johns. He'd given that to Mia.

When he heard the popping sound of a grenade launcher, Josh dove toward the ditch beside the road, tearing the thin fabric covering his knees as he slid across the pavement. The grenade hit, and the Toyota exploded, followed an instant later by a louder explosion when the fuel tank, his ammo, and the extra cans of fuel in the bed blew, launching the Hilux into the air and sending out a shock wave of debris and heat. Instead of ducking for cover, he ran into the trees as shrapnel sliced into his back.

A few yards later, bursting onto a narrow dirt trail, he slammed into another man, knocking both of them down. Josh's peripheral vision picked up the flash of a knife as the other man lunged at him with the blade. Josh spun like a top away from the guy, avoiding a knife wound.

Muscle memory kicked in. Leaping to his feet, Josh used a bent elbow to knock the guy's knife aside. Then in one sweeping step, he was behind the man, grabbing the top of his head from behind. Running his hand forward over the guy's forehead, his fingers dug deep into both eyes. Holding the head like a bowling ball, he yanked back but felt the guy already twisting to break free.

Sliding his SEAL blade from its scabbard with his right hand from his waist-belt, he didn't have time to go for a better target higher up, so he went for the man's liver, buried the blade in it, and twisted.

Letting go, he dropped the already dying body as it bled out. The guy had a walkie-talkie clipped to his belt. Josh took it and hurried further into the trees away from the trail before he turned north, moving parallel to the roadblock. He didn't have time to look for Adrienne. He could only hope she'd made the same decisions he was.

When he was halfway between the burning Toyota and the trailer, he dropped and crawled to the edge of the trees, where a perfect target presented itself. He didn't know how many armed thugs they were up against, so he had to risk taking out as many as possible to infect them with fear and panic.

He saw three men bending over the guy with the shattered leg. The nearest target, an exposed bum, was by the wounded man's feet. The second target was slipping a belt around the leg above the bloody wound. Number two's head lined up with the first target's butt. The third man was sitting cross-legged by the casualty's head, cradling it on his lap.

Josh aimed at the center of the butt crack of the first target and lined the shot up so that one round would take out all three men. The bullets he used were black-tipped NATO rounds capable of penetrating three-quarters-of-an-inch of RHA armor from a hundred meters.

With the Toyota burning and making a lot of noise, Josh didn't expect anyone to notice the muzzle flash or hear the shot. He squeezed the trigger and killed all three, as he'd planned. Now he had eleven rounds left.

Staying flat, he slithered back through the trees until he was on the far side of the trailer, away from the burning wreck.

Returning to the tree line to discover what was behind the roadblock, he thought, *Cocksuckers!*

The bandits had brought their families with them. He counted ten armed men among them and too many women with children lounging behind the trailer. In gone-crazy Venezuela, it seemed for some that crime had become a family affair; kidnapping and looting were their business.

The women and children were scrambling to fold up

blankets and pack plates and food into hampers. *Jesus,* he thought, *they were having a fucking picnic.* They probably had expected a leisurely day of robbery and kidnapping before they went home to watch some fake Russian reality TV show if they had a dish antenna and a generator.

There were two pickup trucks parked closer to the trailer. Then there was the tractor for the eighteen-wheeler and several motorcycles. Running in a crouch, Josh headed toward the bikes. When he saw Adrienne huddled behind one, relief joined his adrenaline surge.

She was watching a skinny adolescent boy with an AK-47 standing in the center of the road, between the road block and her position. The boy was watching what was going on. Beyond the trailer, a pillar of dark smoke spiraled into the sky from the burning Toyota.

Adrienne saw Josh and without a sound mouthed, "This bike has the most fuel." She grinned and moved her head so he could see that she was already busy hot wiring it as he had taught her.

Before they escaped, he had to disable the other bikes and trucks. Staying low, Josh started slicing tires with his blade. Between each bike, he glanced at the kid with the AK-47. Someone shouted from the trailer, something about paying attention, and the kid turned. When he spotted Josh, his mouth dropped open. Before the boy could react, Josh heard the heavy crack of his sniper rifle firing as Adrienne shot the boy, killing him instantly.

Sprinting toward the corpse, Josh scooped up the AK-47 and ran to the front corner of the truck tractor to slice open the front right tire. Hearing running noises headed his way, he shouldered the automatic rifle, stepped into the road, and fired into the angry mob until the thirty-round clip emptied.

As he retreated, he dropped the weapon. Women and children were screaming. He heard shots and felt two rounds hit him, one below his right shoulder that felt like a through-and-through and another one that grazed a hip.

He didn't feel any pain yet. That would come later once his cortisol-adrenaline rush was over. Before that happened, they had to be gone.

Adrienne was already on the dirt bike with her hands on the handles, goosing the engine, watching him over her shoulder. His sniper rifle was slung across her back. When he leaped on the seat behind her and wrapped his arms around her waist, she pulled a wheelie and they raced north along the curved road, hearing rounds snapping past them.

The curve in the road that had hidden the roadblock also served the same purpose now, and they were soon out of sight and picking up speed.

There were two pickup trucks he hadn't disabled. They had just ruined a family picnic and seriously put a dent in their criminal enterprise. Without a doubt, the survivors were going to be really pissed.

If Josh and Adrienne were going to evade them, they had to leave the road as soon as possible. Once out of sight, they'd have to find a place to stay while he treated his wounds and assessed the situation. With over twenty percent of the country's population gone, there had to be some place they could hide.

"We have to find an abandoned house, out of sight of the road," he said in her ear. Without turning to look at him, she nodded.

"We have to find it sooner than later," he added. "I'm shot and might bleed out." He felt her stiffen in alarm.

"You shielded me?" she said. "Didn't you, *Padrasto*?"

Calling him her stepfather left him momentarily speechless. He remembered making that promise back in the barn. And he knew if they survived, he'd deliver...somehow. He whispered in her ear, "Yes, *filha*, I did."

CHAPTER 21

ADRIENNE WAS DESPERATE to get off this hazardous highway with its treacherous potholes and find a place to hide before the bandidos caught them. She'd barely met Josh and didn't know him, but he'd risked his life to save her and then treated her like she was special. No one had ever done that before, except for Mia, and until recently she didn't even know that Mia was Purple Tomato, one of her most steadfast YouTube fans.

The stolen dirt bike purred as Adrienne frantically glanced left and right, searching for the perfect side road to take. Before he'd passed out, Josh whispered in her ear what to look for. "It has to be a gravel or dirt track just wide enough for a small truck that leads out of sight into the countryside. It has to be overgrown with weeds. That means no one has recently used it. Our objective is to find a deserted farm out of sight of the main road. The tricky part will be to leave no evidence that we were there, no tire tracks. If you can't, you'll have to walk back and brush them out, do whatever it takes."

Not long after hearing his slurred words, she'd felt his arms slipping away from her waist where he'd been holding on. They'd been moving fast, and she almost lost him. She'd barely grabbed his hands and pinned them to her belly.

To keep him on the bike, she leaned forward to shift his weight to her back. It wasn't easy driving the bike bent over at almost ninety degrees with her chin almost touching the handlebars and his weight crushing her. She could hardly breathe. It also didn't help that the sniper rifle slung across her back was digging into her flesh.

If he slipped left, she had to tilt the bike to the right to keep him balanced on the rear seat. Then when he slid in the other direction, she leaned the bike left, an almost impossible balancing act, all the while fearing she was going to lose him, her heart pounding like a terrified mouse.

After Adrienne stopped the 250cc bike, she knew he was alive because of his shallow breathing on the back of her neck. *Gracas a Deus por isso*, she thought. But she didn't know how to survive in a strange land so far from home. She'd lost everything: her bank account, her apartment, her beloved doll. Pappi made her watch as he hacked Sky into little pieces with an ax. He'd always been a *bastardo sujo*. It broke her heart watching that. Sky might have been a doll, but she was the only one she trusted with her secrets.

As long as Pappi lived, she'd never be safe. If he found out she'd escaped the *traficantes de escravos*, he'd never give up the hunt to find and kill her.

Fearing the engine might not start again, she left the bike idling.

Once off, it wasn't easy holding Josh in place with one hand while unhooking the two stubborn bungee cords holding a cloth satchel behind the seats, wondering without a hint of guilt if it belonged to the young boy she'd killed. Such was life, kill or be killed. Pappi had been an enforcer for one of Rio's most violent favela gangs. When she'd still been a child, he'd forced her to go with him to learn how to torture and murder people.

She almost tossed the satchel away but changed her mind. What if there was something useful in that heavy bag, something to help keep them alive? She opened it, poked around, and found several small water bottles under other stuff. As thirsty as she was, Josh needed the water more. Because of his blood loss, he had to hydrate, so before mounting the bike again she stood beside it and patiently trickled an entire bottle into his mouth, losing only a few drops. As the minutes ticked by in her head, she started tapping one nervous foot, repeatedly glancing down the highway, expecting the *banditos* to appear.

Getting back on the bike would not be easy since Josh had fallen forward across her seat and his head was hanging over the handlebars. Grunting and groaning, Adrienne strained to lift him. She cursed under her breath, not wanting to risk him hearing. "*Maldito inferno!*"

After all, she knew men expected women to be *gentil e educado*. Papai beat her every time that kind of language come out of her mouth, and she'd been a boy then. And she never told Papai when she was a boy that she thought of herself as female. But he found out anyway when someone told him she performed on the streets for tourists dressed as a girl. That was when he started using his *charutos* to burn that girl out of the little boy she'd been then.

Adrienne slid the sniper rifle from her back to her front before squeezing under Josh. Once on the seat, she used her back to push him upright. By then she was breathing heavily and drenched in sweat. After catching her breath, she used the short bungee cords to fasten him and the satchel to her body. One cord under their arms and the other around their waists with the little metal hooks digging painfully into her flesh.

"*Maldito inferno!*" she mumbled. If she hadn't been riding a similar bike for most of her life, she'd never attempt this. After buying her first bike with money earned busking, she'd been a *mostrar*, risking life and limb and loving every moment. Now she looked back on that time and wondered how she'd survived.

Tying them together probably wasn't a good idea. If she lost control of the bike and they tumbled, he'd land on top and one of her legs would end under the bike, maybe broken and shredded, and they'd be in fucking hell for sure then.

Precariously balanced, she drove the bike onto the road and then heard the roar of engines coming fast from behind, getting much louder as they closed the distance. She hissed, sounding like a wildcat, "*Bocetas vis!*"

Gripping the handlebars and leaning forward, she fed gas to the engine, and the bike took off like a cheetah, leaving black tire tracks and smoke behind them. With Josh's weight added to her, the acceleration yanked them back, threatening to pull them both off the bike. It took every ounce of strength in her arms to hold on.

Then she saw a side road that matched Josh's directions as they shot by it at almost 100 kph. "*Filho da Puta!*" Adrienne roared. "*Foda-me!*" There was no way she could turn around and get out of sight before the bandits caught them.

Both sides of the road were lined with trees. When Adrienne spotted what looked like a footpath, wide enough to barely let the bike through, without thought she aimed toward that dark slot and increased speed, literally flying as they left the road with the wheels off the ground. By the time the front wheel hit the path inside the trees, Josh's dead weight was pulling her back, again threatening to yank them off the bike. With every ounce of strength she had and then some, she held on until the muscles in her arms were bulging as her sweaty fingers started slipping off the bike's handles.

Once they were several meters down that narrow path, racing by the shadowy trees in a blur on either side, she applied the brakes. Then Josh's weight reversed, threatening to push them forward off the seat and slam her into the handlebars before slinging them through the air to land in front of the bike. Now the *maldita* rifle barrel was digging into her chest, and that bag squashed between her legs and belly hurt too.

She won that battle but didn't know how. Once the bike came to a stop, Adrienne used her legs to keep it from falling over.

"Wow!" she heard a feeble voice say in her right ear. "That was great driving! Did you learn that from YouTube too?"

With her body trembling from shock and exertion, she twisted to see Josh's blurry eyes and calm expression. "You awake?" she asked.

"Maybe," he replied in a weak tone, "unless we're both dead and this is hell."

"How can you joke like that?" she said, annoyed.

"Why not? You did it when me and Shani disarmed that bomb under your cage."

Still shaking, Adrienne released the tight bungee cords holding them together and slipped off the bike. "You got food?"

Josh zipped open one of his vest's pockets and fished out a couple of energy bars. She took one and read the label, "Soldier Fuel energy bar." She handed it back. "You eat while I check your wounds."

He grinned. "I have more."

"Don't eat them all."

They both turned at the sounds of noisy vehicles racing past their hiding place.

A moment later, he broke the silence and said, "Help me off the bike. I'm feeling weaker than a hooked tuna after hours of fighting to be free."

A moment later, she had him on the ground, back against a tree, his legs sticking out in front. She took off his vest and shirt until he was naked from the waist up. The sight of the scarred battle-map covering his skin caused her to shudder. The injuries from the slavers and her Papai's *charutos* paled in comparison.

Josh was still oozing blood from the fresh wounds, the inside of his shirt caked with it. She opened the satchel. Removing a couple of clean pullover shirts from the top, she found some candy bars, more small water bottles, toothpaste, a toothbrush, and plastic bags with more snacks. She took the food out and set the bags on the ground between her and Josh.

"What's that?" he said, pointing at one bag with a shaky finger.

She opened it and sniffed. "Seeds from spicy hot peppers."

"Taste one, and if it burns that's good. Then grind them to powder and stuff that into all my open wounds." He pulled out his SEAL knife, offering it to her. "Use my knife's tang as the grinder. If you can find a rock or something else flat and hard, that'll get the job done."

Later, after she started turning the chili seeds into powder, Adrienne asked, "What's this do?"

"In the wounds, the capsaicin from the pepper seeds will cause the blood to clot faster, destroy germs, and speed up the healing process. It'll also relieve the crippling pain I'm feeling so I can function better." His eyes drifted away from her, avoiding eye contact.

Sensing something wrong, she said, "What?"

"I won't be much help. I've been wounded enough to know when I'm useless. Once we stop the bleeding, it's going to take time to regain my strength. I'm sorry."

She grinned and returned to grinding the pepper seeds. After patching him up as best she could, she had him drink more water before they climbed back on the bike.

More than an hour later, they'd reached an abandoned farm at the end of the weed infested gravel road she'd spotted earlier.

"How far do you think we are from that highway?" he asked

"Over three kilometers," Adrienne replied. "This place isolated, like you want." There were no other houses in sight.

She drove the bike around the house to the back and stopped between it and a barn. With the engine off and the kickstand down, she helped Josh get off. Together, with him leaning on her, they walked around the house and returned to the bike.

Josh said, "This place is sealed tight. Plywood sheets over the windows. I'll bet all the doors are double locked and maybe even nailed or screwed shut. Whoever lived here was hoping they'd come back one day and didn't want to make it easy for thieves to loot the place."

"So how are we going inside?"

"We aren't, not today." He looked at the barn. "We'll get in there, hide the bike, and spend our first night in the loft. Tomorrow we'll break into the house. Before we sleep though, I want to brief you on the mission, where we're going, and what we have to do when we get there. Do you know Morse code?"

"What's that?"

"Hmm, I was hoping you'd learned that from YouTube like you learned to shoot, but no biggie. I'll teach you all you'll need to know."

"Why bother if you already know?"

"Because in a special ops team, everyone cross trains. And now that you and I are a team, we're going to stay here for a few days, and I'm going to teach you how to survive if something happens to me."

Hearing that Josh considered they were a team thrilled her, but she hid her feelings.

After they discovered the barn doors were all locked from the outside with hefty padlocks and barred on the inside, he asked, "Did you learn how to pick locks from YouTube?"

Adrienne shook her head.

"Then I'll teach you."

"Maybe that lesson can wait," she said and pointed up. One of the loft doors hung partially open.

"How are you going to get up there without a ladder?" he asked.

She pointed at the sturdy, round rails between fence posts enclosing an acre-sized garden choked with weeds. "Looks like each rail spans three posts. One pole six meters long is more than enough for me to climb and get inside."

"What if you fall?" He looked concerned.

"I won't. I trained in gymnastics, ballet, and popular Portuguese and Euro dance forms. My legs stronger than most people, and I have perfect balance." She stuck a hand out. "First, give me one energy bar."

After she'd peeled the wrapping off a GoMacro Bar and ate

it, chased with water from one bottle in the satchel, she said, "You go to shade and rest." She handed him another water bottle.

Josh studied the distance to the tree she'd indicated. He scratched his head, looking troubled, and said, "I don't have it in me to crawl that far on my own." She could tell by the tone of his voice and posture that he hated admitting that.

Adrienne helped him reach the shade before going to work, using his SEAL knife to get one of those hefty fence rails loose. She wanted to be inside the barn before dark. Glancing at Josh, she noticed he'd fallen asleep, his chin resting on his chest.

CHAPTER 22

THE BRAZILIAN SPECIAL forces troops rushed Mia and Esther inside the hangar. More than one medical team worked there, giving the children physicals and treating those who needed it. The doctors and nurses immediately shifted their attention to the two shooting victims. One group hurried to Mia's side and the other to Esther.

With a restless murmur, the children followed but were stopped by the special operations troops who formed a perimeter around the two cots isolated in a back corner of the hangar.

"No closer," the officer in charge said. The curious children stood on tiptoes and craned their necks to gain a better view of the bloody victims.

One girl asked in Portuguese, "Are they dead?"

Another added in the same language, "Who is it?"

"It's our savior, Mia Chanson," a third girl said. "I know it's her. The last time she performed in Rio, I was close enough to the stage to see her face. In Venezuela, I saw her again when she washed and dressed me. She risked her life to save us. She's a saint." The girl's eyes were swimming in tears, and she broke down sobbing.

A moment passed as the word spread. Many of the children were Mia's fans.

One young girl, standing behind the others, forced her way through the crowd to the front. Once she saw the bloody figures on the cots, she kneeled and made the sign of the cross. There was a hushed silence followed by a rustle of movement as most of the children also got down on their knees to pray.

Everyone heard the girl's prayer. "In the name of the Father and the Son and of the Holy Spirit, dear Father, we present before You those who are victims of a shooting. We ask that You touch their hearts. Lord, heal their brokenness." She covered her face with both hands, and fresh tears escaped between her fingers, dripping to the floor.

The weeping spread through the hanger until the children were crying and consoling each other.

This scene greeted Shani and Cheéte when they entered the hangar. Pushing through the crowding children, they reached the medical teams working on Mia and Esther.

Esther, covered in blood from a visible shoulder wound, was still bleeding profusely. Mia was also covered with blood spatter on one side, from the chest down. When Shani saw Mia's chest rise and fall, she said in Hebrew, "She's not dead."

"Not yet," Cheéte said.

Shani glared at him.

Holding up his hands in surrender, he said, "Where there's a heartbeat, there's hope."

"Much better," Shani replied, and her focus was back on Mia.

When Mia abruptly sat up, everyone gasped, even the

doctor beside her who leaned closer and gently explored Mia's torso with her fingertips. Once done, she urged Mia to lie back down and whispered in her ear not to move. "You might have fractured ribs on that side. We won't know until we take x-rays."

The doctor stood and reported, "There's a hole in her clothing but no wounds. The blood is not hers." Using a sterile stainless-steel probe, the doctor leaned over and inserted it through the ragged hole in Mia's shirt, discovering the deformed slug of a spent bullet. To keep Mia warm, a nurse spread a blanket over her and tucked it around her neck and head, covering most of her.

The doctor held up the malformed slug to examine it. After a moment, she said, "I've seen nothing like this before…Is she Wonder Woman with skin of iron?"

Mia replied in a barely audible voice, so only those closest heard. "Please, don't start spreading rumors like that. Gal Gadot is Wonder Woman. Not me. I know her, and she's a good-hearted, kind, and generous person."

Shani leaned closer to Cheète and said, "I think Josh is responsible for whatever stopped that bullet."

"She's wearing his bullet resistant undergarment bodysuit. Something he got from DARPA for this mission," Cheète said. Startled, he glanced around to see if anyone heard him.

Mia shifted and focused on them. With a frown, she said, "Keep it down. If I can hear you, so can others." She gestured for them to come closer. A moment later, Shani and Cheète were hovering beside her, their faces inches apart.

In a barely audible whisper, Mia said, "The underwear Josh made me wear is a composite of carbon fiber and a boron nitride-reinforced material."

"Never heard of it," Cheéte said.

"Well," Shani said, "if it saved your life, it's worth whatever it cost him. The hole in your blouse shows the round would've hit your heart if it had gotten through."

"During our raid last year on that nasty Nazi ranch in Montana," Cheéte said, "we all got to wear the latest lightweight armor still in development. No one told us what they were made of, and DARPA had us turn them in when the job was over. I suspected Josh got to keep something, but I wasn't sure what."

Shani jabbed him in the side with an elbow. "Keep it down," she hissed. "Maybe DARPA doesn't know he has it."

Cheéte took a moment to think that over before nodding. "Yeah, that makes sense. Josh stole this expensive carbon-boron body armor out of love." He whistled. "That's a lot of love. I wonder how much."

Shani shook her head. "How would you know, lust man? You have three wives and no telling how many girlfriends. Back in Venezuela, I saw the way you were ogling me. Don't even try."

"Honest," he replied, "I love all of my wives. That's my curse. I can't live without them."

"You know that love thrives on truth and trust," Shani said. "Because you keep your wives a secret from each other, you risk losing them all."

"Knock it off," Mia said. Her voice croaked, followed by coughing. Wheezing, she added, "You two sound like adolescents too immature to admit you like each other. Stop dancing around the way you feel."

Shani's face flushed. "No way," she said. "He's old enough to be my grandfather." She avoided looking at Cheéte.

Sounding offended, he said, "I'm not that old!"

Shaking her head, Mia said, "I want to know how Esther is doing."

The baby-faced doctor with the enormous eyes tending Mia was struggling to hide a grin when she said, "Your friend is alive but unconscious. The slug that didn't reach your heart entered her right shoulder at an angle and exited her left side a few inches lower than the entry wound before hitting you. It was quite a blow, and we'll transport her to a hospital as soon as the air ambulance arrives."

"What is your friend's name?" a junior nurse asked in Portuguese. She was holding a pen poised over a form on a clipboard.

Shani stood from where she'd been kneeling beside Mia's cot and replied, "Our unconscious friend's name is Mia Belle-Chanson."

The nurse wrote it down. When she looked up, she asked, "Isn't that the name of the famous French singer and producer? I have a cousin who is madly in love with her and her music."

"I'm also a fan," the doctor said.

Guessing what Shani was doing, Cheéte looked at Mia and held a finger to his lips. She nodded, revealing she understood. She gestured for him to get closer, and when he did, she whispered in his ear. "That ruse will not work. I'm taller than Esther."

"No reason to be concerned," he replied. "Esther is unconscious and will be covered with a blanket on the way to the hospital."

Mia frowned. "Her complexion is dark but not enough to pass for me, especially if any paparazzi get a photo of her."

"Then we'll have to make sure that doesn't happen," he replied.

Shani had stepped away for a moment to talk in private with the doctor. Finished, she rejoined their huddle. “Your doctor is going to cooperate,” she said. “It seems her uncle is General Costa. One of his younger brothers married her French mother. Tomorrow, with her help, every major newspaper and news show in the world will report an assassin hired by sex traffickers shot Mia Chanson, and they’ll think you’re in a private hospital in Brazil under heavy guard, struggling to live. That may get the assassins off our asses long enough so we can sneak you out of this country and back to France.”

Mia shook her head. “No, that will put Esther in more danger. I will not leave Brazil without her. If it wasn’t for her, I’d be dead. Esther placed herself between me and that building. I want my combat team in that hospital to guard her. If she dies...” Her voice broke, and she closed her eyes.

The young doctor was on the other side of the cot between Shani and Cheète. “I have a suggestion,” she said.

Mia slipped a hand out from under the blanket and offered it to the doctor, who took it. “It would be nice to know your name and something about you.”

“My name is Celeste Costa. I’m a big fan of yours, and I’ve been in Brazil for almost two years finishing up a surgical residency program here. Before coming to Brazil, I spent several years in the medical program at the *Universite de Lyon* in France.”

“What’s your idea?” Shani asked.

“Correct me if I am wrong,” Celeste said, “but if you’re really Mia Chanson, and I don’t doubt that you are...I mean, I’ve heard the rumors that you have been freeing sex slaves, so what has happened to you here makes sense. Anyway, I’m willing to arrange a Jet Rescue Air Ambulance to evacuate you and your wounded friend from this airport to French Guiana and from there to France. I date a nurse who works for them, and Jet Rescue is more than capable."

"We don't know you," Shani said.

Mia reached out with her free hand and gripped Shani's wrist. "What choice do we have? We have to get out of Brazil. I trust her. If Doctor Celeste goes with us, we'll do what she suggests."

Shani thought for a moment, then said, "Doctor, I want you to call your uncle. I have to talk to him before we do anything."

CHAPTER 23

INCHING INTO CONSCIOUSNESS, Josh's first impression was confusion. Light-headed with eyes closed, he couldn't remember where he was. Still, he was aware of one thing, lips covering his mouth that were not his with an aggressive tongue shoving something gooey into his maw.

That seemed too yucky to be real. Still, it occurred to him he might be hallucinating. Maybe he'd gotten drunk and was in a whorehouse. But he'd never done that before.

When he opened his eyes, the world was fuzzy. In that blur, he saw what looked like a shadowy head above him. Turning to the side, he gagged on a gooey lump stuck in his throat, ejecting it, followed by a fit of coughing.

"*Obrigado, querido Deus,*" a relieved voice said. "He lives!"

That voice sounds familiar. Since his mouth felt like the driest place on earth, he said, "I'm thirsty and want to sit up."

"*Desculpa,*" she said as a weight left his abdomen. He realized she'd been sitting on him and had said sorry in Portuguese.

The girl helped him sit with his back against something

rough. "Here," she said, and Josh felt the familiar shape of a plastic bottle slip between his parched lips followed by a trickle of warm water.

After swallowing several times, he struggled to breathe through his nose. No matter how hard he tried, he couldn't get a full breath. With little strength, he pushed the bottle away. "Who are you and what happened?" Getting those words out cost him too much energy. *Damn, I must be in awful shape,* he thought.

"Adrienne," the voice replied. "They shot you yesterday. Tell me how to fix *ferimentos*."

She wanted to treat his wounds. Her name repeated itself in his thoughts while he struggled to retrieve memories that had gone AWOL. It was the Portuguese that finally helped him remember she was from Brazil and he'd helped free her and others from traffickers. "What am I leaning against?" he asked.

"Hay bale," she replied.

"We're in the barn, right?"

"Yes."

Knowing that guess was right helped him remember more. "Well, hell, that's better than waking up to discover I'm stuck in the Atacama.... How about a little water to rinse out my eyes so I can see better?"

He felt her hand on his chin, tilting his head back before she flooded his eyes with water. Then she used a cloth to dab away the excess.

He squinted, focusing on her expression. "When I woke up, I swear you were kissing me." He made sure his voice sounded conversational.

Adrienne's skin tone was the same as Mia's, and when Mia blushed her face became slightly darker. That was how he knew Adrienne was embarrassed. He watched her eyes glance down, away from his, as she processed his words. Then her blink rate increased, warning him she was having a nervous reaction. "Not kissing!" she said. "I no like boys that way."

"What were you doing with your tongue then?" he asked.

The words flew from her mouth. "Keeping you alive! Feeding you!"

He wanted to laugh but decided not to. "Then you were stuffing food in my mouth like a momma bird feeds her chicks, right?"

Once she translated that, she relaxed. "Yes," she replied.

In his condition, she might've killed him doing that. Since it was apparent she didn't know, he let it pass and said, "Good. In my condition, I need a momma hawk."

"For my chicks, I am fearless," she said, determined.

"Well, in that case, Mama Hawk," Josh continued, "tell me what I missed since we arrived here on that borrowed bike. I remember how you were going to get in the barn through the loft but not what happened next."

"First, you eat." She held up the open package holding what was left of an energy bar.

She'd been chewing the bar a bit at a time to make it easier for him to swallow. Most Americans would have freaked out upon discovering that, but he'd been through a lot worse. He nodded approval. "You don't have to force feed me anymore. I can chew now."

She kneeled beside him instead of returning to her first perch on his stomach and fed him one bite-sized chunk at a time. Feeble. It took a while before he swallowed the last bite, followed by more water and coughing.

Since he was incapable of standing on his own, she helped him, acting as his crutch, and led him to the rear of the barn where she pointed at a 1956 Chevrolet half-ton pickup truck sitting on blocks. "When I had motorbike," she said, "I did maintenance. I fix this too."

"YouTube?"

Without missing a beat, ignoring his quip, she nodded. "I learn much from YouTube. Engine looks okay, but battery and tires are missing. I search but not find."

"Without the battery and tires, this old Chevy won't be much use," he said.

"This way." She guided him slowly out of the barn to the house until they reached a set of stairs leading down to a sturdy, locked cellar door with top, middle, and bottom hasps and heavy-duty padlocks. "If there are tires and battery, I think they in there."

"Do you know how to pick locks?" he asked.

Her excitement fled, and her head drooped. "No," she replied in defeat. "I *inspecionada fora* of house more than once. Every door triple locked. All windows with wood planks covering them, screws holding them to window frames."

"No problem," he said. "I know how to pick locks, and I'm going to teach you. You'll open all the others first. This basement door will be last."

She looked at him with a question.

So, he told her, "I suspect that two of the three doors into this house are also locked from the inside, and the way in will be through this basement entry."

"Why not pick first?"

"I want to make sure I'm right, because if that's the case the door that lets us inside may be booby-trapped, and we'd be more vulnerable down there at the base of those stairs in front of that very sturdy door."

He saw she was doing some serious thinking as her eyes darted back and forth from him to the cellar door.

"Let me guess," he said. "You're wondering how we're going to disarm the trap if there is one?"

Looking relieved, she nodded.

"I've done stuff like this before but do not trust myself to do it in my current condition. That means you have to do the work. Since this is a farm, I'm guessing the trap will be a shotgun aimed at that door, rigged to fire when it opens, nailing whoever is standing where we are now." When he saw her alarm, he added. "And I'll be by your side every step of the way. But we need tools. Did you find any?" He hoped they weren't locked in the basement.

With a serious expression, she said, "Door at back of barn with lots of old-fashioned tools on other side, but door also padlocked three times."

"How do you know there're tools in there?"

"Empty knot holes in walls. I peeked, saw tools, no shotgun."

"That's good to know." He grinned. "Let's get started, Mamma Hawk."

As she helped him return to the barn, he could tell from her body language that her mood had lifted. A good thing.

I've been wounded too many times over the years, he thought. *Most were minor, but a few were serious, and one was bad enough to be airlifted from Ramstein Air Base in Germany to the Brooke Army Medical Center on Fort Sam Houston, the only Level 1 Trauma Center the DOD has. My back and neck are hurting like hell, my skin's cool to the touch, I'm sweating, and I'm having trouble breathing. This may be worse. With no chance of proper medical care, I might check out at any time.*

Before they reached the door inside the barn to the

toolshed, he decided he had to teach Adrienne as many survival skills as possible. The longer he lived, the better chance she'd have to reach the GPS location in time to hook up with the Oath Group team on the trawler.

If they couldn't get the truck running, she'd have to use the borrowed motorcycle and go alone. In his condition, he'd only slow her down and get her killed or worse. He wouldn't let that happen. This girl deserved to live more than he did.

Tears filled his eyes because he knew she'd refuse to go without him. That meant he had to give her no choice and put a bullet through his brain first. He was glad that the last message he'd sent to Captain Forest, before he lost the satphone when the Toyota blew up, included what he wanted for Adrienne if anything happened to him. If she made it to the meetup point along Venezuela's coast, the Oath Group would take care of her, and Forest would talk to his grandmothers in San Francisco, so they'd become her family.

Once they reached the toolshed door, he needed time to gather enough energy for the next step.

"Do you pick locks with fingernails?" she asked after a long silence.

"Pull up my right pant leg and remove the ankle holster with my back-up-weapon and put that around one of your ankles," he said. "Since I'm helpless as a newborn chick, Momma Hawk has to have one of my firearms on her at all times. I'll still have the automatic in my shoulder holster and some of my throwing knives. Where's the rifle?"

She pointed at the hay bale where he woke up. The rifle was resting lengthwise on top of it.

When she finished moving the ankle holster and its pistol to her left leg, he said, "Good." He pointed at an empty twenty-liter plastic bucket on its side several feet away. "You can't support me and learn to pick locks, so I'll sit on that after you get it over here. Now help me reach the wall so I can lean against it. If you let go, I'm going to collapse."

Once she had him sitting on the upside-down bucket, he said, "Pull up my other pant leg and run a finger around the inside rim of that boot until you find a slit to an inside pocket that holds my lock picks."

She was a quick learner and had all three locks open in less than an hour. Inside the tool shed, they found what he wanted, a vintage hand auger with an excellent assortment of drill bits. Thank God whoever the farmer had been maintained his tools properly. Every tool and bit Josh inspected was in excellent shape. He selected a bit that would let Adrienne drill a two-inch round hole in the wood cellar door.

"I'm going to teach you how to break down your weapons, clean them, and put them back together until you can do it blindfolded in less than a minute."

"Why waste time?" she said. "Let's see if tires and battery in cellar first."

"Not until the afternoon sun is on that side of the house," he said. "Weapons first."

Her body drooped.

Noticing her reaction, he said, "Listen to me, Momma Hawk. I have a plan, and we'll be leaving this place before noon tomorrow. But for that to happen you have to do all the work. Got it?"

"I thought we stay until you better."

He made sure not to look away or change expression before he said, "Plans change. We leave tomorrow."

He knew he wouldn't get better, only worse. Since his tactical wristwatch would guide her to their GPS location, he wasn't worried. The Oath Group team's instructions were to hang around for seven days off the coast, checking that spot before dawn each day, and the trawler's arrival should be in three days. His original plan had been cutting their meet-up time close. Now, with his failing health, they didn't have that luxury.

"Hand me your pistol," he said.

"It not mine," she replied.

"Now it is. Call it a survival gift."

When he had the automatic on the bench in front of them, he said, "This is a 9mm Glock 43 subcompact semi-auto pistol."

Less than an hour later, she was blindfolded, breaking down the sniper rifle and reassembling it, as she had done with the Glock. She was bright and learned fast.

By 13:00, he was sitting near the bottom of the stairs, watching her use the auger to drill two holes near the top of the basement door. She was standing on the upside down twenty-liter bucket he'd used in the barn as a stool. One hole was to let light in, and the other was for her to see what was inside.

By 14:00, the shotgun trap Josh had anticipated was disabled, and they were inside the cellar where they found shelves half-filled with properly persevered fruits and vegetables, dried jerky in jars, many types of dried herbs and spices, five tires for the Chevy, and the truck's battery along with four twenty-liter cans of gasoline. On top of one tire was a portable manual tire inflater.

Poor Adrienne, he thought. *She's going to be really sore tomorrow morning.*

"This is too easy," she said, as they stared at the treasure.

"No reason to worry," he replied. "I was born on a ranch in Montana and grew up there. When we arrived, this place looked like it had been well maintained. That's why I was thinking the odds were in our favor that we'd find most of the stuff we'd need. Nothing wrong. It turned out better than I expected."

Josh didn't tell Adrienne that these lucky breaks also worried him. It was his experience that when things went too smoothly an unexpected clusterfuck was waiting to drop a ton of toxic turkey shit on him when he least expected it.

"Okay," he said, "Now you get to fix me." He pointed. "Get that duct tape over there, and the jar that looks like it has more dried hot pepper seeds in it."

CHAPTER 24

SOON AFTER THE Oath Group's trawler left the Cayman Islands, the boat had a new name fitting one that was supposed to have a Cuban crew. The trawler was now called Fidel's Gran Palo, and the ensign flying from the stern flag pole wasn't the Stars and Stripes. It was the Cuban national flag with three blue and two white horizontal stripes and a red triangle bearing a white, five-pointed star at its center.

The Oath Group had twelve combat teams, numbering 144 troops. There were also a few hundred support personnel recruited, as they were honorably discharged from military service. They had handpicked every man and woman after a thorough vetting process that included background checks through the CIA, FBI, NSA, and DIA. Their loyalty was to the U.S. Constitution and not an individual or political party.

The twelve teams comprised former Green Berets, Army Rangers, Navy SEALs, Delta Force, and troops from the Marine Raider Regiment.

Hugo was one of six, a split A detachment, the number often used for special recon missions. He grew up in Dona Ana

County, New Mexico, between Las Cruces and El Paso, Texas. He and the others knew that since they were planning to capture a Russian from Caracas, a hornet's nest, that meant this mission was one of the most dangerous to go on. If they failed, no one would rescue them, and no one would know what happened or where they were buried—if they were buried—so failure was not an option.

Two years earlier, Hugo had retired from the U.S. Navy as an E-9 Master Chief Petty Officer and team medic in the SEALs after serving for twenty-two years. Now he was a defense contractor with Josh's elite private Oath Group.

During the five-day cruise from the Cayman Islands to Venezuela, the six former SEALs had repainted the trawler from white to battleship gray to make it harder to spot. The blackout curtains they'd installed ensured no light revealed the boat's location.

When *Fidel's Gran Palo* first arrived at the GPS coordinates Josh provided, it was midnight with no moon and only a few stars were visible through the clouds. Hugo was in the pilothouse, steering the boat. The other five were outside on watch. As the trawler cruised slowly parallel to the beach, the dark mountains loomed menacingly on the other side of the sand.

When they'd been several miles out at sea approaching Venezuela, they'd seen only a few scattered lights along the forested, mountainous coastline. The closer they got, the darker their destination became. It was apparent that no one lived near this isolated area.

The trawler had been running without lights for hours when Oscar, the team leader, killed the primary engine, switching to battery power. Captain Forest, Josh's #2, bought this boat knowing it had six lithium-ion batteries capable of providing two days of quiet power without the need to run the generator. The sudden silence claimed the night, and Hugo left the pilothouse, climbing to the flybridge to watch for Josh's signal.

They loitered near this spot for one hour, waiting. If Josh didn't signal, they'd return to international water and return at the same time the next day to try again. Hugo focused on scanning the strip of beach and the mountain slope above it that was their GPS meetup location.

The other four members of the team wore night-vision goggles, watching for threats. Forest had warned them that piracy off the coast of Venezuela had increased because of the country's crises. They'd all read the piece from the BBC that was published in January reporting on "Venezuelan pirates—the new scourge of the Caribbean."

One paragraph stood out: "*It's sadly reminiscent of the piracy crisis in Somalia a decade ago, where jobless fishermen took up arms to prey on passing ships*."

With the threat of pirates, each man carried an MK47 assault rifle-grenade launcher with integrated computer-assisted fire control and programmable ammunition. If any bloodthirsty pirates made an appearance, they wouldn't live long enough to regret it. Of course, the trawler's primary weapon was way more lethal. Aaron and Ethan had installed that as they waited to hear from Josh.

When the hour wait ended, Oscar turned the trawler north, and they left the coast for international waters to try again another day.

THE SECOND DAY had been a repeat of the first. On the third day, three hours before daybreak and minutes after arriving for their hour vigil, the minutes dragged until Hugo spotted a tiny blinking green light halfway up the mountainside above the beach. With a surge of energy, he counted four dots for H, a pause, another dot for E, another break before the dot, dash, dot, and dot of an L. Then another L followed by a stop before the final three dashes for the O.

"HELLO."

Hugo pointed a pencil-thin green laser to the right of that spot on the mountain and clicked it on-and-off three times, the verification signal. He slipped the laser into a pocket and turned to climb down to the enclosed wheelhouse when another green flash caught his attention, and he turning back, watching as Josh flashed three dots, three dashes, and three dots, giving the distress signal for SOS.

Reading that, Hugo sucked in a breath and held it. Then, after a brief break, he saw two dashes signaling an M. He waited for more flashes, but none came. That meant Josh needed medical care. If there had been a threat, Badger, Josh's call sign, would've ended the signal with a T to warn them.

Knowing there was no threat was a relief. At least they'd probably go ashore without someone shooting at them, but what was Badger's condition?

The two going with Hugo, Simon, and Louis joined him on the boat deck behind the pilothouse to get the Zodiac ready. A two engine, fifteen-foot, five-inch-long military inflatable. Its two motors were a Suzuki 70 HP gas engine and an all-electric 80 HP for silent running. There was a crane on the boat deck to lower the Zodiac to the water.

Hugo said, "Badger has a medical emergency. Simon, go

below and get one of our T3 Medical Backpacks and let Oscar know." Simon scrambled out of sight down to the main cabin while Hugo and Louis hooked the Zodiac to the crane, swung the inflatable out over the water, and lowered it to the surface.

Louis was the junior man on the team. He'd only served six years in the Navy, the last five as a SEAL.

Hugo admired and respected Badger, but Roy Benavidez, a Green Beret legend that earned the Medal of Honor after being wounded thirty-seven times while saving eight men from certain death in Cambodia in 1968, was his number one role model. Like Roy, Hugo's mother was a Yaqui Native American and his father was a Mexican American farmer. Whenever Hugo faced a challenge, he always asked himself what Roy would do. Benavidez let nothing stop him from doing his duty. Hugo's hero had died in 1998 at age 63.

"What the fuck do you think happened?" Louis asked, interrupting Hugo's thoughts. "Do you think Badger had a run in with a Bolshevik blood-sucking leech?" The man grinned, expecting a laugh.

Hugo shrugged, ignored the second question, and denied Louis the reaction he craved. "We won't know until we reach him, but we'll be ready for anything. Badger probably ran into trouble on his way to the coast, or he would've warned us that there were hostiles nearby. Venezuela is a failed state, a super clusterfuck, and anything could've happened. Still, we know he's alive and alert enough to send the signal."

"Sounds like Somalia all over again, right? But since we only have a boat, there won't be any Blackhawk down." This time, Louis provided his own laughter.

"Your guess is as good as mine," Hugo replied as Simon returned and handed Hugo the medical backpack. Although

Tier One Special Ops teams cross-trained so every member was a medic, only Hugo had gone through the training to become one. To save lives, Special Ops medics did surgery in the field.

Once the three were on the water in the Zodiac, they used the silent electric motor to reach the shore and then pulled the heavy inflatable up the beach into the trees, where they hid it under a canopy of cut branches and foliage. Finished, Simon used a broken branch with lots of foliage on it to erase the slug trail leading from the water to the Zodiac's hiding place.

Just as they were slipping into the rainforest, they heard a loud gas-powered motorboat racing toward the trawler. A spotlight lit up their boat.

"Shit on a shingle!" Louis said. "Fucking pirates, but one thing we can count on, Blackbeard and Johnny Depp won't be with them!"

"No big deal," Hugo replied, determined to ignore Louis's corny, wise-guy cracks. "Our guys will take care of them. Let's get moving. We have to climb this mountain to reach Josh. He's located halfway to the top. With that medical SOS signal, I don't think Badger will be coming to us."

"How many times has he been wounded?" Simon asked.

"Don't know," Hugo said. "I've never been in the field with him. When he was with the SEALs, we weren't on the same team, but I heard his body looks like a battlefield."

As they started climbing the steep slope, swinging their eighteen-inch machete blades through the thick foliage, they heard voices shouting in Spanish for the trawler to surrender or die. Several AK-47s fired into the air as warning shots.

Then their trawler opened up with the M134 Minigun that had been mounted to the bow of the boat before they'd arrived. It was a six-barrel electrically operated weapon that fired up to six-thousand 7.62mm rounds per minute. When it wasn't in use, they stored it in a watertight storage compartment under a nearby deck hatch. The belts, with thousands of rounds of ammo, were in another compartment next to that one. The silence that followed with no return fire from the AK-47s told them the outcome.

"Scratch one pirate boat and crew," Louis said, and for once Hugo joined the laughter as they slashed their way higher up the steepening slope. After a moment, he held up a hand to stop and keyed his encrypted, hand-held portable two-way radio and called the trawler. "Report," he said.

"Threat eliminated," Oscar replied. A Navy SEAL sniper, he'd retired as an E-9 Command Master Chief Petty Officer at sixty-two, outranking Hugo.

Hugo keyed the radio and said, "From what we know about these pirates, most of them don't work alone. When that bunch doesn't report in, they might send someone else to find out what happened to them."

"No matter who or what they send, we're ready," Oscar replied.

CHAPTER 25

CHEÈTE NOTICED A grim-faced General Costa entering the hangar as Shani's satellite phone buzzed. As she focused on the screen, that meant her psychic radar was impaired. A good thing, as far as he was concerned, since he saw her as a walking-talking feast for hungry eyes.

As Costa made his way through the crowded front half of the hanger toward the back, attracting almost everyone's attention, Cheète took advantage of the momentary distraction for a sneak peek of Shani, who stood several feet from him.

He liked what he saw but didn't enjoy her glares when she caught him looking, so he kept it brief. When Mia noticed, she'd grin. She knew him better than most and didn't judge him as others did. Heck, when he'd visited France, spending time with Mia and Josh, she'd point out women he'd like to *étude*.

Cheète refused to deny himself the pleasure of at least looking, even when the object of his interest didn't like it. Mia wouldn't give him away, but his wife detested when he looked at other woman, giving him hell every time she caught him.

So, refusing to be denied a harmless pleasure and to avoid getting caught, he'd become an expert at stealthy glances.

But his admiration was cut short when he saw her expression transition to one of dread, sending a chilly warning down his spine.

What the hell? He thought. He'd never seen Shani bothered by anything. She was a role model of fierceness that Cheète admired more than he enjoyed her moody beauty. In an instant, he feared the worst.

Then she looked up, and their eyes locked. The dread he saw in them looked even worse. His first thought was, *Dear God, not Josh. Who else could it be?* His friend was the one who stayed in the lion's den. A glacier of melting ice flooded his stomach. Shani gestured for him to join her.

He figured the only reason she'd want to tell him first would be if Josh had been captured or was dead. It couldn't be anything else. So she wanted him to break the bad news to Mia instead of her.

If true, what a FUBAR that'd be!

Damn, maybe that's why the general looked so sour. He knows. Cheète disliked being the one to break this kind of news to a parent, child, wife, or lover that their significant other had been captured, killed, or maimed.

When Cheète reached Shani, who'd moved further from Mia's cot for privacy, he positioned himself so she'd have to turn her back on Mia and Costa, giving him time to avoid being the bearer of bad news if the general already knew.

"What wrong with you?" Shani asked. "You look like a child caught sneaking into a freezer for ice cream."

Ignoring that barb, he asked, "What did you read on your phone?"

She tapped the screen and turned it toward him. "I don't

want to say it because someone might hear me. This has to be kept between us."

He started reading the text. Before he was halfway through, he knew why it was so important to Shani. Mia was a sensitive person and what was in this text might break her. He knew her that well. After all, he was in Haiti with Josh when they'd rescued Mia and her friend Celeste from the traffickers. And he'd helped find a French family he knew to adopt her so she could escape her toxic parents.

When he finished reading, feeling lightheaded, he asked. "What if the general already knows?"

"Impossible," Shani said. "Costa has his intel sources, but not for this."

"Explain."

"That alert came from Tamar, one of my closest friends, but she's still with Kidon, and it's apparent to me she's on a Mossad mission to assassinate someone in Russia's largest and most ruthless criminal group. She risked her life to send that warning. And what happened to Celeste and the Spanish film producer hasn't been reported in the news yet. The general is focused on what's happening in his country, not France or Spain."

Cheète nodded. "Makes sense, but I don't understand why you're telling me if you want to keep this a secret."

"I need your help to make sure Mia doesn't return to France. We have to hide her in another country. Poisoning Celeste and murdering the producer was bait. The Russian bratva will be waiting for her if she returns home. I also don't have any contacts in this part of the world to help me sneak her out of Brazil. But I think you do, right?"

Cheète thought for a moment before replying, "I've been out of this game for decades, but I know how to reach a former

Marine pilot in this part of the world. He's a strange duck, an asset SOCOM and the CIA have used for decades. Before Josh and I became a Scout Sniper Team, they sent my previous teammate and me to South America on a mission. That's when I first met Jimbo..." He stopped, looking stunned. "I've already said too much. That operation was classified and still is. But if you want to sneak out of Brazil, Jimbo would be our guy, and I know he can make it happen. He has two choppers and a float plane. The choppers don't have the range to reach us, but the plane does. If we provide the GPS position, he'll land on the river and pick us up at that location. Then he'll fly us wherever we want to go in the Americas."

Shani placed a hand on Cheète's arm, stopping him, and nodded toward Mia. "We can talk more later. I want to hear what General Costa has to say."

As they reached the cot, Cheète tuned in to the general.

"Now that we know who one leak was, everything we do and say from this time forward must be shared with no one outside of this small group. Understood?" Costa said.

One leak, Cheète thought, alarmed. *There's more? This is getting worse by the second.*

"I'm sorry, General," Shani said, "but I didn't hear what you told Mia."

With a sigh, Costa replied, "The link we discovered was one of the crew members on the C-130. What I didn't yet share with Mia is that his family was kidnapped soon after the rescue mission was approved, before we were in the air on our way to Venezuela."

Mia gasped, grabbing everyone's attention. "That's what they did to Aya, my housekeeper and cook. They kidnapped her family before we left France and forced her to spy on me in Venezuela."

The general kneeled, moving closer to Mia, and lowered his voice. "That is very concerning. I'm thinking the information that brought you to Venezuela to rescue those children was bait for a trap." Costa gestured for the others to come closer.

A moment later, he continued, "There's more you must know. First, I want to say that Celeste's plan to use the air ambulance is excellent because Mia can't return to France with her film crew. That would put all of their lives at risk. The Jet Rescue flight also can't be booked in her name. We have to find someone we can trust who wasn't involved with our rescue mission, because there are probably more informers."

"We can trust my boyfriend, Remy," Celeste said. "He's a nurse with Jet Rescue."

Mia held up a hand, catching the general's eye, and then in a wary tone asked, "What else did you want to tell me?"

From Costa's expression, Cheète thought it was more bad news and hoped it wasn't about Giselle. Like Shani, he knew Mia well enough that if she found out her best friend had been poisoned and was in intensive care, nothing would stop her from returning home. Holding his breath, he waited for the ax to fall.

"You mentioned your housekeeper Aya was also being blackmailed," the general said. "That may explain what she did on the flight to Manaus."

"What did she do?" Mia placed a hand over her mouth.

"Aya jumped out of the Brazilian rescue helicopter while in flight," the general said.

"She's dead!"

"No, no, no!" the general replied in a rush. "She's not dead. If the pilot hadn't been flying so close to the surface of the Rio Negro River, she would be. Once she hit the water, a fisherman in a small boat rescued her before she sank."

"Unless she knows her family is safe, she may try again," Mia continued. She turned to Shani. "Do you have my phone? I want to call her."

The general said, "Don't give her the phone!"

Mia stared at Costa. "Why not? I have to let her know, so she doesn't try to kill herself again."

The general shook his head. "Aya and your film crew think you're near death in an undisclosed hospital. Getting you safely out of Brazil and back to France depends on secrecy, at least for now."

Cheète felt a rush of relief and could see the same reaction in Shani's eyes. Maybe they still had a chance to save Mia from herself, but he needed to reach Jimbo as soon as possible to make the arrangements.

"Then I'll hold a press conference." Cheète heard Mia say. "That way my film crew and Aya will know that it's Esther fighting for her life, not me."

"That's the other news," the general said. "Your friend Esther is out of surgery. She'll live but..."

"*Mon Dieu!*" Mia protested, "Not a 'but.' I hate that word." She blushed and then said, "I'm sorry, please go on."

Dr. Celeste provided that answer. "Esther's spine wasn't shattered, but the bullet was close enough to cause paralysis from the waist down. She can't walk. She needs surgery, and the best surgeon for that is in the UK."

"Then I want to hold the press conference here before we leave," Mia said. "You must know a Brazilian journalist who can be trusted to hold the story until we're gone." Then she added in a rush, "Too bad you don't have news about Josh and where Adrienne went." It was apparent from her expression that she was troubled.

He hoped his friend was okay, but the risks Josh took in

combat were more dangerous than Cheète's addiction to women like Shani. If Josh didn't stop and settle down soon with one or both of his loves, his last heartbeat might arrive sooner than later.

A moment of silence followed when Cheète saw Dr. Celeste and her uncle exchange a glance, followed by a nod from the general. Then the doctor said, "We can trust my cousin Patricia, one of my uncle's grandchildren."

With apparent pride, Costa cut in. "My granddaughter writes a column for the tabloid, *Super Notícia*."

"It's a paparazzi-gossip column, Mia," Celeste added, "but she's talented, and we can trust her to hold the story until you're gone."

"She arrived in the city this morning to cover the story of Mia being shot by an assassin," Costa continued. "With your approval, Mia, I'll send a car to pick her up and bring her here. She doesn't need to know why."

"I don't know her," Mia said.

"Like me, she is also one of your fans," Dr. Celeste replied.

Then Shani spoke up, startling Cheète. "Is this the Patricia who was one of Mia's super fans that got the free pass to her last concert in Rio?"

When the doctor and her uncle nodded, Cheète understood what Shani was doing, so he added, "That means Patricia will be loyal to you, Mia. She'll hold the story." He noticed Shani was struggling to hide her relief.

They all turned to Mia, waiting for her answer. Eventually, she nodded. "That makes sense. Let's do it."

"I'll have Patricia here within a half hour," the general said as he slipped a mobile phone out of a pocket and made the call.

I have to use the head," Cheète said, leaving the others to visit the hangar's bathroom.

"Me too," Shani said and followed.

Cheète saw this as an opportunity to reach out to Jimbo through Forester in Idaho and arrange the pickup some place north of the city along the Rio Negro River. The expatriate pilot would find someone with a power boat to deliver them to the GPS coordinates. The crusty bastard had contacts all over Central and South America. He'd make the call in the bathroom.

With the arrangements made, they returned in time to see Patricia enter the hangar with one of the general's junior officers as an escort. Shani tugged on his sleeve, and he leaned closer to hear her whisper, "She's wearing Mia Belle-Chanson merch. This is going to work. Do you think we might have to drug Mia?"

Knowing Mia's intense love and loyalty to her closest friends, Cheète replied, "I think that might be a good idea. But we should play it by ear. Drugging her should be a last resort."

Cheète and Shani knew where Jimbo was going to fly them, but they didn't know the exact location. Captain Forest said he'd make the arrangements to have the pilot land in the Caribbean to meet an Oath Group trawler near Venezuela with a team of frogmen aboard. It wasn't surprising that an Oath Group Team of former SEALs was working in a hot spot like Columbia and Venezuela. The captain had volunteered no information beyond that, and Cheète hadn't asked, understanding the importance of "need to know" for black ops missions.

CHAPTER 26

JOSH AWOKE TO the hypnotic hum of tires on pavement and wondered how long he'd been out this time. His neck was stiff, and he wiped drool off his chin with the back of a hand. He craved water, but that could wait until he caught up with what he'd missed.

To get his thoughts straight, he focused on their ride, glad the motor wasn't rattling or clanking. It was a sixty-year-old Chevy pickup truck, and he didn't know what shape it was in.

Adrienne sat ramrod stiff, barely looking over the top of the dash, both hands on the steering wheel at the nine and three o'clock positions, a serious expression scrunching her features. His Garmin tactix Bravo, with its black face and olive drab nylon strap, looped around her right wrist.

"First you give me Glock. Then you give me watch. Why?" she'd asked when he handed her the Garmin.

He sort of lied. "You're driving, so you need it more than I do." He was relieved when she accepted that. What he didn't add was that if he died before they got there that watch would guide her the rest of the way. If she had to return to the farm, it would take her back there too.

Learning how to use that watch had been another of her survival lessons.

"How long did I sleep?" he asked.

"About two hours." Her eyes never left the almost empty road.

"Where was I when I dropped off?"

"You tell me about your grandmothers. How Grandma Cat in trouble for beating racist assholes then stealing motorbike. Clay was lawyer that kept cat out of *cadeia*. That was first time they met." She was grinning. He liked that expression better than the serious one.

He worried about her running out of gas in a country with massive oil reserves but a shortage of fuel. She'd started with a full tank and one twenty-liter can of gas in the truck's bed with the rest of the supplies she'd scavenged from the farm.

To meet the Oath Group team on the trawler, she'd need to refill the Chevy's gas tank at least once. He also didn't know how long that truck had been sitting there. With age, gaskets and fuel lines might leak.

Getting the pickup running had been hell for Adrienne. He'd used what little strength he'd had popping the clutch, while she did the pushing until she was drenched in sweat and gasping for air. On the seventh try, the damn engine turned over and died seconds later. The thirteenth time had been the charm. He'd wondered if that thirteen meant the angels were on her side.

"Are you going to tell me how they fell in love?" she asked.

What about the battery? he thought. *Did the solution of boiled water and four tablespoons of Epsom salt revive the damn thing?*

Holy fuck, what if that didn't work? It was his responsibility to make sure she'd make it.

She punched his arm. "Hey, where you go?"

"I heard you," he said, "but my mind is cluttered."

"Cluttered?" she said, glancing at him briefly, worry lines creasing her forehead.

She didn't know what cluttered meant, and his Portuguese was sketchy. "Cluttered, in my condition, means I get confused. Sorry."

"Oh, yes," she said, "if I was shot as many times as you were, I'd be *confusa* too."

He told her how Cat and Clay had fallen in love. When he finished, she asked him how he'd met Rachel and Mia.

NEXT TIME HE awoke, it was night, and he asked, "How much gas is left?" He couldn't remember how far he'd gotten with his Rachel and Mia stories before he blacked out from exhaustion again.

"Don't know," she said.

Agitated, he asked, "What do you mean you don't know?"

She took one hand off the steering wheel and tapped the gas gauge with a calm fingertip. "It stopped working. Needle stuck halfway, mileage indicator also."

"Sorry," he said. "I'm cranky." He couldn't think of Portuguese for cranky. "Ah, *temperamento.*"

She nodded. "I be cranky too if I shot like you."

Jesus Christ, when was she going to get angry at him for something? "What about the Garmin?" he asked. "How far do you have to go to reach the GPS location for your meetup with my team?"

Her right arm shot out so the watch face hovered an inch in front of his eyes. "I'm driving!"

He had to rub his eyes and then squint. What the Garmin revealed caused his heart to flutter in panic. It was almost midnight. The Chevy had to be running on fumes. *Calm down*, he thought. *She doesn't need to know what I'm thinking. If the motor dies...*He couldn't finish the thought.

"You're almost out of gas," he said. "Pull over so you can pour the last can into the truck's tank. But keep the engine running."

"I know. Battery, right?"

"Correct." *Smart kid*, he thought. *At least one of us is thinking rationally*.

Moments later on the road again, he asked, "I don't remember where I left off with Rachel and Mia's stories."

She told him, and he continued.

After telling her, he said, "You have to stop for gasoline."

"Where are we going to find *combustível* at this hour?"

It took a moment to gather his scattered thoughts, and he didn't like the solution he came up with. "You'll have to steal it." They were driving past buildings, and there were scattered parked cars.

"How about one of them?" she asked.

"No, you need a sure thing. Let's find a big house with a party going on."

"What?...That's *estúpido*."

He liked that she'd called his idea stupid. "That's exactly why it's perfect," he said. "I think it's Friday or Saturday, so if we find one of those, no one will expect it will happen to them. People with money in Venezuela are high in the government. Most of the private sector rich people left the country when the thugs took over."

Off to the north between them and where Caracas was on the other side of a mountain range, he saw scattered lights in what looked like a hilly residential area. "Let's drive up there and see what we find. Do you remember what I taught you about siphoning gas?"

"How could I forget? First time, I get mouthful. Yuck!"

"Good." He saw a sour expression appear on her face. "I mean, I'm glad you remembered. The second time, you stayed gasoline free, right? You're a fast learner."

"The third, fourth, and fifth time too," she snapped. "Why did you have me do it so many times?"

To keep you alive, he thought. *I don't want you to forget what I'm teaching you after I'm gone.* Then he asked, "How many times do you listen to and rehearse a new song before you perform it?"

She snorted. "*Droga,* you *complicado,*" she said.

He didn't want to grin but did. "Thank you for the *complemento*. I don't speak fluent Portuguese, but I know that you just said I'm damn tricky. In my world, that is an *ativo*."

IT WAS 0300 when Josh found what he was looking for, a big isolated house in the hills sitting on a large lot at the end of a narrow road. Adrienne had parked under the spreading branches of a tall tree. The paved road curled down the hill to the house where a closed gate blocked entry to the driveway. Instead of a fence around the rest of the house, there was a line of trees standing at attention like an army of silent sentries.

"There's no *festa,*" Adrienne said.

"Can't have everything," he replied and pointed at a lit

window on the second story as a shadow passed in front of it. "That and the five cars in the driveway say a big family lives here." There was a covered carport on the west side of the house and a three-car closed garage on the east side. "If you look at the back of that carport, you'll see two pumps."

"That spot looks like day," she said.

"That's good."

"Why good?" she asked, keeping her agitated voice down. "I will not expose myself like that."

"Behind those two pumps, it's dark. The lights are only over the parked cars. You're going to sneak around behind the carport, select the pump with gasoline, and pick it if there is a lock. Stay in the shadows and you'll be okay."

"What if there are dogs?"

"Pray there aren't any," he replied. "If there are and they are noisy, mean mutts, quit and return. We'll keep looking."

"I'll have to carry the heavy cans up the hill," she said.

His pointing finger shifted further west, away from the carport and the house. "See that clump of trees next to the road about twenty yards outside the gate? Take the filled cans there. Once we have all four, you'll return here and drive down to get them."

"What if I get caught?"

"I'm a sniper. From this seat, I've got you covered."

She stared at him, doubt flooding her face.

"You're thinking I might pass out again. What have you been taking for energy? I've seen you chewing something."

Her lips twitched before she twisted around toward the driver's side door and reached down out of sight, hefting a small hemp sack in the air between them. "Roasted coffee beans I find in cellar."

Josh blew out a big breath. "I've never done that before." He made a sour face.

She snorted. "You afraid of bitter coffee beans?"

"I didn't say that. I'll do it. That doesn't mean I have to like it."

"Me too," she said. Then with a toothy grin that melted his heart she lifted another bag and shook it at him. "Beans taste better with chocolate. I also find jars full of Hershey Special Dark Bars, very popular in my country. Do not eat them all."

"Hand me the sniper rifle before we launch our stealth attack," he said.

She snorted. "This is *louco*."

"Welcome to my world," he replied.

CHAPTER 27

"CHANGE OF PLANS," Hugo said, speaking through an encrypted two-way radio to the trawler. "Cruise out about thirty miles and hang out in international waters. We'll meet up somewhere out there when it's time to rendezvous."

Venezuela claimed its territorial sovereignty reached over seventeen miles out to sea, further than the UN agreement that set the limit to not exceed twelve nautical miles. Venezuela wasn't alone. There were a few other countries that didn't agree with the rest of the world, and the US was on that short list.

"Roger that," came the reply from the trawler. A few minutes later, he listened to the burble of the engine as the boat left until he heard it no more.

It started raining as Hugo and his two teammates got ready to climb the steep, heavily forested slope. It was the rainy season and hot, so it wasn't unexpected. Rainfall along this coast averaged about sixty inches annually. Farther inland, closer to Brazil and the Amazon rainforest, the downpour reached more than a hundred. Venezuela, being near the equator, was also hot all year, at least at lower elevations.

During the cruise from the Cayman Islands, Hugo and his team learned what they could about their destination. Henri Pittier National Park covered about a thousand square kilometers.

There were many insects here, explaining why they wore combat clothing treated with insect repellant. They'd also applied DEET lotion to their exposed skin before leaving the trawler. So far Hugo was thankful that the bugs were keeping their distance.

In the heavy rain and darkness, they couldn't see what they were hacking through but were aware of the towering trees. With the steep, slick surface, it was a risky climb. One slip meant losing control and tumbling down the slope, bouncing off trees, breaking bones, rupturing organs. Most people would think what they were doing was impossible, crazy even, but that wasn't the reason. They'd all been SEALs. Their motto, "The only easy day was yesterday."

The plan was to set up a trail of ropes tied to trees so they'd be there when they'd need that support the most.

Soon after they started toward Josh's GPS position located halfway up the mountain, they hacked limbs from smaller trees and used their serrated, razor-sharp combat knives to slice away the foliage, ending up with sturdy eight-foot climbing sticks. Before moving higher, they anchored the poles below them and pushed, taking two-to-three steps before securing their footing and pulling the pole up to repeat the maneuver.

"Even with ropes, it won't be safe bringing him down in this fucking muck," Simon said as he tied off the first hundred-foot rope to a tree.

"We can slide down," Louis added, laughing. "Turn our butts into toboggans and hold the rope as we go."

Hugo was used to Louis's odd sense of humor, so he ignored him. "We'll deal with Josh's medical condition first," he replied, "and then figure out how to get him to the beach safe, hopefully when it isn't raining."

"When do you think that'll happen?" The tone of Louis's voice revealed he didn't expect a reply, and Hugo ignored him again.

Hearing the noise of multiple outboard motors, Hugo caught Simon's attention and guided his eyes to one of the taller trees lurking in the rain close by. Simon nodded, handed his climbing staff to Louis, pulled himself up to the nearest branch, and vanished. He'd scale the tree until he found a spot with a view of the beach where they hid the Zodiac and use his night vision gear to see what was going on. If the pirates came ashore, they might stumble on their inflatable or the first rope where it was tied to a tree near the beach.

A quiet moment slipped by before Hugo asked Louis, "What, no monkey joke?"

"Hey, what can I say?" Louis replied. "I look more like a monkey than he does." He flashed another silly grin.

Hugo couldn't help but smile and shook his head. "You're hopeless," he said.

"That's what all the girls say too."

This time they both laughed.

Hugo wasn't too concerned about the Zodiac being discovered. They'd dragged it off the beach well beyond the tree line, covered it with brush, then cleared away their tracks in the sand. The rain was also helping erase any trace they might have missed. And with the ebb tide, any floating debris and bodies from the destroyed pirate boat should've been carried out to sea.

As they waited for Simon, Hugo estimated they'd climbed one hundred steps since leaving the inflatable. Each step probably gained them a foot of elevation. Josh was about fifteen-hundred feet above sea level. Fourteen hundred to go. He used the back of one hand to wipe away the slick sweat from his brow. His wide-brimmed rainforest bush hat protected him from the rain, not his perspiration. Despite the downpour, it was muggy and hot.

Hugo expected Josh's injuries to be serious. Even daunting terrain like this wouldn't stop him. If Josh couldn't walk, he'd crawl. As long as he had the energy to move, no matter the level of pain, no matter the risk, he'd keep moving. That SOS meant he was well beyond his endurance limit. Even if the injury wasn't a lethal wound, losing too much blood could be fatal too.

Hugo shrugged. That harsh reality held true for everyone serving in one of the Oath Group's combat teams. Josh had carefully recruited and hired only men and women who thought and fought like he did. That way, he'd ended up with 144 troops who were fearless and dedicated, just like Roy Benavidez, Hugo's role model, who'd earned an MOH saving eight men. Roy had been stabbed or shot thirty-seven times on that rescue mission.

"Stay here and wait for Simon," Hugo said. "I'm going to keep climbing to gain more elevation. We don't know how bad Josh is injured, so every second counts. Once Simon returns, you two will use the ropes I deploy to climb faster and safer. I'm leaving my backpack and most of my gear here. Bring it with you. Drag it behind you if you have to."

"Hey, Roy Boy, if you run into a pizza joint up there, I want..."

"I know," Hugo said, interrupting him. Louis was from New York City. "You want pineapple with your cheese, sausage, and beer?" Hugo thought Louis was an urban savage.

Slipping out of his backpack, Hugo freed up a two-hundred-foot coil of static rope. Selecting a nearby tree, he tied off one end to its trunk about waist high and fastened the other end of the line to a carabiner attached to his climbing harness. He selected one more two-hundred-foot coil of rope, looped it over a shoulder, and left.

A static rope was the best choice for this terrain and weather because it didn't stretch. Every ten steps, Hugo stopped to check his GPS location in relation to Josh and, if needed, adjusted direction. When he used up the first coil, he fastened it to another suitable tree and tied the second rope to the same trunk. He'd counted ninety-two steps before using up the first coil. The route twisted through the undergrowth and trees and was getting steeper. It didn't help that he had to hack a trail through the dense brush as he went.

Eighty-five steps later, Hugo reached the end of the second rope and backtracked a bit to find another tree to fasten it to. He'd wait here for the others to arrive with his gear, including more rope.

Hugo found a spot on the top side of one of the larger trees near where he'd tied the rope but first hacked a circular clearing around the space. Finished, he folded himself into a lotus position with his back to the trunk. He downed a power bar from a pocket and washed it down with an energy drink, one of several clipped to his harness. He shouldn't drink this over-caffeinated crap.

Shit, Hugo thought, *no one was safe from PTSD. Even generals.*

Closing his eyes to meditate, Dr. T's voice invaded the

harmony Hugo craved. "You'll make that hell in your head worse if you keep drinking two or more of those a day," she'd say. "You risk more intense mental health problems, anger-related behaviors, and eventually fatigue you cannot slurp away." She told all her vets that. After twenty years in the Air Force before retiring, she finished her PhD and once out started working at a Vet Center. He respected her for that and depended on her support.

True, he knew this junk would probably shorten his life, but without it, he reasoned, death would claim him a lot sooner. On a mission in enemy territory, they sometimes went days without sleep. Hugo grinned, thinking he'd be lucky to reach sixty.

Sensing he was being watched, Hugo snapped back to full attention. Filtering out the rain, he heard what sounded like a cat purring nearby. With the ruthless rain pounding down, the predator had to be nearby. And he knew it wasn't Louis pulling one of his sick jokes. The other two would've alerted him they were arriving to avoid being shot. A few yards from his position, he'd tied a silky ribbon to the rope. That way, they'd know when to signal they were coming in.

This park was home to a lot of birds and animals, like cougars and jaguars. He'd heard cougars before, often too close for comfort, and this sounded like one. An adult male could weigh over two hundred pounds.

Hugo unfastened the shoulder holster under his left armpit and slipped out his Heckler & Koch Mark 23 with its twelve-round magazine. He'd left the submachine gun with his backpack. Without that added weight, he'd made good time.

"You know, fetching feline," he said in a voice that didn't carry far, "you're probably hungry and think I'd make a good meal if you could get the drop on me, but I suggest you go look for something else to chow down on and live another day." He repeated the message in Spanish and again in Yaqui, just in case the wild animal understood one of those languages and not English.

Closing his eyes, he blocked out the rain and focused on the other sounds around him. His eyes were useless at night in this downpour, and he'd left his night-vision gear in his backpack. He frowned, thinking that had been a mistake. After a moment, he heard rustling in the foliage to his right, but it was moving away from his location.

"Smart move," he said. Keeping the .45 handy, Hugo pulled down his wide-brimmed hat to cover his face and tried to cop some z's. The rain didn't relent, but his cap and clothing were waterproof.

His stomach grumbled, reminding him he was hungry. The power bars gave him energy but didn't fill his belly. Now if a snake came along, that was free protein. Hugo didn't care if it was venomous. Cut the head off, skin it, take a bite, chew, and swallow. It was simple. Depending on the insects, twenty to seventy-six percent of their bodies were pure protein. He'd eaten that shit before and would do it again. His favorite snack in the wild were grasshoppers and crickets, but he cooked them first. Over the years, he'd fried, boiled, sauteed, and roasted them. Grubs he preferred raw. Hell, he'd even eaten toasted cockroaches in the wild. But he wouldn't touch city bugs. No telling where they'd been.

CHAPTER 28

HOURS LATER, THE Garmin led them to a narrow dirt road clinging to a rainforest mountainside. Josh stayed in the Chevy, too weak to get out, listening to Adrienne rummaging around in the bed of the truck behind him. He couldn't turn to see what she was doing. Every time he tried, pain rippled through his body, crippling him. He'd battled depression for years, managing it with help from Dr. Tate. Now it was back with a vengeance. He felt empty and hopeless.

He thought the mess they were in was his fault. Wanting to catch the monster that almost killed Rachel, he'd carelessly rushed into a mission without one of his special ops teams and no backup plans. He'd never done that before. That recklessness had almost gotten Mia, Adrienne, and the others killed, and this shit-show wasn't over yet.

His stomach was tied in knots and ached. It also didn't help that his mouth tasted awful from the coffee beans. With him as useless baggage, the odds were against Adrienne making it to the coast. It was time to say goodbye and send her on her way. He didn't see another choice. He didn't have to lie to her...much. All he had to do was convince her to go to the coast alone and meet the Oath Group Team on the trawler.

"What's taking so long?" he called, hating the sound of his feeble voice.

"You will see," she replied.

"I want to talk to you."

"So talk."

"To your face."

"*Porra de merda*," she cursed. "No time for this."

Jesus, he thought, *she sounded like someone on a special ops team*. God, he was going to miss her. Then he laughed, grimacing from pain as he did so. Once he was dead, he would miss no one. That cursed emotion was for the living, the friends and family who might grieve after he was gone. He knew what that was like. He still grieved, survivor's guilt, for all the team members he'd lost.

He didn't fear death, but unbidden memories of his SERE training had triggered a lot of lost sleep over the years, often waking up drenched in sweat, desperately gasping for air. The only person he'd talked to about what happened during Survival, Evasion, Resistance, and Escape training was Dr. Tate. It was one of those courses you wanted to forget that refused to leave you alone when you slept.

During SERE, the red team had captured him and waterboarded him in a shed with black widow spiders, their webs clouding the ceiling, crowded with eggs, hundreds of them hanging there watching. When he wasn't strapped to that chair with the cloth bag over his head thinking he'd die as they poured water over his face, there was the loud poetry and music filling that freezing, bare concrete cell so he couldn't sleep. Sometimes, when he awoke in the dark from one of those flashbacks, he heard that freaky recording of *Boots*, a poem by Rudyard Kipling, or *Throbbing Gristle's* post-punk crap, taking him back, shivering on the wet concrete, praying for silence, begging God for the peace that came with death.

That was why on missions he always carried a pill and reserved one pistol round in case he lost or couldn't reach the pea-sized cyanide capsule. If SERE wasn't the real thing, he didn't want to find out what was.

And with all the top secret shit he knew, there was no way he'd risk becoming a prisoner and propaganda tool for his country's enemies. If he'd been with one of his teams, they would've carried him out, even if he was dead. They'd all been through SERE and knew what each of them would do to avoid capture, explaining why special ops teams will fight to the death against overwhelming odds.

"What you want?" she asked, opening his door and bringing him back from those past horrors.

Breathing slowly, he looked her in the eyes. "Show me you still know the Morse code I taught you."

With a sigh, she fished in a pocket and took out the small laser light and showed him she knew what to flash at the trawler. "Now I go back to work."

"Not yet. When my team picks you up, they'll take care of you. I already made the arrangements. I want you to know you're going to be safe in your new life. Cat and Clay will treat you like family."

Since losing the cyanide in the Toyota when the truck exploded at the roadblock, he had no choice but to use the Sig Sauer right after he set the truck on fire to burn his body to charcoal. Leaving no evidence that might be traced back to him and the Oath Group.

Clearly irritated by his silence, she placed both fists on her hips and repeated. "No time for this!"

Unbidden, his eyes filled with tears, and his nose started leaking. "You're not making this easy, okay?" His voice cracked, tears blurring his vision. Good God, why did his fucking emotions have to betray him and turn this farewell into a melodrama?

"I'm trying to say goodbye," he continued, forcing the words out. "The odds are against you making it if you have to lug me through these mountains to reach the coast. That's why you have to go alone." Now was the time for the little lie. "After you link up with the team, you can bring some of them back to get me. That wristwatch will guide you to this spot."

Her silence wasn't what he'd expected, along with her angry expression. Why wasn't she arguing with him? Damn! He wanted—no, needed—a different parting, one that at least ended with a hug or handshake. He tried one more time. "If we don't see each other again, I want you to know that you have earned my deepest respect. I'm proud of you!"

She continued glaring at him. "Finish it, *puta de cu punk*," she said, spitting the words at him like shards of ice. "You lie!"

That shocked him. Drying up the tears. "Okay," he said, fighting anger, wondering why she'd insulted him like that.

Adrienne reached into a pocket and pulled out a handful of bullets. "I'm not stupid, *idiota*," she said and stepped back, pointing at the ground beside the truck behind her. "I'm going to strap you to travois I made using what I found at farm, dragging you. You have no choice. We go together or I stay."

"How did you know what I was thinking?" he asked.

"The look on your face, your eyes. Last time I see that *expressão* in mirror after pai rape me in *buraco do cu* for wanting to be girl instead of boy. I was nine then. I want to slash my wrists. He says, 'I had to know what it means to be woman!' I think *fodê-lo*. I decide to live, not let pai stop me."

What she was telling him felt like a hammer blow to his head. Maybe he was wrong about her not having what it took to carry him across the mountains to the coast. He wouldn't have slit his wrists when he was nine. He would've ended it Hemmingway style, just to punish his dad. He'd been full of resentful anger then, like Adrienne was now. Still, she was half his weight, and she'd never been through special operations training that failed seventy-to-eighty percent of those who tried out.

"Also, every time you talk about reaching coast," she continued, "you make it sound like I only one getting there. So, when you slept, I empty *pistola*."

What? Josh slipped the SIG Sauer from its underarm holster and checked. The chamber and the clip were empty. He hadn't seen that coming.

"You are not allowed to die because you think a girl can't do it. You said we *equipa*," her expression twisted as she dug for a memory, "...a team!" She spat the last word.

Stomping an angry foot on the hard-packed dirt road, she went on, "I refuse deserting you. Even if you die, I drag body so you go home. Understood!"

He held up both hands, palms out. "Okay, I surrender."

Her features softened. "Besides, you haven't told me about your family, what it was like growing up on ranch in Montana. I want to hear that too, because I think it bothers you."

Grinning, he said, "Okay, but before you drag my worthless carcass through these mountains to the coast, roll the truck off the dirt road and down that slope into that thick brush over there." He pointed.

"Why? I hate pushing the truck."

"We can't leave any breadcrumbs behind."

"Breadcrumbs?" she replied, looking confused.

Taking a breath to calm his racing heart, he said, "It's from *Hansel and Gretel*, an old German Fairytale."

Her face brightened. "Yes, understood. I read third year of elementary school. I push the truck."

"May I have my bullets back now?"

"No!" she replied.

"What if we get caught?"

She stared at him for the longest moment. When her confused expression cleared, she said, "I shoot you first. Do not worry!"

CHAPTER 29

WHEN THE SEALS reached the GPS location the SOS had come from, they found Josh dry, alone, and unconscious. The first thing Hugo noticed as he kneeled was Josh's sunken eyes and rapid breathing.

Leaning closer as the others watched, Hugo smelled his rancid breath. "He's severely dehydrated." He placed two fingers over the carotid artery, reporting, "His heartbeat is rapid. That means he's lost a lot of blood and his heart is struggling to move what's left." He'd treated enough wounded SEALs to know.

He placed a hand on Josh's abdomen and applied pressure, discovering it swollen and tight. "He's bleeding internally. And his fever is almost 105. Another three degrees and there's a high risk of brain damage."

Standing under the tarp that kept the relentless rain off of them, Hugo studied the corner nearest him, tied to one of the four trees holding the tarp up. One end of the cover was lower, so the water didn't puddle. He reached up, stretching to his full height, one arm extended. His fingertips were about eight feet from the ground, and he couldn't reach the knotted cord. "I don't know how he managed in his condition?"

Hugo returned to Josh's side. While he was setting up an IV drip to rehydrate Josh, the others cleared more brush away from the area under the tarp.

"Hey," Louis said, pointing at the ground under Josh. "Someone leveled the space under the colonel and dug a shallow trench to channel the rainwater away from him. You can see the scrape marks. And outside of that area, there's a gentle slope."

"Josh couldn't have done that." Hugo leaned closer to Josh's face and shouted, "Are you okay?"

Josh's eyelids fluttered but didn't open. Then he slowly shook his head no.

"Widen the level area and zip our one-man tents together to form a larger unit. Before we transport him to the beach, I have to discover where he's bleeding internally and stop it."

Breaking out the proper digging tools, they went to work. Once they had a larger flat surface, they fastened all four shelters together under the tarp, pegged them to the ground, and carried Josh inside, where they cut off his blood-stained clothing.

"Where's Adrienne?" Josh asked, struggling to breathe.

"Who's Adrienne?" all three SEALs asked.

When Josh didn't answer, Hugo inspected what he could see of Josh's body. When he didn't find any fresh wounds on his front, he said. "Roll him gently on his left side. I want to inspect his back."

That was where they discovered the wounds covered with duct tape. Hugo ripped off one patch, revealing a pale, puckered bullet wound packed with a glob of dark-tinted congealed goop. His eyes met Simon and Louis's, an unspoken question hanging between them. Josh couldn't have applied those makeshift bandages to his back even if he'd been fit. None of them could.

Hugo prodded each patch until Josh jerked and moaned in pain. "This's where we're going to open him up. If fortunate, this will lead to his internal bleeding."

First, they slipped on disposable surgical medical gloves. Then Hugo injected a local anesthetic. During the procedure, Louis hovered behind Hugo, handing him surgical instruments, clamps, sponges, sutures, whatever was called for. Simon, on Josh's other side, held him steady.

Special Ops teams cross-train, so Louis and Simon knew what to do.

"Found the bleeding bastard!" Huge said. "Not as serious as I thought it might be. Looks like the continued seepage was caused by a clotting problem." A moment later, the internal wound sutured, he added, "Let's hope that's it and there aren't any more leaks."

Leaning closer, Hugo said, "Tell me how you feel, Colonel."

"Like I've been fed through a meat grinder." Josh's voice was barely audible.

"Be more specific."

"Ask Adrienne." He sounded like he had gravel in his mouth.

"There's no one else here but us," Hugo said.

"Oh, she's here." He wheezed, still struggling to breathe. "She's watching." His voice faded. "If you fuck up, she'll probably shoot you." Then he forced out, "She's my guardian angel, tougher and meaner than a Marine Corps drill instructor."

All three SEALs jumped when they heard a young female voice speaking accented English outside the tent. "He has terrible headaches, painful eyes, muscle, joint pain, nausea, vomiting."

"What the hell!" Simon said.

Josh lifted a hand and pointed toward the opening at one end of the combined tents. "She's out there with my rifle." His raspy chuckle sounded crazy with him ending up winded. "I'm freezing!"

Hugo thought, *But he's hot to the touch and drenched in sweat.*

"Maybe he's hallucinating," Louis mouthed.

"Then who was that voice from, numb nuts?" Simon asked.

Wide-eyed, Louis shrugged.

Hugo shook his head. "You two stay with Josh. I'll go find Adrienne." He crawled out from the cover of the low-slung, connected tents into the rain and searched the trees above him with his eyes.

"Adrienne," he called, "by now you know we're here to rescue Josh. We have rations if you're hungry." Hugo didn't know where she was.

"Behind you." It was the same voice he'd heard before.

Hugo turned, thinking, *Jesus, how did she sneak up on me like that?* He saw a mud-covered, slender girl holding Josh's sniper rifle with the barrel pointed at the ground. When he stepped closer, he smelled her unpleasant sweet-and-smoky scent.

"I'm the team's medic," Hugo said

"I know," she said. "Josh told me."

"Please come inside so I can make sure you're okay."

Once in the tent, with bright light from small battery-powered, LED lanterns, Hugo sponged the muck off her body and discovered she didn't have many cuts or insect bites, something he'd expected since they were in an old-growth tropical rain forest near the equator.

"How did you keep the insects off?" he asked as he handed her one of his extra, long-sleeved, camo-colored t-shirts. On her, Hugo's spare shirt turned into a sack dress, ending below her knees.

"Something Josh teached me," she said. "I smashed hot peppers and made paste to cover our bodies." She grinned, her teeth glowing pearly white in the lantern light.

Hugo pointed at Josh. "Did you cover his wounds with the duct tape?"

She nodded.

"How am I going to turn duct tape into a joke?" Louis said.

Adrienne glared at the SEAL. "Not funny, Louis!" She spat at him. "Josh talked about you being a clown."

"Sorry." Louis held up both hands in surrender, struggling to hide a shit-eating grin, and said, "Gaping at plucked duct tape, a fake cake not to bake."

After a moment of silence with three pairs of eyes staring at him, Adrienne said, "That's awful."

Hugo and Simon burst out laughing. Louis looked sheepish.

They all turned to Josh when he snorted laughter then grimaced from the pain it caused. It was apparent that every move hurt. Then an alarmed look flashed across his face. "Did you hear that?"

"Hear what?" Hugo asked, his muscles tensing for action.

Without a word, Simon slipped outside the tent.

Josh's watery eyes shifted from face to face. "Just our neighbor. I wished she'd turn that damn music down." With a groan, he closed his inflamed eyes.

"Hey, Colonel," Louis said, "If you want me to, I'll go talk to that guy."

"It is female," Adriene corrected, "but don't get ideas. Josh says she has mean son-of-bastard boyfriend."

Licking his parched lips, Josh added. "Adrienne says most of what I see, hear, and dream isn't real."

"Did you dig all the rounds out?" Hugo asked Adrienne, pointing at the other duct taped wounds on Josh's back.

She shook her head no. Her eyes, filled with concern and what couldn't be anything but love and admiration, had shifted to Josh. After a moment, the words rushed out of her. "There was a roadblock. Our truck blowed up with Captain Thiago and most of Josh's gear. He killed some. I got one. Then we stealed a motorcycle. I drived. Josh behind me, holding on. That's why he is wounded. After that, we found farmhouse where he teached me to improvise."

"What did you pack in the wounds?" Hugo ripped off another patch of duct tape to reveal a healing slash from a knife.

"Dried black cobra peppers," she replied. "He teached me to ground them into powder and pack the wounds with it, that capsaicin numbs nerves."

"How the hell did he know that?" Simon asked.

"Mia taught me," Josh said and started coughing.

"Mia is Josh's French girlfriend," Louis added.

"I know," Adrienne replied. "I also know Josh married Rachel months ago because Mia said no. Rachel was Josh's childhood girlfriend. I also know Rachel was shot in San Francisco soon after the wedding and is in coma. Josh shared everything."

"Stop with the questions," Hugo said and flashed Louis and Simon a warning. "Can't you see the effort it takes Josh to respond?"

Josh raised one hand and said, "It's okay. Keeps my mind occupied and my demons at bay."

Hugo understood. He had his demons too. "Got it."

"Did those peppers give you a hot time?" Louis asked.

Without saying a word, Josh squinted with one eye closed, giving Louis a dirty look. Adrienne speared him with a frosty glare.

Louis squirmed before he tried again. "How hot were they?"

"Hotter than jalapeños," Josh replied. "But only if you eat them."

"Good to know," Hugo said. He was concerned Josh might have a malignant virus, since highly infectious diseases that could be controlled with vaccines had returned with a vengeance after Venezuela's health care system had collapsed several years earlier. They needed to get him to a civilized hospital.

"As soon as this rain lets up, we're going to move you to the Zodiac and meet up with the trawler. You need better medical care than we can provide."

Josh shook his head. "No, we have an appointment to keep with the Russian in Caracas. Did you bring the interrogation kit?" He struggled to sit but failed. "You have some mod tabs, right? Give me one." Modafinil had replaced Dexedrine as the "go pill" armies around the world used to deal with battlefield fatigue.

Hugo didn't want to give Josh a mod tab. Not in his shape.

"Forester had a case delivered to us in the Cayman Islands before we set sail," Hugo replied. "He didn't say what it was for but said you'd know what to do with it."

Hugo tore off the last patch of duct tape below Josh's right back shoulder, exposing a nasty-looking bullet wound.

"Dat slug is still there," Adrienne said. "I tried but didn't find it."

Hugo went to work. After cleaning the area and painting it with an antiseptic solution, he said, "Scalpel." Louis handed him a fresh blade, and Hugo used it to reopen the inflamed wound.

He handed the scalpel back and said, “Forceps.”

After digging deep and finding the slug, Hugo closed the wound, treated the area with antibiotics, and covered it with a dry, clean dressing. During all the cutting, Josh hadn’t revealed the pain he had to be feeling, not even a flinch.

“We still have to get the Russian,” Josh said. “And I’m going.”

“That isn’t a good idea,” Hugo said. “You need care I can’t provide.”

“I’m willing to take that risk,” Josh replied. “This is for Mia. If I die before we conclude the mission, I expect the team to carry on without me.”

Adrienne cleared her throat loud enough to grab their attention. Every eye turned to her, even Josh’s. “I know where the Russian is hiding,” she said. “Josh goes on boat to hospital. We get him.”

“No!” Josh protested, struggling to sit up again but failing. “I’m going. All I need is a mod tab to get my strength back.”

“No argue,” Adrienne replied in a no-nonsense voice. She stamped a bare foot and placed fists on hips. “You are in no shape.... Clear?” Her eyes drilled into Hugo’s. “What you say?” The unspoken message was, “you better agree with me.”

“Josh has to go to a hospital,” Hugo said and was surprised when that earned him a grin from the girl.

Josh sighed. “Jesus, you two are stubborn. Okay.” The tone of his voice showed he’d surrendered. “But, just in case, I’ve already promised she can join the Oath Group. If anything happens to me, I want you guys to make sure she becomes one of us.”

A moment later, he added, "She's a natural. If she doesn't join the Oath Group, another outfit will recruit her. I don't want that."

CHAPTER 30

AS THEY WAITED for a break in the downpour, with Josh's vitals monitored regularly, they'd learn if he was still bleeding inside. But when the rain stopped, the clouds and the lingering earthy smell warned there was more to come.

They had to go, and the SEALs and Adrienne started down the mountain using the ropes placed on the way up. With Josh sedated and tied to a sled they'd put together with branches and rope, they made good time rappelling down the mountain and arriving before the ebb tide reversed.

When they'd started down, Hugo worried Adrienne wouldn't be able to keep up or might injure herself, but she raced ahead until she vanished from sight. As Hugo and the others reached the tree line at the bottom of the mountain, they found her curled up, napping.

The SEALs looked at one another, wondering how she could sleep like that considering what she must've been through the last few days keeping Josh alive. During the wait for the rain to stop, Josh told them Adrienne had built a travois, tied him to it, and dragged him behind her from the other side of the coastal range to the spot where she flashed the SOS to the trawler, something else he taught her.

Before anyone moved, Adrienne opened her eyes. Hugo nodded his approval for her level of alertness and then used his night-vision gear to search the short stretch of beach that appeared empty. But he knew that couldn't be trusted.

"Stay with Josh," he said to the girl.

Without protest, she slipped Josh's rifle off her back and took up a prone position with an open field of fire in front of her.

As the three SEALs double-timed into the open and across the sand to the Zodiac's hiding place, Hugo thought about what Josh had said, that her shooting skills were almost equal to his.

Satisfied nothing had been disturbed, they cleared away the foliage covering the inflatable rubber boat and carried it out of the trees to the sea. Simon tied a bowline knot to the craft and fastened the rope to a tree with a knot that could easily be untied remotely. Once the Zodiac was loaded, Louis settled in the bow as the lookout. Simon and Hugo, with the laconic girl helping, carried Josh across the sand to the water and hoisted his unconscious weight into the center of the boat.

With everyone on board, the loaded inflatable now weighed over two-thousand pounds.

"Those fucking pirates better not show up," Simon muttered as he gripped his weapon.

"I have a few gifts for them if they do." Louis grinned, revealing a flash of white teeth in his camo-painted face. He hefted his combo grenade launcher machine gun like a trophy. "What about you, Adrienne?"

They'd also painted her face with camo; she'd demanded it.

"I rather cut off their *testículos*, but I do what Josh teached me, shoot them full of holes from chest to neck, hip bones to pelvis."

For a moment Hugo wondered if she was Roy Benavidez reincarnated. Then he noticed the girl had vanished. What the hell? Looking around, he saw Adrienne had slipped out of the boat and returned to the beach. God, she moved like a ghost. "What are you doing?" Hugo called.

"It time for Louis, Simon, and me go to Caracas and capture Russian," she replied.

Hugo thought he should've told her what the plans were. "First," he said, "we take Josh to the trawler and arrange for a med evac somewhere closer to Mexico. Then we return pretending to be Cubans and go hunting for this Russki."

Without expression, Adrienne rejoined them. Once on board, she sat beside Josh and held one of his hands with both of hers.

Hugo stayed in the stern beside the motors and yanked on the anchor rope, releasing the knot from the tree. When he started the silent electric 80 HP engine, Simon squeezed past him and pulled in the line, trailing the inflatable. Finished with that, he resumed his position in the bow beside Louis.

Simon watched the northeast quadrant while Louis focused on the northwest. The outgoing tide moved fast, and they made good time. When Hugo felt the brief slack period before the tide reversed direction, they'd reached the open sea where tidal currents didn't have as much of an impact but the waves were choppier and higher than their craft. Once they left the tidal currents behind, Hugo switched to the noisy gas engine.

A half-hour later, Louis signaled a warning that a pirate boat was approaching from their port side.

Hugo killed the Suzuki and switched back to the electric. The pirate's loud engine also gave that boat's location away.

Details? Hugo signaled. He glanced at Josh to make sure the colonel was still sedated. It wouldn't do to have him wake up in the middle of a violent flashback, screaming his lungs out as he'd done a few times on that mountain. What he saw caused his eyebrows to lift in surprise. Adrienne had crawled on top of Josh and spread herself out to shield him if they came under fire. She also had Josh's sniper rifle aimed at the pirates. Her courage and willingness to risk death to protect Badger caused a lump in his throat. *God damn*, he thought. They must have been through some kind of hell to bond like that.

He blinked away his tears and turned to check the other two SEALs.

Louis was using night-vision gear to track the pirate. In a barely audible voice, he said, "It's an open boat about twenty to thirty feet long, and it's riding high in the water and moving toward us."

Hugo frowned. "Shit, I didn't expect them to be out here looking for targets in weather like this. Fucking bastards!"

"Maybe they're still looking for the ones we sent to hell," Simon replied.

It started raining harder, the downpour, darkness, and choppy waves helping to conceal them.

A moment later, Louis signaled the pirates were going to cross their bow in ten beats. They crouched lower. Hugo turned off the electric motor, letting the inflatable drift.

As the sound of the pirates' motor grew louder, the rain became a drencher. The other boat passed in front of them, close enough to jump from one to the other. It was a long wait until Hugo couldn't hear them anymore. Then he fed power to the silent electric motor, moving them in the opposite direction.

A moment later, Hugo asked, "Louis, did you see how many there were?"

"I counted five."

Simon nodded agreement.

"I can't hear them anymore," Hugo said. "How about you guys?"

They listened for a moment before shaking their heads. Thinking of the girl as part of the team, Hugo checked for her reply. He'd spent a lot of time in third-world countries where most children weren't pampered and treated the way they were in the United States.

When she saw him looking, she nodded, her expression still serious.

"Good." Hugo fired up the louder gas engine and also kept the electric motor running. Once they were racing and bouncing through the storm and chop at a steady 50 knots, he said, "It's time to contact the trawler and find out where they are."

Simon made the call. After he had the trawler's GPS location, he told Hugo to make a course correction to the northwest.

A few hours later with the showers still pounding them, they pulled up to the trawler's stern swim deck. Once Josh was aboard, they moved him and his deadly defender to the forward cabin. Everyone left but Hugo, who stayed with her and Josh. But a few minutes later, Louis returned, replacing Hugo.

ADRIENNE THOUGHT IT ironic that Louis, the SEAL team's wannabe comedian, had been assigned to monitor her. Before he left the cabin to join the others somewhere else on the boat, she heard Hugo tell Louis it was his job to monitor Josh, but there was no reason for that since she was there. After all, she was the one who dragged him through the rugged coastal mountains, the challenge of her life, since Josh had to be over twice her weight.

Leaving the truck they'd found inside that abandoned farm's barn and liberated had been her worst living nightmare. But when she ran out of road and had no choice, they'd left it behind. And as far as she was concerned, she was the one responsible for catching the Russian who wanted Mia dead, while Josh went to his grandmothers' house in San Francisco to recover from his wounds.

Josh had told her that was where he always went to heal. Still, according to Hugo, he'd have to go to the Palo Alto VA Medical Center first.

"But," she'd protested, "Josh said he often went to the Walter Reed Medical Center for surgeries after being seriously wounded."

"That was before we left the military," Hugo had replied. "Now we use the VA, and Josh listed the Palo Alto VA for his go-to-place to be stitched back together. Don't worry, the VA Medical Center has more beds than Walter Reed and access to some of the best doctors in the world from Stanford's hospital."

Focusing on the cutup again, it was apparent from his expression that the gagster was uncomfortable being in the same room with her since she'd made it known that she didn't care for his disastrous humor. Josh had told her all about the SEAL team and mentioned that Louis was a funny stand-up comedian when he was using the jokes his twin brother wrote for him. Knowing that, maybe she should've given him a break.

So, since she wanted to discover what the others were talking about and what this jester probably already knew, she had to find out from him. She was convinced the SEALs knew something they didn't want her or Josh to know. After all, no matter what Josh said, they hadn't earned her trust yet.

What could that be? Adrienne asked herself. The answer was simple: Mia's safety and Rachel's health. Either Rachel was worse or better. As for Mia, maybe the Russian had gone into hiding or added more bodyguards.

As much as she hated and feared her papai, she'd learned a lot from him. How to torture people, how to scare them *sem cocô*, and how to get information out of someone who doesn't want to give it to you by tricking them.

She also knew Louis was the youngest of the six-man team, meaning he was probably at the bottom of the pecking order. Still, he was a SEAL, and from what she'd learned from Josh that meant something.

"I'm sorry. I was mean about your humor," she said.

That earned Adrienne a grin. "I've been thinking about that. How about adding, 'do not screech from plucked duct tape?'"

Oh, querido Deus, Adrienne thought, but she made her face light up and laughed anyway. "That's more like it," she added.

And when she saw the blush changing the color of his face, it was apparent to her he craved attention, so she pounced. "Have you performed on YouTube's Comedy Central Stand-Up?" she asked.

"There's comedy on YouTube? I didn't know that." Now

there was excitement glowing from his eyes. This tough SEAL was about to be putty in her hands. "How many views does it have?" Then he stuttered. "I mean, people watch it, right?"

"Of course. I watch," she replied. "Stand-up already has almost one billion views, and Josh will be happy for you when you hit it big there. He'll also be pleased to hear Rachel's health has improved." Adrienne didn't know if this was true, but that didn't matter. What counted was saying it with conviction, as if she already knew. Louis's reply might tell her what the facts were, and even if her ploy had been wrong she'd still have the answer she wanted.

"Yeah, we know," he replied without taking time to think. "When he finds out she came out of her coma, his spirits will lift a lot. Everyone in the Oath Group thinks so too. We're happy for him."

Without missing a beat, Adrienne said, "I think you need to do something with word 'tape' to improve joke." His grin grew wider. He didn't know she was faking it.

"I can do that," he said. "I just need a few minutes with my rhyming dictionary."

"Too bad the Russian slipped away," she said, tossing out her next trick. The truth might be that Josh's Captain Forest ordered the SEAL team to stand down and bring Josh home instead, but she couldn't ask. She had to make it sound like she knew what was going on and give him a chance to correct her if she was wrong.

But his expression sobered, and he said, "Yeah, and our source doesn't know where he went."

It took an effort to hide her shock. She hadn't expected her subterfuge to turn out correct. That was the last thing she wanted to hear, that the Russian had gone into hiding or left the country. What a clusterfuck, as Josh would've called it.

It was apparent she was now headed to San Francisco and Josh's grandmothers. Adrienne worried they wouldn't let her stay with them while Josh's wounds were treated at the VA hospital. Sure, he'd promised they'd take her in and love her, but before Mia and Josh saved her life, she'd learned the hard way never to trust anyone...ever. Trust always led to sorrow, beating herself up for being a fool again. She hated being the fool.

Fodendo um, she cursed herself as her eyes filled with tears. She didn't want anyone to notice. When it was her against the world, she had to bury such weakness.

CHAPTER 31

OSCAR SAT IN the captain's chair in front of the trawler's wheel, facing aft. He'd been an E-9 Command Master Chief Petty Officer when he retired at sixty-two. Hugo and two others sat on a bench near the back of the pilothouse behind a long narrow table, eating nuts and sipping black coffee. Derrick stood off to the side in the shadows, leaning against the aft bulkhead. Only Lewis wasn't there.

"We're expecting a call from Captain Forest with details about Badger's med evac," Oscar said. "What condition was the colonel when you reached him?"

"He was sleep deprived," Hugo said. "You saw the girl with him when we came aboard. If it hadn't been for her, he would've died in Venezuela. After we treated his wounds and got him to sleep, he had one hell of a flashback. Whatever he was hallucinating, it turned him into a bloody fiend. I thought my demons were bad, but his are in a whole nother league."

"Shit," Simon added, "stands to reason. Josh was a fucking snake eater longer than all of us." Simon took a sip of coffee and set the mug down with a clunk to underline what he meant.

"I first met him in the SEALs," Oscar said. "The colonel has itchy feet. He can't stay in one place long, and he's also drawn to combat like plaque to teeth."

"I've heard the reason Badger retired was because they were going to make him a full-bird colonel and assign him to the Five-Sided Puzzle Palace," Ethan said.

"That's not the main reason," Oscar said.

The three behind the table stared at him, waiting. Oscar shrugged. "Don't look at me. I'm not a useless oxygen thief. What I know is his business, not yours. This is need to know, and everyone here just wants to know."

After another moment of silence, Simon continued, "Well, on that mountain, when the colonel went kinetic, it took all of us to restrain him, including the girl. That's why we sedated him. I don't know how Adrienne managed when they were alone. Jesus, she's one tough cookie, and Badger wants the Oath Group to train her and make her one of our us."

"Sounds like someone I'd want as my wingman," Derrick said, his cacao black skin blending into the shadows. DELTA Force recruited Derrick out of the SEALs to serve with Josh on the same team. Derrick was a man of few words, who craved combat as much as the colonel.

"Next time Badger's awake, maybe we should contact Doctor Tate and have her talk to him," Ethan said, who sat at the table with Hugo and Simon. He'd served twelve years in the Navy, six as a SEAL.

"You know how Doc T works. She'll want to be here. No way that's going to happen." Oscar rubbed his bulbous nose before continuing. "She's the one who called Captain Forest with the news that Josh's wife came out of her coma, and the doctors discovered Rachel was pregnant."

"What else did you learn from Forest?" Hugo asked.

"That this was shaping up to be one strange operation, like something from Mission Impossible. The target was staying in the penthouse of a forty-story building."

"Don't tell me we were going to tightrope walk from another building to the target. That shit's for Hollywood." Simon tore open an energy bar wrapper and broke off a bite. Before he put the chunk in his mouth, he added, "Caracas is a cluster bomb ready to explode. I for one am glad that Russkie moved to another hidey-hole or fled the country."

Oscar chuckled. "There wasn't a tightrope. Josh was planning to have that expat pilot he's used before fly us to the penthouse from the mountains surrounding the city, grab the Russkie and fly out, all at night. And our mode of transportation was going to be a camouflaged, foldable hot air blimp with an electric motor."

"You're joking, right?" Hugo said.

"No," Oscar replied. "We all know how Badger loves trying out stuff like that in combat. He bought this thing on a whim from some startup company years back, and it's been in storage at the potato farm. Forest shipped the thing to Columbia for that expat pilot to get ready."

"How were we going to keep this blimp a secret from over two million people as we flew over Caracas?" Hugo took a sip from his steaming mug.

"Since that mission's scrubbed, that's history. What isn't is what else Forester told me." He fell silent, wanting to see who'd succumb to curiosity first.

Hugo shook his head. "I'll bite. Out with it, Senior Chief."

"The Oath Group people in Idaho want revenge for what the Russians have done to one of our own."

"Badger's wife and the fetus are okay, right?" Simon asked. "No damage?"

"Patience, Padawan," Oscar said. "There's more to unwrap. Once you have all the facts, you'll understand. And what I tell you next does not leave this cabin. Captain Forest made that clear. He wants to keep Badger out of the loop until the doctors release him for active duty."

"Jesus, everything we do is on a need-to-know basis. No one else ever needs to know," Hugo said. "That's how it's always been. If it wasn't Rachel, it must've been Mia."

Oscar guffawed. "Well, it isn't her, and I'm one of the few who knows what she does when she isn't saving children. Now you'll all know. When we're done here, Ethan will take you down to the salon and show you the interview a journalist had with Mia in Brazil. Reuters picked it up, and its spreading through the EU like an airburst from a 203mm killer shell. In the interview, Mia doesn't mention Badger or the Oath Group, but she names the fucking Russkie and the mob he works for. That's why the idiot probably returned to motherfucking Russia with his tail between his legs."

"So, if it isn't Mia, why does the Oath Group want to go after the Russian mob?" Hugo asked.

The red mike on the encrypted radio buzzed. "That's the call we've been waiting for," Oscar said as he picked up. "Big Stick here, over."

"Popsicle Dick here, over," Captain Forrester's voice crackled from the speakers set in the ceiling above the trawler's control panel.

"We hear you loud and clear, Popsicle," Oscar said. "This line is secure, over."

"In a few minutes, a Grumman Albatross will arrive at your GPS location. When the pilot signals he's there, send up a flare so he can find you. Transfer Badger, Adrienne, and Derrick to the seaplane. Derrick knows his orders. Once they're gone, sail Big Stick to Sea Hawk Island (the code name for the Errol Flynn Marina in Jamaica). After you drop anchor, you'll receive further orders, over."

"Roger, over."

"Over and out," Forest said, ending the call.

Everyone turned to Derrick, who shrugged, using two fingers to show his mouth was zipped. "Need to know," he said.

"I know the colonel's call sign is Badger, but why does Forest call himself Popsicle Dick?" Simon asked. "He's taller than anyone in the Oath Group and is built like a tank."

"That also is on a need-to-know basis," Oscar replied.

"What else were you going to tell us before Forest called?" Hugo asked.

"The Russians poisoned Celeste, and she died this morning in a French hospital. But that's not all. Charles Tweet, the billionaire the FBI arrested after our raid on that Montana militia ranch a few months ago, got out on bail and somehow transferred his ankle monitor to a body double. He's in the wind. It seems he had an escape tunnel from his Florida estate to another house across the street that one of his LLCs owned."

A moment of numb silence filled the pilot house before Hugo said, "No wonder the Oath Group is on the warpath and Popsicle Dick doesn't want Badger to know what's going on until he's combat ready. With Mia's best friend Celeste killed, that's the straw that will break the Russian bear's back."

"Yes," Oscar said. "Does anyone want to place bets that the Oath Group won't wage a war of terror against Russia's bratva leaders? My bet when it's going down will be New Year's Day ushering in 2020, when those whoring gangsters are partying and guzzling vodka. That's when their guard will be down the most. The logistics are going to be a nightmare. Badger should be operational by then. He's in his element when planning complex missions like that."

"He's better than anyone," Derrick said in his raspy-whispery voice. "I'm all in for that shit."

No one said a word as they chewed on the new information.

A moment later, Oscar waved a hand to dismiss them. "Ethan, go to the flybridge and keep watch for that Albatross. When the pilot makes contact, fire off a flare. Hugo, have everyone else prepping Badger and his guardian angel so they're ready to transfer as soon as that flying boat arrives. Dismissed."

He swiveled his chair around to stare out the rain-spattered windows that looked over the bow as the others left the wheelhouse. The rain was still coming down hard, and visibility was only a few hundred yards with a low ceiling. He thought the pilot of the seaplane must be a fool or great at what he does to risk a landing in this weather.

CHAPTER 32

DURING THE RIDE north to Venezuela's coast to meet the Oath Group team on the trawler, Josh told Adrienne a lot about his two lovers and his family. After all those stories, Adrienne felt she knew them better than they knew themselves.

Still, she didn't expect his grandmothers to accept her with open arms. They'd be suspicious. *Who's this girl who bewitched our grandson?* They had no reason to trust her.

Before Mia and Josh risked their lives to save her, she'd learned to trust no one. Even a few of her YouTube fans turned out to be *falso. Esboçado,* only interested in what she could do for them.

After the SUVs left Travis Air Force Base, the closer she got to San Francisco the more Adrienne expected the worst. *Querido Dues!* She hated meeting strangers. It seldom turned out well.

Eventually, thanks to the serious silence inside the Tahoe, she fell asleep.

Adrienne jerked awake when the SUV stopped. Opening

her eyes, she saw a garage door lifting in front of the Chevy. She glanced through the side window at the front of a three-story Victorian house, painted olive green with dark-red trim and black-paned windows. Even though it was still night, the motion-activated lights under the eaves had turned the sidewalk and street in front of the home to daylight.

The second Tahoe pulled in behind them, blocking the driveway.

Josh's grandmothers must be próspera? she thought. Adrienne preferred common people. She didn't trust those who had too much *dinheiro*. With wealth came temptations, often leading to corruption.

Once the garage was open, she shifted her gaze back to the front and saw two armed men appear from inside. They flanked the SUV, scanning the street. As the Tahoe glided forward onto the steep ramp leading under the house, the two men kept pace with them as they pulled inside, always facing the street. Then the reinforced metal door reversed direction, sealing them in. Once down, the inside lights flicked on, also as bright as day.

She wondered why there were so many serious-faced armed men. Protection from rival gangs, maybe? Now she was wondering if San Francisco had favelas like Brazil's cities. Since she'd never planned to leave her country, she knew little about the United States.

All she'd ever wanted was to be a girl, be free of her family, and sing. Only when she performed did she feel alive.

Maybe Josh's grandmothers were *mentes criminosas*, who hated traffickers. Josh couldn't have told her everything about his family. Why would he? He'd probably only picked the good things to share. Maybe this Oath Group Josh led was a very dangerous *gangue*.

Porra, she thought, *what choice do I have?* Then she realized she'd be better off with Josh's people than her family. After all, if they hated traffickers, they couldn't be that bad.

At the bottom of the ramp, the driver turned into a spacious underground garage and stopped behind several parked cars. Two women waited on the other side of the parked cars in front of a metal door set in a cement wall. One was black like Adrienne, and the other woman wore men's clothing, blue jeans and a long-sleeve slip-on shirt without a collar. The serious Caucasian woman had white hair standing up like a bristle brush, tight on the sides and high on top.

The black woman seemed to be Dr. Tate, and the older one was Grandmother Cat. They fit Josh's descriptions. If this was Cat, her torso, arms, and legs were covered with colorful tattoos, what Josh called body art. But clothing hid those areas. That disappointed Adrienne. She wanted to see.

She wondered where the others were: Josh's sister Suki and Grandmother Clay, upstairs or at that hospital where the *helicóptero* took Josh? When she watched him fly away, a void opened inside of her. Feeling alone and helpless, it had been a struggle to keep the tears locked inside, to show no weakness.

The driver, Mia, and Shani left the SUV. Adrienne stayed behind and felt like shrinking into a prune, as she watched the older woman walk forward with welcoming eyes and grip one of Mia's hands with both of hers, keeping at an arm's distance. That had to be Cat. Josh said she wasn't a hugger like his other grandmother, Clay.

When Dr. Tate started toward the Chevy, Adrienne's stomach knotted, and she shifted her gaze to her knees. *What if they don't like me?*

Then the door opened and Dr. Tate said in a welcoming,

pleasant tone, "You must be the hero I've been wanting to meet…Thank you for saving Josh. I'd miss him if he were gone."

Adrienne discovered she'd been holding her breath. "How did you know that?" she asked.

"I have my sources," Dr. Tate replied and held out a hand. "Come on, let's go for a walk. I want to hear all about how you and Josh met. You talk; I'll listen. I might ask a question now and then if that's okay."

"It's still night out," Adrienne said, and thought, *How does she sound so genuinely cheerful?*

"Best time to go for a stroll," Tate replied, "and I prefer empty streets."

Adrienne couldn't argue with that. The only time she liked crowds was when she was performing for them. With her fingers tingling, Adrienne took Dr. Tate's hand and then found herself beside the woman, who was only a few inches taller than her. That was the only thing she hated about transitioning, the drugs that stopped her from growing, keeping her looking more like a child instead of the woman she wanted to be. Her pai was six feet tall. She thought she'd at least have reached five-two or three by now, not stuck at four-eight.

"We'll have to go upstairs and leave by the front door," Dr. Tate said. "Don't mind our two chaperones. Whenever we leave the house, we have to take them with us because of a criminal who escaped police custody a few days ago, an evil man who might try to hurt Josh's family and friends to get to him."

Curious, Adrienne asked, "Are you going to tell me more about this *criminoso* who wants to hurt Josh?" If she knew who the man was, maybe she'd get to him first.

"I'm planning a long walk, so we'll have plenty of time for me to answer your questions."

Once they were outside on the sidewalk, Dr. Tate said, "You first. I want to hear all about your adventures with Josh."

Adrienne laughed. "What happened wasn't fun. We weren't playing games."

Tate stopped under a lonely corner street light, stepped back, and inspected Adrienne. "That jacket looks like it would fit someone three times your size, and what do you have under that...a big man's t-shirt. I think we'll do some shopping while we're out. It's always cold here this early in the morning, but that coat should keep you warm enough."

"I know nothing about this city," Adriene said. "I grew up in Rio with over thirteen million."

"San Francisco isn't that big, a seven-mile square with less than a million," Tate replied. "I think you'd like Urban Outfitters. Not that far, just a couple of miles, or we could walk to the Richmond District, about the same distance. It's early, so we'll stop for coffee and a snack first. You look like you could add a few pounds, but be careful or you'll end up like me with a fire-plug figure."

Adrienne giggled. Then said in a shy voice, "I'd like that."

As they walked, the story poured out of Adrienne, and she forgot there were two armed men following them for protection. It was easy to talk to this woman. Now she understood why Josh depended on Dr. Tate for his sanity. He'd called her a PTSD whisperer.

Adrienne still wasn't sure what that meant but was learning. This woman was crafty at getting her to open up about what had happened after her *pai* had sold her to the traffickers.

When dawn crept over the city from the east, spreading like honey toward the Pacific, they found a warm coffee shop and settled around a corner table away from the main entry. The two men sat with their backs against the two walls, watching everyone in the shop with a glacial look that issued warnings to keep their distance, leaving the nearest tables empty.

That impressed Adrienne. Even her *pai* couldn't do that, the *maldito bastardo.* She wanted to be dangerous, just like Josh and his men.

"During our stroll, you never mentioned Brazil," Dr. Tate said. "What would have to happen for you to go home?"

A moment passed as Adrienne sensed a bubble of muted silence settling around their table, shoving the other voices away from them as she retreated to a safe place, escaping the brutal reality of her past.

"My pai has to die." Her voice sounded meek, barely audible, as goosebumps raced up her arms and she shivered as if death were in the *retaurante* with them.

That one question had unlocked the vault in her mind where she'd imprisoned those demons so they couldn't haunt her. Removing her hands from the warm comfort of the coffee mug, she twisted her suddenly icy fingers into a Gordian knot before adding, "If I go back to Rio before he dies, I must kill him." *As long as he lives,* she thought, *I'll never be safe...anywhere.*

"What about now?" Dr. Tate asked in a voice as smooth as the coffee Adrienne was drinking, pulling her back to reality. "When you were telling me what happened to you and Josh in Venezuela, it sounded like you felt safe with him."

The emotions that flooded her when she heard Josh's name drove out the arctic cold that had invaded when she'd thought of her brutal *pai.* If she could only tear that *cadela desumana* out of her head, as if he'd never lived.

"I miss Josh. He is my only amigo," Adrienne replied in a

fragile voice, and with that admission she turned inward, attempting to shut the world out again.

"What would it take for you to feel safe while Josh is recuperating from his wounds?" Dr. Tate asked.

That's a good question, Adrienne thought, and the darkness receded a bit. "I think..." Her voice faltered before she gained the courage to continue. "I do not trust cities, too many people. Evil hides in shadows and crowds. To be safe, I need to go to the Oath Group's potato farm in Idaho, learning how to be warrior like them. Josh said I was natural. He promised they'd teach me, watching my back."

After saying that, she relaxed as her *demônios* returned to the dark recesses in her mind where she preferred them. With a sigh of relief, she reached for the welcome warmth of the coffee mug and wrapped her hands around it, thinking, *This San Francisco coffee tastes so much better than all those bitter coffee beans I ate in Venezuela to stay awake,* and her eyes flooded with tears of relief.

"WE HAVE TO talk, Mia," Cat said as they hooked arms and entered the house through the underground garage door. Tate and Adrienne went up the stairs first and out of sight. Shani hung back.

Cat and Clay had first met Mia and Josh in France years ago. They'd spent a month together visiting France, Germany, Italy, Switzerland, Spain, and Portugal. A few years later, they'd returned for another visit, France again but this time touring Sweden, Norway, and Finland.

"Shani, you go upstairs with the others," Cat said. "What I want to discuss with Mia is for our ears only." Then she guided Mia into what had to be a fortified safe room across from the opening to the stairs leading up, and closed the heavy, vault like door, sealing them in.

This was Mia's second trip to the United States. Before returning to France, she'd visited San Francisco one night to see Rachel in her hospital room but hadn't called Cat or Clay. She'd wanted to check out Josh's high school sweetheart and new wife, the woman she lost him to. Seeing Rachel in that hospital bed looking helpless did something to her she still didn't understand. Instead of seeing a rival, she saw someone she wanted to know better. They had something in common. They both loved Josh.

"I know what you want to talk about," Mia said. "I don't hate Rachel."

"Hmm, I was sort of thinking that might be the case," Cat replied as they both took seats around a small table at the back of the safe room in what looked like a corner kitchenette. "Captain Forester explained why you can't go home because of the damned Russians, and you're welcome here. But I also want to know what you're planning to share with Rachel when you meet her. She hasn't been released from the hospital yet, but when she does, she'll be staying with us. That girl's been through hell with more to come. She isn't like you, and it will not be easy for her to rebuild her strength and accept that Josh has another lover."

"What do you have to drink?" Mia asked. She didn't want to rush into this conversation, because she'd had little time to think about what she wanted to do.

"Bourbon, beer, or wine. We keep a supply here just in case."

"Do you have any of that Bordeaux you carried home from France the last time you visited?"

"We do," Cat said. "Three bottles." She got glasses from a cupboard and a room-temperature bottle of wine, handing that to Mia and setting the glasses down. "You do the honors." She opened and closed her hands, clenching them. "The arthritis is stealing my ability to grip things. Old age is a thief."

"On the flight to Travis Air Force Base, Josh's man Derrick told us about Charles Tweet giving the sheriffs the slip." As she talked, Mia watched the older woman closely. For a woman with rugged features, Cat had warm, expressive eyes. She seldom gave away her emotions verbally, but her eyes revealed a lot.

"For Rachel, what have you been thinking?" Cat asked.

Good question, Mia thought and let the fresh inklings flooding her mind do the talking for her. "I want to be her friend, help her recover, teach her how to understand Josh, so they will always be free to laugh when they're together." She wrapped both hands around the top of her head and continued, "Josh carries a lot of darkness in here, and she has to not only be his lover but his best friend, his partner, who knows the signs when he needs her most just like he will learn hers. And I owe him my life. That's why." Her arms dropped to the table, and she felt tears filling her eyes. Some escaped, trickling down her cheeks.

Cat reached across the table to take both of Mia's hands, and the grip was comforting.

That's when Mia knew Cat didn't bring her into this room to grill her about her intentions regarding Rachel but to learn what Mia needed. This house was where Josh must have learned to be as insightful as he was. She knew for a fact that he hadn't learned that in Montana from his parents.

CHAPTER 33

CHEÈTE'S FLIGHT FROM Travis Air Force Base in California to Malmstrom Air Force Base in Montana landed a little after midnight. He'd been fortunate an Air Force C-130 was headed that way and didn't hesitate. Only service members, retirees, and their families were eligible to fly free.

The last few days were a blur. Slipping out of Brazil on Jimbo's Albatross. The rough flight north out of South America to meet the Oath Group's trawler somewhere in the Caribbean between Columbia and Mexico. The instrument landing on water in bad weather and almost zero visibility. He still didn't know how Jimbo pulled that off without killing them.

Then there was the hop from the trawler to the Cayman Islands, where they switched from the Albatross to an Oath Group C-130 that flew them to Travis Air Force Base. Soon after arriving, he parted company from the others.

Still, he'd watched a sedated Josh leave first with Derrick literally glued to the colonel. They flew out in an air ambulance to the VA hospital in Palo Alto. The three girls climbed into the first of two black Oath Group Chevy Tahoe SUVs for the fifty-four-mile drive to San Francisco. Each vehicle came with two armed men.

Hours later, as he walked down the Air Force C-130's ramp into the familiar Montana weather, Cheète was running on empty, craving caffeine, but the coffee had to wait. He'd already booked a car with his Visa card before leaving California. The Enterprise location in Great Falls was a short walk from Malmstrom's main gate. But the rental agency didn't open until 0800, so he bagged a bunk on base to catch some z's before the last leg home, a 300-mile drive south. At dusk, he'd eat on base before walking into town to pick up the rental. After all, the Air Force always had the best chow, the Marines the worst.

When his family picked him up at the Enterprise in Bozeman, his kids would swarm him with hugs. Arriving home, he'd have his wife tell the kids to go outside and play with their friends before he towed her into their bedroom, locking the door.

Later, after a long hot shower to scrub off the mission, he'd sleep for the rest of the day. The next morning he'd awake to the welcome scent of bacon, pancakes, fried potatoes, and scrambled eggs. His mouth was already watering. His wife and daughters were incredible cooks.

Before he fell asleep, he wondered what Charles Tweet was up to since the billionaire had escaped custody.

A few hours later, he awoke drenched in sweat from a flashback reliving the night he'd saved a young Ukrainian girl from being murdered by Tweet. The billionaire knew Cheéte and Josh were behind his downfall. What if the asshole was still in the States seeking revenge?

Sweet zombie Jesus, he thought. *I should've paid attention.*

Derrick guarding Josh. The armed escort in the two SUVs for the girls. I screwed the pooch. Credit cards can be traced. I should've paid cash for that rental.

He called his Crow warriors on the reservation, waking them up. Like him, they'd all served in the U.S. military.

Cheète reacted as if he were being hunted by the fugitive billionaire's thugs in Great Falls. That meant not picking up the rental he'd reserved with his credit card. So a little after dawn he asked around base until he found an airman first class named Peter who was on his way home to Spokane for his annual thirty-day leave. Peter refused money, saying it wasn't far to the Great Falls Transit Center, where Cheète planned to pay cash for a one-way ticket on a Greyhound bus to Billings.

He'd learned soon after retiring through counseling at the Billings Vet Center to recognize when his PTSD had been triggered. He also knew if he did nothing, paranoia would overwhelm his rational mind, causing delusional and dangerous behavior. It'd happened before. That was why Cheète's mind boiled with solutions to the imagined threat that he refused to ignore.

The longer he stayed off the grid, the better his odds were to avoid discovery. His first move had been to remove the battery from his mobile phone and store both in a button-down pants pocket. His second was to pack up most of his gear, including his dismantled sniper rifle, and ship them home to the Crow Reservation south of Billings. That left him with two weapons, his backup pistol in an ankle holster and a Marine Corps Ka-bar in its sheath hanging down his back, hidden under his long sleeve shirt and windbreaker.

Since he was flush with cash after the Oath Group had paid him at Travis for his time spent in Venezuela and Brazil, he didn't need to use the credit card to pay for the bus ride. Still, it sucked that his no-show fee to pick up the Enterprise rental was going to cost him a hundred dollars. He'd considered canceling, but if Tweet's people were tracking him online, they'd start earlier looking elsewhere.

"You didn't mention what branch of the service you were in," Peter said as they left Malmstrom Air Force Base and drove west down 2nd Avenue into Great Falls.

Forced to stop planning, Cheète replied, "I was attached to the 2nd Marine Raider Battalion when I got out."

"What was your MOS?"

"Scout Sniper...Hey, is there a place to eat near the Transfer Center?"

"Tracy's about a block away," Peter replied.

"Any recommendations?"

"My favorite is the BBQ pulled pork sandwich. They make their own bread, butter pickles, and the Coca-Cola sauce is to die for."

Cheète smiled. "That sounds interesting. If it ain't too much trouble, cruise by the bus depot so I know the route back and drop me off at Tracy's. I had morning chow a few hours ago, and it's almost noon. After eating, I'll walk back to the depot and wait for my ride."

"Sure thing," Peter said.

Cheète noticed Peter glancing at him with curiosity before asking, "What was it like being a Marine Corps sniper?"

"Most of my missions were special ops, so I can't talk about them. Classified shit. What do you do in the Air Force?" Cheète didn't know this guy and wasn't about to trust him. If he did the asking, then Peter would do most of the talking. The less this guy knew about him, the better.

"Tactical Aircraft Maintenance."

That told Cheète that Peter was probably an REMF. "Now that sounds more interesting than what I did," he said. "Spending hours or days in concealment doing nothing but waiting for a target that might never show."

"No shit." The guy sounded interested. "What do you do if you have to take a leak?"

"Roll on my side, whip it out, and make sure I'm not pissing in the wind. Tell me more about the specifics of your job. It sounds better than lying around waiting to shoot someone's face off."

An abrupt laugh, almost a bark, escaped from Peter before he replied, "I perform special pre and post-flight inspections of aircraft and use automated technical data to diagnose and solve maintenance problems if there are any."

After Peter dropped Cheète off in front of Tracy's, he decided to find a place to buy a burner phone. Then he'd reconnoiter the Transit Center and the surrounding area before returning to the restaurant for chow. To kill some time, he went inside and studied the menu. Since he considered himself operational, he wasn't about to eat something that might punish him later. He decided on the Kicken' Chicken Wrap. The Santa Fe Chicken Salad looked good too. Then he left, planning to return. Staying too long in one spot was risky. He didn't feel safe in cities, preferring a rural setting where his ghillie suit blended in.

Once he had the temporary phone and activated it to call home, he got the answering machine. Not wanting to leave a digital trail, he hung up.

He was tempted to activate his regular mobile to check for messages but decided against it. If he was right that the fugitive billionaire was coming after him to get revenge for catching the degenerate being a kiddy fiddler, he had no choice.

He'd read Tweet's CIA profile and learned that the thuggish billionaire lived for revenge.

Cheѐte had removed his share of high-profile foreign sociopaths and psychopaths who were deemed dangerous to the United States. Before each mission, he'd read their profiles. Nothing was ever their fault, even when caught in the act. They had nothing but scorn for the justice system and their victims and didn't lose sleep having witnesses eliminated. Tweet was that type.

After he looped back to the parking lot across the street from the Transit Center, Cheѐte stayed in the shadows, hiding behind trees and watching from a distance. After fifteen minutes, he left in the opposite direction and did some window shopping downtown, where he found a store that sold MAGA and Trump hats. Deciding a dark-blue Trump 2020 No More Bullshit baseball cap would make a perfect disguise, he bought one. He also picked up a cheap pair of mirrored sunglasses. Wearing Trump's lying BS on his head, he felt like a traitor, a perfect disguise.

Returning to the Transit Center parking lot from another direction, he stalked about, checking the parked cars. When he found the unmarked Chevy Suburban with U.S Government plates, he felt his precautions had been justified.

Maybe the driver of this car was one of those corrupt agents working for Tweet. Last year the billionaire had paid off Homeland Security Agents to hunt for Josh. They ended up arresting General Graves at that hospital in Billings instead. Those bastards had delivered LG to the Nazis in that militia camp. The Oath Group had rescued the retired general a few days later, but too late. He died soon after from the damage to his body. During the recovery mission, Josh had killed the two who'd tortured his mentor and friend, and one of them had been Tweet's only daughter.

Even though the Oath Group had emptied all of Tweet's secret offshore accounts, the billionaire still had resources in the United States, so he had the financial means to keep those corrupt bastards on his dark payroll.

While Cheète was scanning the inside of the locked government car for evidence, he sensed movement across the street in front of the Transit Center and ducked behind the SUV, watching over the top of its hood. The baseball hat shaded his features. A Chrysler sedan that looked like another government vehicle had pulled to the empty curb in front of the main doors. Two guys got out to talk to another one who'd just come out of the building. After a moment, the third guy shook his head and pointed across the street at the car Cheète was hiding behind. The Chrysler left and number three jaywalked to the parking lot.

Keeping low, Cheète scuttled in the opposite direction until he'd put several cars between him and the SUV. For a moment, he considered sneaking up behind the guy as he was unlocking the door to his ride and slitting his throat but rejected it. Too risky. And what if the government agent wasn't in Tweet's pay?

The triggered temptation to kill the guy was strong and took an effort to resist.

Once the man drove off, Cheète left the parking lot, returned to Tracy's, and ordered. Looking relaxed and sitting with his back to the windows without looking over his shoulder once, he ate and planned his next moves, deciding against the bus or flying to Billings.

Moments later, he also dismissed the idea of hiring an Uber driver, not wanting anything to do with a public company linked to the internet. If he did that, it was a sure thing that information would be in a database that might trigger an alarm for any federal agents or hackers working for Tweet who were monitoring the internet searching for him.

Instead, Cheète contacted a member of the Little Shell Chippewa Tribe that lived in Great Falls, a man he'd known early in his Marine Corps career, another Scout Sniper, eighty-two now, who'd retired twenty years before he did.

Waagosh considered himself an "ogichidaa," a warrior. They'd stayed in touch. Sometimes Waagosh visited the Crow reservation south of Billings, or Cheète went to Great Falls. They'd find a remote and sheltered rural area and shoot a few hundred rounds at distant targets, betting on who'd get the most center hits.

Last time they talked, his old friend sounded like he could use some thunder in his life. After all, there was a lot of truth that "old soldiers never die." He understood, because that was why he'd jumped at the chance to go with Josh to Venezuela. An old soldier was never too old for a good fight, better than getting fat and lazy in a rocking chair. Better than going fishing.

To get his old friend's phone number, Cheète had to put his mobile together and activate it. When it linked to the internet, there was an alert telling him of several messages from his wife. They were all from her mobile, minutes apart. Oddly, it wasn't like her to be that impatient. Maybe she couldn't make it into Billings to meet him once he arrived.

Cheète selected the first message and felt the hairs on the back of his neck tingle and his stomach knot when he heard Tweet's rancid voice instead of his wife's. "I have your family, asshole," the voice said as Cheète's face turned numb from shock. "If you don't call back in twenty-four hours, they'll vanish, after my men take turns raping your lovely wife and I ride your daughters like they're wild mustangs. That's on you for fucking up my life." The recording ended.

With heart thudding, he checked the time of the first message and breathed a sigh of relief since he still had a few hours before the deadline. Then he found Waagosh's number, got out his burner phone and made two calls: one to his team on the Crow Reservation with new instructions and then his old friend. When the Chippewa warrior answered, Cheète asked, "You up for a hunting trip shooting two-legged varmints with your ancient M40? You'll need your ghillie suit too. As scrawny as you are, I'm sure it still fits."

A few minutes later, he used his regular mobile and called his wife's number. Tweet answered. "About time," the evil bastard said.

"What do you want?" Cheète replied. He already knew the answer but wanted to hear it.

"I want you to take me to where that traitorous coward Josh Kavanagh is hiding."

That meant Tweet didn't know Josh was being treated for his wounds at that VA hospital in California. Good! Cheète decided to do whatever he could to keep the degenerate from finding out while saving his family at the same time. "Only if my family is free and I know they're safe," he said.

"You're not in a position to make demands," Tweet replied.

With rising anger, Cheète struggled to stay calm and in control. "Since I know what makes you tick, I also know that my wife and children will die along with me and Josh. The only way you get us is if my family is free and I know they're safe. No rapes. No torture. This is how it will go down. I will come to you. Once you have me, you let my family go. Once they're safe, one of my people will call and let me know. Then," he lied, "I'll take you to where Josh is hiding on the reservation."

"No way," Tweet said. "Not until I have you and Josh."

God, Cheète hated that slug's deep baritone voice. Last year, after saving the Ukrainian girl from the pervert, he remembered how good it felt kicking that toxic dickwad in the gut. The girl, the same size as his twelve-year-old daughter, had long cinnamon-colored hair and vivid green eyes. Even after getting caught raping the girl while planning to murder her, the monster had the gall to attempt bribing them to let him go.

"Your word isn't good enough," Cheète said. "You do it my way or Josh and I will hunt you down anywhere you go. With our resources, we'll find you, even if you are hiding in Russia, North Korea, or Iran. And once you have me, if you attempt to torture me to find out where Josh is hiding, my people will alert him. He'll be in the wind before you can fart."

Cheète listened to a long silence before continuing, "You're thinking about how my people are going to know what you're doing to me. I'll tell you. After I'm with you and know my family is safe, my guys will expect a call from me every fifteen minutes. One missed call and Josh will vanish. You might kill me and my family, but you won't have Josh, and he'll find you." After a spine-tingling pause, he finished, "You will never know how you died. It could be a bullet from a mile or two away, explosives, poison, or Josh slips up behind you to cut your head clean off. He loves his knives. Once he's holding your head in his hands, the last thing you might see before your brain is dead will be his smile."

Cheète knew Josh had killed no one like that with a knife, and he wasn't sure Josh would get close enough to decapitate the man, since snipers killed from a long distance and then slipped away like ghosts, but it sounded too good to leave out since Charles Tweet was a coward.

CHAPTER 34

WHAT A SUPER-sized clusterfuck, Cheète thought. At least my family's safe. During the swap to save his wife and children, he hadn't expected Tweet's thugs to drive him to a small private airport and a waiting bird. Now they were in the air circling the cabin on the Crow reservation where the billionaire thought Josh was hiding.

Cheete hadn't planned for that and had no idea how he was going to get out of this mess.

"Hey, there's a dead man in here, Boss," the Russkie's accented voice said over the helicopter's radio.

"Is it Kavanagh?" Charles Tweet shouted from up front in the seat next to the pilot. The fool was shouting as if the guy at the other end was deaf.

They'd strapped Cheète in a rear seat with zip ties trapping his hands behind his back and double cuffs hobbling his legs at the ankles. His hands had gone numb during the eighty-mile flight from a private airport.

"He's belly down in the bed, Boss," came the reply. "We'd roll him over and have a look, but we don't know him."

"How do you know he's dead?" Tweet asked, a scornful, superior tone to his voice. He covered the mike and mumbled. "Dumb-ass Russians."

"He stinks! And he's not breathing. And when we pulled the blanket off, he was covered in bruises, like someone kicked the shit out of him."

"Well, that sucks!" Tweet said. "If someone got to Kavanagh first, I'll make that asshole suffer."

"What if it isn't him, Boss?"

"Maybe it isn't. Treasonous cowards like him have enemies. I'm not the only one. Maybe he killed this guy. If he's outside taking a walk, maybe he'll be back to get rid of the body, and we'll grab him then. The idiot says he walks a lot. I'll have a look. Maybe I can ID him." Tweet held up his left hand, thumb down, telling the pilot to land the bird.

Cheète had been holding his breath and, with some relief, let it go. He knew the idiot Tweet was referring to was him. The bird had been circling the cabin at a high altitude. The tattooed bruiser beside Cheète held a thermal sensor scanning the land below for heat signatures that might show a trap. His tats signaled he belonged to the Russian mob and held an inferior status. That he was a bone breaker, spending more time in prison than out.

Cheète kept his face expressionless and his eyes glued to the back of the Tweet's thick, sunburned neck. No matter what happened, once this bird landed, the billionaire was cooked.

A dozen of Cheète's Crow warriors were down there with his Chippewa friend. They were dug in and concealed with camouflaged, thermal blankets made of Mylar foil, blocking their heat signatures.

The plan had been to lure the billionaire's convoy into a

trap. Cheète hadn't thought of the kiddie fiddler flying in after his thugs had arrived to secure the area.

I was stupid! he thought. *What would Josh have done? He'd have a laser-guided MANPAD ready to knock the bird out of the sky.*

Still, his people were all sniper qualified. They'd agreed that Waagosh got the first shot, taking off Tweet's head with an explosive round. Then the others would shoot out the tires on the five Cadillac Escalades so no one escaped. If any of Tweet's thugs in the cabin didn't surrender, Cheète had an IED planted inside.

When the bird dropped straight down, Cheète leaned to the side and glanced out the window. *My mess just got worse,* he thought.

The five white SUVs formed a half circle in front of the cabin, and the bird was landing between them and the only door. Waagosh wouldn't see the target since the corrupt billionaire was about as wide as he was short, reminding Cheète of a banana slug.

The cabin's walls had to be at least sixteen-inches thick, and all the windows had solid wood shutters, all closed. By shooting out the tires and disabling the bird, his men would trap Tweet's crew, but that cabin was a solid bunker. It might turn into one hell of a fight with casualties on both sides if Cheète allowed it to escalate that far.

He was so preoccupied with his thoughts that he didn't notice the Russkie slip out of the bird until the muscle-bound ape reached in and grabbed him by the throat, yanking him roughly out his side.

"What the…" The bruiser shoved Cheète from behind, cutting off his last word.

"Move, idiot!" The man shoved him again, and this time Cheète fell hard on both knees.

Tweet was already in the cabin.

Before Cheète stood, the gangster grabbed a handful of his shoulder-length hair and dragged him inside, his feet kicking up dust.

"I can't tell if it's him," Tweet said. "The photos I saw were from 1994, when he graduated from bootcamp."

Thinking of his wife and daughters, his friends, and the other women he loved, Cheète said, "If you flip him over, there are about a dozen combat scars on the front of his body." That was a lie. Josh had scars on the front and back, but this corpse didn't have any. This young Crow Indian, not even twenty yet, had died a few days ago, tossed to the side of a road out of an old white Ford van driven by neo-Nazis after they beat him to death because he'd dared to admire one of their women. His friends said all he'd done was look. After murdering him, the racists had gone into hiding.

With Tweet's drivers and pilot still outside, there was thirteen in the small cabin, counting Cheète and their boss.

Everyone was staring at the body on the bunk bed, where Rachel and Josh had spent most of their honeymoon. No one moved. The smell of rot filled the air.

Tweet said, "Go ahead, idiot. Why should we soil our hands? You turn him over."

"How can I do that with my hands zip tied?" When no one moved, he continued. "Are you pussies sacred of me? Twelve to one." He cackled, prodding the tycoon's ego.

Tweet nodded, and Cheète's handler cut his hands free.

As Cheète stepped toward the bunk, he thought, *Good, at least I'll be the one who kills these bastards. Josh and my warriors will take care of my family and keep them safe.*

Knowing his death was going to be fast and painless, he suppressed a victory grin, reached down, and rolled the body over.

The cabin exploded into splinters.

After the dust settled, Cheète's Crow warriors found only six bodies. The wood shrapnel from the explosion had shredded the SUVs, knocked the bird on its side, and killed the men outside. Everyone in the cabin had been obliterated. Cheète's team hadn't fired a shot.

THE FIRST THING Josh noticed when he awoke was another warm body against his left side. When he opened his eyes, the brightly lit room blinded him, and he closed them again. "Who's there?" he asked.

The reply was a barely audible grunt, a familiar sound he'd heard before, telling him he had to be back in the states, but where? The last thing he remembered was being on the trawler off the coast of Venezuela with one of his SOF teams.

"Is that you, Audie?" Josh asked to make sure.

This time, Audie Murphy, a large Golden Retriever, barked softly followed by happy panting and a thumping tail.

Audie had been LG's PTSD service dog. After General Graves died, he became Sukie's guardian angel. Since then, Audie and his younger sister had been inseparable. Blinking his eyes to clear the blurriness, Josh turned his head to the side and saw Audie's friendly, furry face. "Hey, Boss," he said. "If I had a choice about who greeted me when I returned to life, it would be you."

Audie's tail continued thudding against the mattress, and he peeled back his lips in a dog grin.

Thinking of LG, his lost mentor and friend, Josh's eyes filled with tears. "Are we alone?" he asked.

This time Audie replied with a whimpering grunt that told

Josh they weren't alone. LG had trained all of his PTSD service dogs and also taught them how to reply to simple questions. That was how he knew what Audie meant.

Josh bobbled his head to the right until he saw who was sitting there. "Hello, Suki," he said. "Why didn't you let me know you were here?"

"I didn't want to interrupt," she replied, grinning.

"So...where am I?"

"The VA hospital in Palo Alto."

"That must mean I'm going to live, right?"

"Maybe," she replied. "Your doctor isn't very forthcoming. Audie seems to understand what she's thinking though."

"Audie's trained to sense and smell human body language," Josh said.

"You don't have to tell me that. Audi doesn't let me out of his sight, and without him I'd be dead."

"I understand," Josh said. "Audie saved me from myself a few times too."

"From what Adrienne said, you had one of those moments in Venezuela."

"True, is there anyone else here I know?"

Suki nodded. "They're in your doctor's office debating what to do with you."

A slight electric warning rushed through his body. "What the hell does that mean, little sister?"

Suki laughed. "I can't answer that. I'm not one of the deciders."

Forewarned, Josh asked, "What's this doctor's name?" He held his breath, hoping it wouldn't be her.

"Everyone who works here calls her general this, general that. I'm not sure she has a name."

Holy fuck, Josh thought. She was supposed to be retired.

Looking at Audie, he asked, "Is Suki talking about Doctor Hard-Ass?"

Audie stared at him for a moment, blinked, and crawled closer, putting a comforting paw on his chest, before saying a gentle woof.

"Oh, dear God, not her," he said.

"Explain, please," Suki said.

"The first time Hard-Ass operated on me was in Germany at the U.S. Army hospital in Landstuhl, near Ramstein Air Base. That's when I was a SEAL. The second time was at Walter Reed. I was in Special Forces then. The third time was at Brooke Army Medical Center in Fort Sam Houston, Texas, when I was with Delta. I should've died from those wounds or at least ended up crippled. She's the surgeon who brought me back from the brink, a miracle worker, but she's as mean as they come."

"Well, good morning to you too," a familiar voice said from the door. "My memories of our previous times together aren't the same as yours. I remember a stubborn SOB who made my life as a doctor stitching him back together as difficult as possible. I recall the last time I saved your sorry ass and patched you up so you could get shot again. You started calling me Deb just to piss me off after I said you could call me Cliff."

"Shit," Josh said. He felt his face blushing as he turned and saw the now retired two-star Army general wearing scrubs. She was smaller than Grandma Cat and thinner. "What the hell are you doing at a VA hospital?" he asked.

She came over to the right side of the bed and slipped the ear buds for the stethoscope around her neck into her ears and listened to his heart and breathing. A moment later, she pinned him with her hard pewter-colored eyes, and replied. "When the Army made me retire at sixty-four, I went to work for the VA. I'm like you. I don't intend to ever stop doing what I love. Even though you refuse to admit it, that's what you and I have in common. In the field, you save as many as you can, and I kept them and you alive. Here we go again."

"I take it you're involved in deciding my fate? What was the verdict?" Josh asked.

"Your Oath Group wanted to keep secrets from you until you had totally recovered. Dr. Tate and I had a different opinion. We won. There will be no secrets."

Fearing the worst, Josh felt his face blanch. "I'm ready," he said.

"The rest of the jury has to be here first," she replied, turning to the door. "And here they are."

Dr. Tate, Captain Forest, Rachel, Mia, Shani, and Adrienne came through the door one at a time. Mia was pushing Rachel's wheelchair. Derrick was last, and he closed the door, placing his back against it. Josh knew that his mouth was hanging open in shock as he stared at Rachel and Mia. When Mia locked Rachel's wheelchair, she moved up beside his wife and placed a comforting hand on Rachel's arm. Rachel covered that hand with one of hers.

What the fuck! he thought.

The silence in the room would have filled a tomb until he saw Rachel's lower lip quiver and her eyes fill with tears. That was when he knew he was going to hear the worst kind of bad news possible.

"Okay," he said, his voice breaking. "who's going to start this shit show?"

"That will be me," Dr. Cliff said. "We have decided that until I release you ready for duty you belong to me. And after all your surgeries, Derrick and Adrienne will be in charge of your physical therapy, reporting directly to me about your recovery."

Josh looked from Derrick to Adrienne to Dr. Tate. "Okay...How long do you think that will take?"

"Knowing you, I estimate six to nine months," Dr. Cliff replied. "You should be ready to return to the field and get shot again in early 2020." She turned to Dr. Tate and said in a clinical tone, "Now you get to lower the hammer."

"Dear God," Josh said. "Your bedside manner still needs improvement. This is why I call you Dr. Hard-Ass."

"That's enough," Dr. Tate said. "You two can continue your banter later." She pulled a chair closer to the hospital bed, sat, and started talking.

Josh thought when he'd lost LG that was bad, but what he was hearing now was worse. They'd lost Cheète and Giselle. Esther was recovering from a sniper's bullet in the UK and might never walk again. And the Russian Bratva was still hunting for Mia. The only good news was seeing Rachel out of her coma, but he didn't know what to think about her being pregnant. He wondered if he was going to see his grown son and daughter soon.

Thank you for reading ***Never for Glory***. If you enjoyed this action thriller, or even if you didn't, please visit the novel's Amazon page, and leave a brief review or star rating. Your feedback is important and will help other readers decide to also read the book.

In ***The Patriot Oath,*** he fought for his country. Now he's home and engaged in the deadliest of battles. If you like war-hardened heroes, action-packed fight scenes, and powerful political agendas, then you'll love Lloyd Lofthouse's gripping adventure. Visit https://www.amazon.com/dp/B0991S8DZ1 to buy the first thriller in this series today and continue reading!

Join the Josh Kavanagh Thriller series email list to get your first-free short story and to be notified when ***Fiddling with Death***, the next novel in the series is released or contact me at ***lloydlofthouse@gmail.com*** with questions or comments. After twenty-four years, how will Rachel react when she meets the man, she thinks abandoned her?

ACKNOWLEDGEMENTS

There are many people who have had a direct or indirect hand in the making of the **Josh Kavanagh Thriller** series. Rather than trying to list everyone (and thereby setting myself up for failure and mortally offending the people I don't mention because there are so many), I will simply thank you all: the talented host and authors that belong to the ***Brentwood Writers Critique Group*** (the city in Northern California, not the community in the southern area of the state), the VA Martinez PTSD support group, where the idea for the series was born from a prompt in 2018, and Imbue Editing (https://www.imbueediting.com) for the cover, the final edit, and launch promotion.

Printed in Great Britain
by Amazon

60690247R00167